P9-CMY-151

THE REVENGE OF MAGIC

ALSO BY JAMES RILEY

The Half Upon a Time series

Half Upon a Time

Twice Upon a Time

Once Upon the End

The Story Thieves series

Story Thieves

The Stolen Chapters

Secret Origins

Pick the Plot

Worlds Apart

THE REVENGE OF MAGIC

JAMES RILEY

ALADDIN

NEW YORK LONDON TORONTO SYDNEY NEW DELHI

This book is a work of fiction. Any references to historical events, real people, or real places are used fictitiously. Other names, characters, places, and events are products of the author's imagination, and any resemblance to actual events or places or persons, living or dead, is entirely coincidental.

ALADDIN
An imprint of Simon & Schuster Children's Publishing Division
1230 Avenue of the Americas, New York, New York 10020
First Aladdin hardcover edition March 2019

Jacket designed by Laura Lyn DiSiena
Interior designed by Mike Rosamilia
The text of this book was set in Adobe Garamond Pro.
Manufactured in the United States of America 0119 FFG
2 4 6 8 10 9 7 5 3 1
This book has been cataloged with the Library of Congress.
ISBN 9781481485777 (hc)
ISBN 9781481485791 (eBook)

This one, like everything, is for Corinne

THE REVENGE OF MAGIC

- ONE -

JUST MINUTES BEFORE THE ATTACK IN Washington, D.C., Fort's father was embarrassing him at the Lincoln Memorial.

"President Forsythe Fitzgerald," his dad said, pointing at the spot each word would go above the giant seated statue of Abraham Lincoln. "I feel like we're going to need a larger statue, though. These ceilings are high enough to fit that head of yours, but you're definitely going to need a bigger chair."

Fort rolled his eyes, but a grin popped out anyway. "I'm pretty sure that they don't let twelve-year-olds run for president," he said. "I think I have to be an adult, and that's when you said I was going to be leading a mission to Jupiter. And curing cancer, I think? The version of me in your head really needs to make up his mind."

"You'll do all of that and more!" his father shouted. Other

visitors to the Lincoln Memorial began to look at them, making Fort blush. "There's no time to be lazy, not with all the amazing things you're going to accomplish! And don't forget that I still want a flying car, so I'll need you to invent that too."

Fort tried to pull his father to a less crowded area, but his dad wouldn't move. "I will, if you just talk *less loudly*," he murmured as two girls slightly older than Fort stared at them, whispering. Fantastic.

"Um, I'm pretty sure as an adult, I can talk as loudly as I want," his father said. "But stop pushing us off topic, Fort. This is your future we're talking about! You're going to be a great man someday, and I for one can't wait to take pictures in front of your statue as children gaze up at it adoringly!" He waved at the two girls. "See? We've already got two volunteers!"

The girls both broke into wide smiles, and Fort felt his face burn with the heat of a volcano. "I'm sorry about this," he told them. "He thinks it's funny to embarrass me wherever he can."

"It's not *not* funny," one of the girls said.

"Intelligent youths around here!" his father shouted in response. "Listen to them, Fort. I hear that children are our future."

"*I'm* your future," Fort hissed at him. "Because once you're old, I get to decide which nursing home to put you in."

"Low blow, young man," his dad said, then pointed at Lincoln. "Do you think our beloved sixteenth president would have spoken to his father that way? And he's your personal hero!" He leaned closer to the girls conspiratorially. "When my boy here was in diapers, he'd stroll around in a top hat and make us all call him Fort Lincoln."

One of the girls snorted, while the other turned away to hide her laughter. Fort wondered how easy it'd be to spontaneously combust. "He's making that up," he told the girls, his face getting even hotter. "And we really need to be going."

"Oh, we have plenty of time," his father said, taking out his phone. "Besides, I think I have pictures of that in here. Girls, do you want to see?"

"I'm just getting really tired," Fort said, yanking his father by his arm toward the steps of the memorial. "Maybe we should head back to the hotel?"

"Nonsense!" Fort's father shouted. "Why, we haven't seen Einstein yet. Did you know there's a statue of Einstein right off the National Mall, Fort? And the Gettysburg Address!" He pointed at the speech carved into the wall of the Lincoln

Memorial to the left of the president. "Look at this. Two hundred and seventy-two words. Short and to the point!"

A slight tremble shook the memorial, like a heavy truck was driving by. Fort looked around nervously, but the tremor only lasted a few seconds, and no one else really seemed bothered by it.

"I think President Lincoln is waking up," his father whispered to him with a grin. "Did you know a second man gave a *two-hour* speech before Lincoln at Gettysburg?" He handed Fort a brochure with the Gettysburg Address written out in multiple languages. "I don't see that speech carved in marble, do you? If that's not proof that shorter is better, I don't—"

A second tremor hit, this one more violent. Several people shouted in surprise around the memorial, and Fort almost lost his balance, barely avoiding dropping to his knees on the marble. He looked up at his father in alarm. Was this an earthquake? What was happening?

His father reached over to steady Fort as the trembling stopped again. "Ladies, maybe you should go find your parents," he said to the two girls they'd been talking to, then turned to Fort. "Are you okay, kiddo?"

"Totally fine," Fort said, pretending his heart wasn't still racing. "It was nothing."

"That's the spirit," his father said, though he looked a bit shaken too. "But maybe we *should* head back to the hotel and grab some dinner. Einstein can wait. After all, time is his relative, I think. Probably a cousin."

Fort couldn't even bring himself to roll his eyes. Instead, he shoved the Gettysburg Address brochure in his pocket, and started to make his way through the now-unsettled crowd toward the stairs. As he reached the top of the steps, something strange caught his eye in the distance.

The Lincoln Memorial was surrounded by a circle of roadway, with the Reflecting Pool stretching out from the memorial to the Washington Monument almost a mile away.

But even from that distance, Fort could see lines of people quickly leaving the monument in every direction.

That wasn't a great sign. But the strangest thing about it was that as far as Fort could tell from this distance, all the tourists were running from the monument in single-file lines, each person moving at the exact same speed.

"Dad, do you see that?" Fort asked, turning around just as a third tremor struck, this time much worse than the last two. The stone of the memorial leaped straight up, throwing Fort a foot in the air. He landed hard as the stone cracked beneath him in a jagged lightning shape all the way down the steps.

"Out!" Fort's father shouted, pushing the girls toward the exit before grabbing Fort's hand and yanking him down the stairs.

They made it down to the street circling the memorial, with horrifying noises coming from behind them. The shaking grew more intense, and now people by the Reflecting Pool were running off, again in single file, one behind the other, not even looking as they crossed the street. Fortunately the cars had all stopped and the passengers had exited their vehicles, merging smoothly into the lines of fleeing tourists.

As odd as all of that was, even stranger was that no one was screaming in fear, yelling for a friend, or even saying a word. Instead, they were all deathly quiet, moving in unison like some sort of flash mob they'd been choreographing for months. The sheer silence of those fleeing sent a chill down Fort's spine.

A horrible new cracking noise erupted across the Reflecting Pool, like rock scraping against rock, and Fort's father shouted something, but the grinding stone overpowered his words. Fort turned to find people near him pointing at the Washington Monument, and *they* were all screaming. That at least felt more normal to Fort than the eerie silence closer to the monument and Reflecting Pool.

"Look out!" someone yelled as a car came speeding around the circle, right toward a large group of tourists. One of the two girls from above had just stepped in the path of the car, but the other yanked her out of its way as the car roared past.

"Off the road!" his father shouted, and pushed both Fort and the girls onto the lawn to the side of the crumbling Lincoln Memorial. "We have to get out of here!"

"My mom's still in there!" one of the girls shouted. "I need to go find her!"

"I'm coming—" the other girl started to say, then abruptly stopped, turned, and ran off toward the side streets.

"Megan?" the first girl called after her. "Where are you going?!"

Fort's father looked back up into the Lincoln Memorial, then down at Fort. "Wait here," he said. "Don't move until I get back! I'm going to go find their mother."

His father took the cracked steps two by two, pushing up against the crowd like he was swimming up a waterfall. Fort waited for a moment, then ran after him, followed by the remaining girl.

"Look!" someone shouted behind him.

"It *can't* be real," someone else said, filming with his phone.

Fort threw a look over his shoulder for a moment, then froze in place, halfway up the steps.

Next to the Washington Monument, something was pushing up out of the ground.

Something that looked like . . . claws.

Claws that were ten feet tall.

- TWO -

"WHAT IS *THAT*?!" THE GIRL NEXT TO Fort shouted, her voice cracking with terror.

Fort couldn't respond, could barely breathe. This wasn't happening. This type of thing only happened in movies, not in real life. Definitely not in the middle of Washington, D.C.

Enormous black-scaled fingers pushed up through the ground, sending grass, rock, and dirt flying in every direction. A muffled roar sounded from somewhere beneath them, and Fort felt it even through the ground shaking.

"You get him, I'll grab her!" Fort heard his father shout from somewhere in the memorial, but Fort couldn't move. Fear pulsated through his body with every racing heartbeat, freezing his feet to the marble steps like he'd been sculpted there.

TV helicopters flew overhead toward the monument, only

to suddenly reverse course as they approached, flying back over the city. Sirens played in the distance too, but somehow never made it any closer. And now the crowds on the monument steps below Fort began to run off in silent waves, as if a command to escape was passing up through them one at a time. But even with the insanely ordered evacuation, the shaking ground made it hard to move, let alone run, and many of them lost their footing as they escaped.

"This can't be *real*!" the girl next to Fort said as one of the clawed hands reached up to the Washington Monument and grabbed it with its hundred-foot-long fingers. The obelisk began to tilt, then topple toward the ground.

When it hit, the ground jumped beneath Fort's feet, and he found himself flying in the air, only to slam into the steps a few feet up.

"Lauren, where is Megan?!" a woman shouted from above him. Fort looked up to find the girls' mother carrying an old man, one Fort had seen earlier in an electric scooter. "Where did she go?"

Lauren started to answer, only to go silent as her eyes glazed over. Without another word, she turned around and ran down the steps, away from her mother.

"Lauren!" the woman shouted, stumbling against the trembling ground.

"Dad?" Fort shouted up.

"Fort, get out of here!" his father shouted from somewhere inside. "I'll be right behind you!"

Fort looked back at the devastation across the National Mall, then turned back toward the memorial and forced his feet to move up the stairs, one after the other. *Don't look at it,* he thought, gritting his teeth to fight through the fear. *You can do this. Dad needs your help!*

He took a step, then another, fighting to keep his balance while trying not to think about the horrific creature emerging from the ground behind him. His father *needed* him, and there was no way he was going to let him down. He had to—

RUN.

The thought hit his mind like a hammer, and Fort instantly straightened up, his mind blank, then turned and ran down the stairs. In the distance, he could see the remnants of the Washington Monument, but that didn't matter. Nothing seemed to mean anything beyond leaving in an orderly fashion.

RUN.

He hit the bottom of the steps and ran toward the line of people escaping—

"Fort!" his father shouted, and somehow, it cut through the fog in Fort's head. He slowed to a stop, then froze in place, one foot hanging in midair.

RUN!

The power of the command crashed over him like an ocean wave, drowning out all his other thoughts, and he started jogging, merging in line with the other runners. But as he reached the side of the Lincoln Memorial, he slowed again, then stopped, shaking his head.

What was he doing? His father was still up there!

A young woman plowed into him from behind, knocking him off his feet. She stumbled a bit, then continued running like nothing had happened. Fort stared after her for a moment in confusion, then looked back up the stairs to find his father carrying an older woman who'd been with the man on the scooter.

Fort pushed himself up and made his way back to the steps. "Dad!" he shouted. "Are you okay? I can help!"

"No, just go!" his father shouted, waving with one hand as he slowly tried to maneuver down the shaking stairs.

Fort ignored him and started crawling up the steps on all fours. As he reached the halfway point, though, the marble beneath him exploded, throwing him off into the grass to the side of the memorial. For a moment, everything went blurry and he couldn't breathe, the air knocked right out of his lungs.

And then two ten-foot tall claws pushed up through the steps where Fort had been standing, and a roar shook the ground, a sound so powerful Fort could feel it in his chest.

A noise like torrents of rushing water thundered behind him, and he turned to find a nightmare rising from the middle of the Reflecting Pool, a giant black-scaled head covered in horns like some sort of crown. The water drained down into the hole it created, and the creature roared again, revealing what looked like row upon row of massive razor-sharp teeth. Its red glowing eyes stared down in fury, and the sheer impossibility and terror of it froze Fort in place. He couldn't even think, let alone comprehend what he was looking at.

More helicopters flew in, this time painted black, and these actually made it close to the creature. A missile rocketed out of one, slamming into its head, but the monster didn't even seem to notice.

"Fort!" his father yelled from above. Fort looked up to find his father on his knees on the steps just below the creature's fingers. The roof was crumbling down all around him, sending huge chunks of marble crashing into the steps.

"Dad!" Fort shouted, and tried to get to his feet, but the shaking was too intense.

The creature's hand pushed the rest of the way out of the stairs, closing around his father and the woman he'd been carrying. Fort's heart stopped as he watched his father disappear behind those scaly fingers.

But then the old woman came tumbling out from between the creature's fingers, crashing to the grass next to Fort, with his father pushing through right after her.

"DAD!" Fort shouted as the creature roared behind him. Something else hissed out of the helicopter and exploded against the creature, but it didn't matter, nothing mattered but his father getting free. He was almost there, half his body had already made it out of the creature's grasp—

But then the hand started pulling back below ground.

"Fort!" his father shouted. The creature's hand curled around him, rupturing the remains of the memorial as it descended back into the ground. "FORT—"

The creature's massive hand disappeared within the earth, and his father went silent.

"NO!" Fort shrieked, and he crawled toward the wreckage, trying to make his way to the hole his father had been pulled into.

NO. LEAVE NOW. *RUN.*

"I won't!" he shouted, not sure who he was talking to, but determined to find his father. "Dad! Can you hear me? Dad!"

He clambered up over the jagged stones, half climbing, half pulling himself toward the hole. A wave of heat swept out of the crack, almost too hot to bear, but Fort pushed himself onward and stared down into the abyss.

"DAD!" he shouted again. . . .

And then something took over, and Fort lost control of his body.

His hands pushed him away from the hole, and his feet climbed him down the rocks. Inside his mind, Fort watched his actions helplessly, almost from a distance, like he was staring down at himself from the wrong end of a telescope.

Inwardly, he screamed over and over, but no sound escaped his lips as his body continued on, jogging him away from danger and into a line with the rest of the silent, fleeing tourists.

NO! he shouted into the void, pushing back with all his strength against whatever force was taking him from his father. He fought and struggled and resisted, his efforts growing in intensity until pain filled his mind and he could barely think, the image of the creature taking his father propelling him to keep battling to free himself, to regain control over his mind, to make it *LET GO*—

And then, abruptly, his body was his own again. From an impossibly long distance, he heard a scream, and it echoed through his brain. It sounded like a girl's voice, and she was in pain, but that didn't matter, nothing mattered except that he was free and could go back to his father. . . .

But a wave of pain washed over Fort, drowning his mind in agony, and everything went dark as he collapsed to the ground, silent joggers flowing around him from every side.

- THREE -

THE ENORMOUS SCALED CREATURE EXPLODED out of a circle of green fire, and Fort couldn't move, couldn't even speak, he was so terrified. Someone, somewhere near him, began to speak in a low, ugly voice, saying things he couldn't understand. Finally he screamed, but the voice didn't sound like his. It was just like the one in his mind, the girl that he'd heard yell in pain—

And then Fort woke up, and this time he recognized his own terrified shouts. Something grabbed him, and he screamed even louder, trying to break free of whatever had taken over his body.

"It's okay!" someone said, and strong hands grabbed his shoulders and squeezed, trying to hold him down. "Quiet now. You're safe!"

Fort fought back for a moment, still screaming, only to

slowly realize that he wasn't on the National Mall anymore. Instead, he was surrounded by various medical machines and screens beeping and glowing around the sterile white room. A middle-aged nurse stood over him, still holding his shoulders and looking concerned.

"I . . . where am I?" he asked, his head feeling like it was full of cotton. "Where's my *dad*?"

"You're at George Washington University Hospital," the woman said. She let go of him and moved to his side. "You were brought here when someone found you passed out over by the Einstein statue. You're lucky to have escaped without a scratch."

"Where's my *father*?" Fort asked, his panic growing. Images began filling his head, a woman carrying an older man down crumbling stairs, his father holding an older woman, a monstrous hand closing around him. . . .

"We'll find him," the nurse said. "Everything's chaos right now, and no one knows anything, but we'll find him. I'm sure he made it out okay."

Fort slowly shook his head, his mouth dropping open. "No," he whispered. "He didn't."

The nurse frowned and sat down on the bed. "Can you

give me your name, and his? He's probably somewhere else in the hospital right now. We'll get you two back together in no time."

In his mind, Fort saw his father being pulled down into the earth before something took him away, a voice in his head that forced him to run. But *had* there been a voice? A girl, screaming in his head? Or had he just heard someone shouting on the street, and he'd just run away in fear, leaving his father to . . . to be taken? He felt his eyes grow wet, and he had to dig his fingernails into his palms to keep from sobbing. "Fort," he whispered so quietly the nurse had to lean in. "Forsythe Fitzgerald."

"That's a bit unusual," the nurse said, smiling gently at him. "Is it a family name?"

Fort nodded. "It was my . . . my grandfather's, my mother's father. He's not alive anymore."

"Was your mother there too, on the Mall?" the nurse asked.

Fort shook his head again but didn't say anything. The nurse waited for a moment, then stood back up. "And what's your father's name? I'll go see if I can't track him down."

The tears flowed down Fort's face freely now. "John," he said slowly. "J.D., sometimes."

"John or J.D. Fitzgerald," the nurse repeated, jotting it down on a clipboard. "Got it. Now you get some rest, Forsythe. Nothing bad will happen to you here. Whatever it was that happened down at the Mall, it's over now. Everything's going to be okay."

The nurse smiled once more as she left. But the smile was a lie, just like everything else. Whatever had happened, nothing was going to be okay. Not anymore.

For a while, Fort found himself alone, and every so often he would drift into sleep, only to wake up screaming from the memory of the creature, or his father yelling his name. After one of these outbursts, two police officers passing by his room glanced in to make sure he was okay, then sat down outside.

"How's the National Security Agency building doing?" one of them said.

"One side of it is completely gone," the other said. "Another of those creatures came up right out of the ground."

"What *are* those things? It's like something out of Godzilla."

"Whatever they are, this was an *attack*. The National Mall and the NSA at the exact same time? This had to be planned."

"You think those *monsters* planned this? They can think for themselves?"

"I don't know. But what are the odds that they just happened to pick those two places in particular? Out of the whole country?"

"Are you kidding? What are the odds that they even *exist*?"

"I'm just saying, someone was making a point. I don't know who, or how they did it, but we better find out soon. I was down there, at the Mall. The military was using rocket launchers against that thing, and the creature didn't even flinch."

"Yes it did. It took off, went back into the ground."

"Not because of anything we did," the second officer said. "It started coming out right in the middle of the Reflecting Pool, only it stopped and retreated all of a sudden. Something was *controlling* that one, same as the one at the NSA."

"If that's true, we're in *huge* trouble."

"Shh," the nurse said, stepping back into Fort's room. "There's a child in here. Go talk somewhere else."

The two officers nodded, then stood up and walked away, though Fort could hear them continuing their conversation a little way down the hall. The nurse gently closed the door behind her, cutting off all outside noise, then approached the bed, looking like she dreaded sharing whatever she had come to say.

"I haven't located your father yet." She sat down on the side of the bed and held Fort's hand. "But it's only a matter of time, I'm sure. I hate to ask, but do you remember where you saw him last? Do you . . . do you know what happened to him?"

Fort bit his lip, his eyes filling with tears as he looked away.

The nurse paused, then nodded. "I see. Do you have a way to get in touch with your mother?"

Fort shook his head. "She . . . she died years ago. When I was born."

The nurse swallowed hard. "Oh, Forsythe, I'm so sorry. What about . . . do you have aunts or uncles, or someone—"

"It *took* him," Fort whispered. "It took him, down into the ground with it. When it left, like the policemen said. It took my father with it." The tears rolled down his face, but he didn't care. He just wanted to let the words out, to let the images free from his head so he didn't have to keep seeing them. "I tried to save him, to follow." The memory of the voice returned, and he grabbed ahold of it like he was drowning and it was a life preserver. "But something . . . something made me leave. I couldn't help myself. It was like I wasn't in control, couldn't even move my own legs. I . . . I could watch, but couldn't *do* anything!"

"You were afraid," the nurse said quietly, squeezing his hand. "Terrified, with good reason. Everyone was, including people much older than you. I'm not surprised you ran. I would have run too. Your father would have *wanted* you to."

"No!" Fort said, his voice getting louder. "I didn't just run. Everyone else did, but I stopped. I was trying to help. I couldn't let him . . . I couldn't just leave him there. But something was in my head and it *made* me leave! It was there, I *know* it was!"

But even as he heard himself, he had to wonder if there really *was* a voice. With everything that had happened, how did he know it wasn't just fear making him get away from the creature? What if he'd just made the voice up to justify leaving his father?

The tears wouldn't stop now, but he fell back against the bed, not sure what to even think anymore. The nurse sighed, then stood up and began fiddling with a needle and some tubes leading into Fort's arm. "I understand, Forsythe. We all have that voice in our head telling us what to do. But you can't blame yourself. You did the exact right thing, getting away. For now, just sleep, and we'll find out what happened to your father in the meantime."

"You *won't* find him," Fort said as the room suddenly began to get fuzzy. "He's gone . . . down into the earth . . . with the monster. . . ."

"Don't you worry about that creature, whatever it was," the nurse said from what seemed like miles away. "There are people who will keep us safe. They'll protect us from the bad things. You'll see."

And then the room went dark, but even as he passed out, Fort knew she was lying.

- FOUR -

"HE'S BEEN HOME FROM THE HOSPITAL for almost six months now," Fort's aunt Cora said, on the phone in the kitchen. "I can barely get him to eat. And now he's been suspended from school for *fighting*, of all things! The other boy made some comment about Washington, pretended to be that . . . that *creature*, and Fort just went berserk. And then after, he said he barely even remembered doing it."

Fort ran his fingers over the brochure of the Gettysburg Address in various languages, the last thing his father had given him, then turned back to stare at the muted television in front of him, showing scenes of the destruction from the attacks six months ago.

First, it panned over the headquarters of the National Security Agency in Fort Meade, Maryland, a black-windowed office building that was now half rubble. One of the creatures apparently had ripped its way straight up through the middle of the building before it disappeared back into the ground. The entire facility was now abandoned, with armed guards surrounding it. A military helicopter even intercepted the press copter, forcing it away from the area.

Then the news turned to D.C., where black domes covered the Lincoln Memorial and what was left of the National Mall, with soldiers guarding the perimeter. Beneath those domes was a massive hole that went, well, somewhere. The government wasn't saying where, or how deep it was either.

But somewhere down there, the creature had taken Fort's father.

"I don't know what to do, Lin," his aunt had continued. "I really don't. I don't think he even sleeps more than an hour or two at a time."

That was true. Every time Fort closed his eyes, he saw the creature emerging from its green circle of fire, coming straight for him while someone shouted in a low, guttural voice in some language he didn't recognize. Whenever Fort tried to scream, it wasn't even his voice. It was a girl's voice, the same one every time.

And then there were the reminders. Everything he saw made him think of his father. Several times a day, Fort found himself imagining his father joking about something, or paying him ridiculous compliments for no reason. Each time it happened, the pain and grief threatened to drown him, and—

A pinch in his hand distracted him, and he looked down to find he'd clenched his fist around the brochure from the Lincoln Memorial, crumpling it. When had he done that? He carefully smoothed it out, then put it down and flipped channels over and over, not caring where he landed.

"There's this boarding school that offered to take him," his aunt said, and Fort glanced in the direction of the kitchen. "The headmaster heard about how my brother-in-law . . . everything that happened. Said he had experience dealing with grief and trauma, so maybe he could help Fort. It sounds almost like some kind of military academy, though. And I don't know if I can just send him away. I'm the only family he has now!"

She was thinking about sending him away? That made sense. Fort nodded to himself, digging his nails down harder. After all, it was at least partly his fault that she had to take care of him to begin with. Cora was his mother's much younger sister and had just graduated college. She'd been broke ever since, paying off her college while working as a waitress in spite of having a degree in computer science. His father's life insurance had provided some money, but not enough, especially when Cora had to skip work to pick up Fort from school after his fight.

First she'd lost her sister, Fort's mother, and now he'd been thrown on her without any warning. And all because he'd run instead of helping his father carry the old woman down, get him off the stairs before—

Fort squeezed his eyes closed and gritted his teeth, trying to force the memories out of his head. Not that it would change anything. His aunt would still have Fort to take care of, something she'd never asked for. All he was doing was making her life harder, just by being there.

Fort turned back to the television to find he'd stopped on a press conference in the White House. Some man in a uniform with a massive number of medals and stripes was speaking, introducing the man next to him, another soldier. Fort frowned and turned the volume on.

"—name is Colonel Charles," the second man said, smiling grimly. "As General Matheson mentioned, I'll be heading up the new joint agency based around these threats. The Thaumaturgic

Defense Agency, or TDA, has already developed specialized deterrents against future attacks, based on the lack of response to traditional weaponry we witnessed in Washington."

Specialized deterrents? What did that mean? What could they possibly do to stop those things?

"Do we know where those creatures came from, and what they wanted?" a reporter shouted.

Colonel Charles stared down at the podium for a moment. "The origin of the monsters is still unknown. Certainly they're nothing we'd seen previously. But leads have suggested a motivating factor behind the attacks. There seems to have been some outside force either controlling them fully, or setting them upon us. We have extensive investigations happening now, but you'll forgive me if I can't provide further information at this time. As soon as it's appropriate, I'll share everything I can."

"Was this a terrorist group, or the actions of another country?" a different reporter asked.

"Will there be more attacks?" another shouted.

Colonel Charles frowned. "The people of the United States should sleep soundly. We have no indication of any further attacks and are working day and night to prevent them from happening again."

"No indication? But you didn't know about the first one, right?" the same reporter asked.

"What do you mean, unknown origin?" yelled a second. "Where could they have come from?"

"What kind of deterrents are you using? How do you know they'll be of any greater use against the creatures if you don't even know what they are?"

"I'm afraid that's all the time I have," Colonel Charles said. "I'll update with further information as the situation warrants."

He walked off to more reporters shouting out questions, and Fort muted the television again, not sure why he'd even bothered.

Six months later, and they still wouldn't say who'd done it, or why. Not to mention that all anyone could think about was if and when another attack was coming. Schools had started holding earthquake drills in case one of the creatures tunneled up nearby. The internet was filled with rumors and conspiracy theories about what the creatures were, where they'd come from, and why they'd attacked. But all anyone knew for sure was that there'd been no warning the first time, so they couldn't expect any the next time.

"Maybe, but you can't live in fear, Fort," his father would

have said. "Because it's not a place. Now *Cape* Fear, that's a real region of North Carolina, so *there*, you can live."

"You shouldn't watch that," his aunt said from the doorway, making Fort jump, thankfully pulling him out of his daydream.

"Are you okay?" she asked. "I know that anniversaries, like six months . . ." She trailed off.

Fort nodded at her, just to show he heard. He'd quickly learned that when he didn't respond, she just asked more questions. He clicked off the TV and slumped back against the couch, closing his eyes. Maybe she'd take that as a hint and leave him alone.

At least then he wouldn't be dragging her down too.

"I'm going to order us pizza for dinner, okay?" she said, and he felt the couch shift as she sat down next to him. "Whatever you want. Let's go nuts. I'm talking, like, *three* toppings."

He shrugged, not opening his eyes. Food didn't taste like anything anymore, so it didn't really matter what she ordered.

"And after that, there's someone I want you to talk to, okay?" she said. "He's . . . well, he's a doctor, but not like that therapist you didn't like. He runs a boarding school, and he says he can help you. He heard about you from, you know, the news, and reached out to me. He said his school might be a good fit."

Fort opened his eyes and gave her another shrug, but this time forced the barest hint of a smile, not wanting her to feel bad about sending him away. At least then she could get on with her life.

She hugged him gently and put her head on his. "I miss them too, *so much*. Your dad and your mom. I'm so sorry you didn't have more time with your dad, or get to meet your mom. They were amazing people."

No. Fort pulled away, realizing he might be making her feel bad, but he just couldn't . . . every time she brought up . . . *no*. He couldn't listen to this, not now. He grabbed the Gettysburg Address brochure and stood up, heading for the kitchen. "I'm going to get a soda. Do you want anything?"

She stared at him sadly. "No, I'm okay."

He nodded and left, passing right through the kitchen to Cora's bedroom, where he turned on her little TV. More news, but it was covering the protests outside the U.S. Capitol, where thousands of people had gathered to demand military action on whichever country had caused the attacks. Assuming anyone even knew. Several of the signs had suggestions, and they only got more angry and bitter from there.

He flipped through the channels, desperate to keep his mind occupied so he didn't have to remember, until he landed on some cartoons, something he wouldn't have to think about. Minutes passed slowly, but eventually he heard Cora call for the pizza, and later, answer the door for the delivery. His aunt had ordered pepperoni, which was fine, since she liked that, and he barely ate more than a slice these days anyway.

"Fort, if you decide you don't want to go to this boarding school, that's okay," his aunt said as she put plates down on the table for dinner. "It's your choice. If you'd rather stay here with me, we'll figure things out. Your dad left enough money for us to maybe find another school around here. Or maybe we can try a new therapist?"

Fort didn't respond. The previous therapist hadn't gotten more than his name out of him, which he felt bad about. But the last thing in the world he was going to talk about was what happened in D.C., especially with a stranger.

There was silence while they both ate, so Fort tried to keep it going by chewing through his slice as slowly as possible. It made her even sadder when he didn't eat anything, so he always forced himself to eat at least a little. It also helped because it meant she wouldn't try to ask him any questions.

The doorbell rang as Cora was putting the rest of the pizza into the refrigerator. She gave Fort a nervous look, then left to go open the front door. From the other room, he heard the deep voice of a man introducing himself, and then, oddly, a girl's voice as well. They moved into the kitchen, and Fort looked up, curiosity fighting its way through the haze in his brain.

A slightly pudgy man around his dad's age came through the doorway and smiled at Fort, who forced a smile back. The man wore a black suit and was holding a black briefcase handcuffed to his wrist, which didn't seem exactly normal for a schoolteacher, but maybe boarding schools were different.

Behind him, an African American girl with short curly hair wearing a green army uniform looked around the kitchen. Her eyes fell on Fort, and she grinned widely, then waved.

"Fort, this is Dr. Oppenheimer," Aunt Cora said, and the doctor stuck out his hand for Fort to shake, which he did. "He's here to talk to you about that school I mentioned."

"That's right," Dr. Oppenheimer said. "And this is Rachel." He gestured toward the still-smiling girl. "She volunteered to give you a student's perspective of what it's like at my school. I've found that can be very valuable for prospective students." He glanced at Rachel, who nodded excitedly.

"Ma'am, can I ask a favor before we start?" Rachel said, dancing from foot to foot. "Would you mind if I used the bathroom? It's been a long trip."

Fort's aunt blushed. "Of course! Let me show you where it is. And you don't have to call me ma'am."

Rachel waved good-bye to Fort as his aunt led her away. Dr. Oppenheimer placed his briefcase on the table and thumbed the locks open. Feeling curious for the first time in months, Fort moved to look inside, but he was disappointed to find a pack of papers filling it.

"You can call me Dr. Opps, by the way," Dr. Oppenheimer said, not seeming to care that Fort was looking. "All the children do."

"Okay," Fort said as the doctor removed the stack of papers from his briefcase, then felt around the bottom. Something clicked, and Dr. Opps lifted the bottom of the briefcase out, then reached back in and pulled out a long silver chain with some sort of round metal ball at the end.

"Silver works better than any other metal at this," he said to Fort as he placed the chain around his own neck. "We still don't know why."

Fort stared at him in confusion. "Better at what?"

"Can I get you anything, Dr. Oppenheimer?" his aunt said, coming back in, then stopping as she saw the empty briefcase and the silver medallion. "Um, *what* is—"

Dr. Opps touched her arm, and Cora instantly collapsed to the ground, like a puppet whose strings had been cut.

"Now," the man said, sitting down at the table as Fort leaped to his feet in shock. "Let's talk about the Oppenheimer School."

- FIVE -

THE SIGHT OF HIS AUNT COLLAPSING to the floor shocked Fort for a moment. But then that moment passed and rage filled his mind, memories of D.C. flashing in and out as he launched himself at the man from the school.

"Don't you touch her!" he shouted, drawing back his arm to punch Dr. Opps. Before he could strike, though, something burning hot slammed into his side, sending him crashing across the room into the opposite wall.

"Rachel, no!" Dr. Opps yelled, stepping out over Fort, hands raised in the air. "Are you okay, Forsythe?"

Fort groaned, rubbing his head, then quickly moved his hands around to feel where he'd been hit, finding his shirt blackened and charred by whatever it was that had struck him. "What . . . what is *happening*?" he said.

Dr. Opps smiled sadly and extended a hand to help him up. "I'm sorry about your aunt. I should have warned you. But we can't have her listening to our conversation. There are things she isn't authorized to hear."

Fort shook his head, not sure *he* was hearing right. "You . . . knocked her out because . . . you're going to tell me top-secret things?"

"I actually encouraged her brain to sleep," Dr. Opps said, helping Fort back into his seat. "Rachel, go find him another shirt, would you? Preferably the same color as this one."

Rachel glared at Fort. "Touch him again, and I burn you to *ash*," she said, then turned and stalked out of the room.

Dr. Opps half smiled. "One of our best students."

Fort stared at him. "What . . . what did she do to me?"

"Let's start a bit further back, shall we?" Dr. Opps said, and reached across the table for Fort's hand. Fort yanked it out of reach immediately, but Dr. Opps just smiled at Fort's nervousness. "No need to be scared. It's much faster to do things at the speed of thought."

"What are you talking about?" Fort said, his hands safely beneath the table.

Dr. Opps held up the ball at the end of the silver chain.

"Our students made it for just this purpose. Wearing it grants me the power to speak to you mind-to-mind." He shrugged. "It's really much easier to explain things by way of memories, honestly."

Fort glanced down at his aunt, who was now gently snoring on the floor. Dr. Opps hadn't lied about putting her to sleep, apparently. But even seeing that, Fort couldn't believe he could hear Dr. Opps's thoughts or see an actual memory. It didn't seem possible.

Then again, neither did the attack in D.C.

He slowly brought his hand up to the table and laid it down palm-up. "You better not be lying."

"Oh, I never lie," Dr. Opps said, reaching for Fort's hand. "There's no need. If I didn't want you knowing something, I'd just erase your memories."

Fort's eyes widened, and he started to pull away, but Dr. Opps clamped his hand down on Fort's, and the kitchen immediately disappeared, replaced by the interior of a car, one stopped above what looked to be an archaeological dig site. Not only that, but the sun was high in the sky, when a moment ago it had been early evening.

"What did you do?" Fort shouted, but no sound emerged

from his mouth, and he realized he couldn't move. Instead, he found himself staring at the steering wheel of the car, where shaking hands held it tightly. But they weren't *his* hands. And in his mind, Fort could hear someone else's thoughts, someone trying to stop the shaking of his hands, trying to appear in control.

Dr. Opps. This was his memory, and Fort was somehow in his mind, seeing everything the doctor had seen and even hearing his inner thoughts!

The man turned to look at himself in the rearview mirror, and inside, Fort almost shouted again in surprise. A man in sunglasses stared back at him, a much younger Dr. Opps, at least by a decade. Fort watched in the mirror as Dr. Opps straightened his hair before opening the car door.

As the doctor stepped out of the car, Fort's new height—the doctor was much taller than him—made the world seem a bit off. As he reoriented himself, he heard Dr. Opps think that he should try to appear unconcerned when he reached the site, just like the government agents he'd seen in movies. But since his hands wouldn't stop shaking, he shoved them in his pockets, where at least they wouldn't be so obvious.

Fort sighed. Between that and the sunglasses, hopefully no one here in Acadia National Park would be able to tell how little sleep he'd gotten, not since early that morning when the news had started coming in from around the globe. . . .

Wait, no. Fort pulled back a bit, realizing he'd been getting lost between Dr. Opps's thoughts and his own. It was *Dr. Opps* who hadn't gotten sleep, after some news from that morning, not Fort. This was so weird, living out someone else's memories and hearing their thoughts!

But maybe he should just embrace it and follow along? It wasn't really that much different than watching a movie . . . a *very* 3-D movie. One where he could also hear the person's thoughts. And feel what they felt. And know what they knew.

Okay, it was nothing like a movie. But still, he didn't want to miss anything, so Fort settled in to watch.

Walking purposefully down the path to the dig site, Dr. Opps tried to keep his pace slow and orderly, but the incline of the path forced him to jog a bit. He frowned, hoping he didn't look too ridiculous in his black suit, now covered in a layer of dust and who knew what else.

"Agent Oppenheimer?" said a woman from below in a green park ranger outfit. She moved up to meet him. "I'm Dr. Lang, National Park Service. Oppenheimer . . . are you by any chance—"

"No relation," Dr. Opps said, showing the ranger his badge. "So, you reported something odd here today?"

Dr. Lang raised her eyebrows. "Odd doesn't begin to cover it. We've found at least three things that genuinely shouldn't be possible. But I didn't think they'd send someone from the National Security Agency?"

Dr. Opps shrugged, trying to downplay the seriousness. "Well, I'm a new agent and I studied ancient languages in college. They probably just wanted an outside opinion."

She frowned at that, clearly seeing through his obvious lie, but gestured Dr. Opps to proceed toward the dig site. She led the way toward an enormous set of five tarps, each at least ten feet long, with four or five archaeologists standing around, waiting for them. The wind blew at the tarps, kicking dirt up and blasting Dr. Opps (and Fort) in the face.

"Sorry about the wind," Dr. Lang said, covering her face with her arms. "It picked up down here just a little bit ago. That's why we covered the find. Didn't want it to get damaged."

Based on what he'd heard from the other sites, Dr. Opps wasn't sure the thing could be damaged. But he wasn't about to share that.

Dr. Lang directed the archaeologists closest to the tarps to raise the first one. "We didn't have any active digs in the area," Lang shouted over the wind as they untied the tarp. "Two students actually discovered the bones while hiking. We think a mudslide uncovered the edges."

Dr. Opps nodded, hoping that two students really had just randomly happened upon this place. But considering the timing, he doubted it.

The archaeologists raised the tarp high, both uncovering the find and giving them a bit of protection from the wind. Lang gestured for Dr. Opps to move in closer, so he carefully picked his way in, stepping over the rope that encircled the site.

"So, Mr. NSA, what's that look like to you?" Lang asked from behind him.

Dr. Opps stared at the bones embedded in the dirt, and for a moment, felt hope for the first time since the calls had begun coming in that morning. "Like some kind of dinosaur, actually," he said.

"Which would be odd by itself, since there's never been a dinosaur fossil found in the park, let alone in all of Maine," Dr. Lang said. She pointed at what looked to be the leg bones of a huge reptile. "And while those do resemble the hind legs of a Theropoda, like a Tyrannosaur, that's not the case here. Because first, *these* bones are only a few thousand years old, not sixty-five million. Second . . ." She nodded at the other archaeologists, who lifted the next tarp.

Long, thin bones ran up from the back of the creature, then separated into extended fingers, like the wings of a bat. ". . . tyrannosaurs didn't have wings," Lang finished.

Dr. Opps's stomach sank into his shoes, and he almost dropped to his knees right there. A *fourth site.* What did this all mean? It couldn't be happening, it just wasn't possible.

"That's not even the weirdest part," Lang said as her colleagues lifted the third one.

"I know," Dr. Opps said quietly, not looking up from the wings. "There's a rider."

The ranger's eyes widened in surprise as the third tarp lifted to reveal a human skeleton seated around the creature's midsection as if it were riding it. "How could you *possibly* have known that?"

He nodded at the fourth tarp. "And I'm guessing there's something in the rider's hand?"

The archaeologists all stared at each other as the wind whipped by them. Finally, one of them coughed uncomfortably.

"This has to be fake, right?" Dr. Lang said.

A nervous laugh escaped Dr. Opps's lips, which he quickly covered with his own cough. "I'm going to need whatever it is the rider is holding."

The archaeologists paused in lifting up the fourth tarp, and Dr. Lang shook her head emphatically. "You can't remove anything from a dig site, Agent Oppenheimer!" she shouted, looking like she couldn't even believe he'd suggested it. "If this is real, it's something we'll need to catalog exactly as found. Winged reptiles that humans *rode*? We've never seen anything like this before. And only a few thousand years old! That's after the pyramids were built. This is *too important*—"

"This isn't the only site, Doctor!" Dr. Opps blurted out, gesturing around. "Do you have any idea what that human is holding? Because *we* don't. All we know is that there were three others exactly like this, all discovered *today* on completely unrelated digs. What do you think *that* means?"

Dr. Lang stepped back, a shocked look playing over her face. "This *has* to be some sort of prank, then. There's no way . . . we didn't even know about this site until a few weeks ago. We couldn't have—"

"Take off that tarp," Dr. Opps said, gesturing at the scientists. "Do it!"

The archaeologists scrambled to do just that, slowly revealing the rest of the rider's bones, moving up the body until two arms were exposed. Just past those arms, a strange reptilian skull, the head of the creature, reared back as if screaming.

Dr. Opps stepped through the winged creature's rib bones, not caring whether he disturbed the site. He picked his way closer to the rider and found the item: something a little over a foot square in the human's hand. Fort couldn't tell at first if the object had always been brown, or if it was just covered in dirt, but as he approached, he saw that there wasn't a speck of dust on it.

Another impossibility.

He bent down and stared at what looked like a leather-bound book in the rider's hand.

"We don't know what the words say," the nearest archaeologist said to him. "Some language we've never seen before. But it *must* have been placed there recently. This leather would have decomposed in fifty years under these conditions."

Dr. Opps nervously reached out a hand and gently touched his finger to the book. When he didn't get electrocuted or anything, he nodded and wrapped his hand around it.

"You can't touch it!" the scientist said, but Dr. Opps just looked up at him, and the man backed away.

Using his other hand, he pried the rider's finger bones off the book, then raised it up out of the dirt. As he did, the words on the cover in an alphabet he'd never seen before seemed to blur, then refocus, now completely readable.

The Magic of Destruction, and Its Many Uses.

Dr. Opps felt a chill sail down his spine.

Out of the four books of magic that had been uncovered that day around the world, this one might actually be the most dangerous—

And then the connection broke, and Fort found himself staring at Dr. Opps across the kitchen table at his aunt's house, thousands of miles away from Acadia National Park.

"So," Dr. Opps said casually. "See anything interesting?"

- SIX -

I WAS . . . I WAS IN YOUR MEMORY," FORT said, his mind still trying to come to grips with what had just happened. "That was you. I was in your *head*!"

Dr. Opps nodded. "That was around thirteen and a half years ago. On that day we discovered several . . . artifacts. The book you saw and three others were all unearthed on the exact same day around the world, Forsythe. None of the digs were aware of each other at first, but my agency put it together."

"You work at the National Security Agency?" Fort asked. "I thought you ran a school."

"The digs themselves were shocking," Dr. Opps continued, ignoring him. "But these books would become a thousand times more important. Not that we knew that at first."

"What's in the book?" Fort asked. "It said . . . magic. *The Magic of Destruction, and—*"

"The books contain knowledge," Dr. Opps said. "Knowledge long lost. But now that we've found that knowledge again, it allows us to do things like, well, show you my memories."

He took Fort's hand again, and the scene shifted to a circular room with descending benches made from stone curving around the room, surrounding a podium in the middle with two books on it. Rachel, the girl who'd arrived with Dr. Opps, was standing in the middle, reading from the same book Fort had seen in Acadia National Park.

Another memory. But this time Dr. Opps looked older and seemed confident, much less nervous for what was about to happen.

Rachel returned the book to the podium and closed her eyes. She raised her hands and formed a circle with her fingers, then mumbled something too quiet for Fort to hear.

Instantly, her hands began to glow, getting brighter and brighter until she held a blinding ball of light in the air between them. Her words grew louder, but even hearing them aloud, Fort couldn't understand them or repeat them. It was like they disappeared from his mind as soon as he registered them.

Rachel turned, energy crackling throughout the room.

Dr. Opps's hair began to rise on end as Rachel opened her eyes, now filled with the same energy that glowed between her hands. She pulled back, then launched the energy at the nearest wall, where it struck with a blinding flash that made Dr. Opps cover his eyes in pain.

It took a minute for his sight to return. When he was able to see, he found that the wall she'd hit was no longer there. In its place was a jagged hole easily six feet in diameter, the wall around it still sizzling with the same energy.

Rachel had been blown back against the other wall and was slowly picking herself up, a huge grin on her face.

"Did you *see* that?" she shouted, jumping up and down in excitement.

Dr. Opps stood, clapping his hands. "Well *done*, Rachel," he said. "Though we're going to have to get that wall fixed now."

Rachel blushed, but her smile didn't fade. "Just imagine this against one of those creatures that attacked D.C. I'll totally destroy it!"

Dr. Opps started to nod, but the memory of the monster in D.C. appeared in his head, and it was like someone had slapped Fort in the face. The image filled his mind, and he began to scream silently inside Dr. Opps's head, only to abruptly find himself back in the kitchen, screaming for real.

Dr. Opps raised a hand. "Calm down, Forsythe. You're perfectly safe."

He stopped yelling as Rachel walked back into the room with a new shirt, staring at him like he'd gone insane. "You're . . . you're going to fight those things?" Fort said to Dr. Opps, not sure whether he was afraid or excited at the idea. "With . . . with magic?"

"Well, *I* will," Rachel said.

"No, she won't," Dr. Opps said, giving her an annoyed look. "Not for several years, if ever. The books we found, Fort . . . they contained formulas. These formulas, when read out loud, unlock previously inaccessible powers within the human body. We think it's a significantly advanced form of quantum communication with the environment and other living things, but yes, the public would most likely see it as magic, if they found out. Many already think that's what the attacks were, some kind of magical creature."

Fort just stared at him. "You run a school to teach . . . magic?"

"No," Dr. Opps said. "I run a school to give our country the power to protect itself from any further attacks like the one that took your father. That's why I'm here, Forsythe. I want you to have a chance to make sure what happened to him never happens to anyone else."

Dr. Opps took his hand again, and this time Fort found himself standing in front of the devastated Lincoln Memorial as the creature attacked an empty National Mall.

"No!" he screamed, and bent over, trying not to throw up as the monster roared. He covered his eyes and shook his head over and over, just wanting it to go away. "No no no no no no no!"

"Forsythe, listen to me!" Dr. Opps shouted over the monster. "This isn't real. We're in your mind, in your imagination. You don't have to hide from the creature here. Give yourself the power that you saw Rachel use. Fight back against it! You can do it!"

Fort clenched his teeth, focusing on the wall that Rachel had destroyed with one ball of energy. If he could do that too . . .

He slowly stood up, though the ground shifted dangerously below him. He opened his eyes, and the clawed fingers emerged from the ground right in front of him. For a moment, he dry heaved, the fear just too great. But reminding himself that this wasn't real, he positioned his hands like he'd seen Rachel do and summoned a ball of energy.

The heat from the magic almost burned him, but that didn't matter. Instead, he just imagined it hotter and hotter, until it scalded his skin. Finally, screaming as loudly as he could, he launched the power at the nearest scaled finger.

The blast tore through the monster's entire hand, and it shrieked in agony. The noise reverberated in Fort's chest, and he felt a chill go through him, though for once, it wasn't from fear.

He could destroy those things. He could get justice for his father.

He could make them feel *pain*.

"That's it," Dr. Opps said, and the kitchen appeared once more. "That's the power I can give you, if you decide to serve your country at my school."

Fort's heart raced with excitement as he replayed the creature shrieking over and over in his mind. But even through the sense of satisfaction he felt, some part of Fort knew this wouldn't be how it'd happen. "You'd never send kids against monsters like that. Why would you teach us instead of adults how to do this?"

Dr. Opps sat back in his seat. "When *I* flip through the books, all I see are blank pages. The books are unreadable by anyone born before the day the books were found, Forsythe. There's a theory that along with the discovery of the books, some sort of power returned to the world on the same day. Whatever the reason, only children born from that day forward have been able to use the information within." He rubbed his forehead. "It took us almost a decade just to discover *that*. And we never even considered the need to teach the magic until the unfortunate attacks in D.C. and Maryland. I opened my school soon afterward."

He leaned forward and showed Fort the silver ball again. "But until our students are old enough to take to the field themselves, we've found a work-around. There are lessons within the books about infusing everyday objects with the power, just like this one. Imagine how safe our country would be if soldiers could use weapons as powerful as Rachel's magic. Or how much more humane warfare could become if we could drop a bomb that put everyone to sleep, like I did your aunt. The possibilities are staggering."

Fort frowned. "So you need us to make you magical weapons?"

"With enemies out there capable of attacks like the ones six months ago, we need all the help we can get," Dr. Opps said, then paused. "I will caution you, however. Whoever orchestrated the attacks might learn of the school and seek to stop us before we're able to protect ourselves. We believe that chance is remote, but the possibility of danger exists."

"Don't worry about that. You'll have me there to protect you," Rachel whispered to him.

"You think those creatures might attack the school?" Fort said, his excitement starting to tumble off a cliff.

"It would be a prime target," Dr. Opps said. "But the school's existence is known to only a few of the highest-ranking members of the military and one congressional committee. And even most of them aren't aware of its location. Beyond the secrecy, though, we have the best protection you could possibly ask for, not to mention that you'll be learning to create defenses yourself."

That was true. And even if the school might be more of a target, was anywhere really safe anymore? Fort nodded. "I understand."

"Then tell me, Forsythe," Dr. Opps said. "Would you be interested in joining my school?"

Fort stood up. He knew the answer but had one last question. "You said my aunt couldn't know about any of this. What happens if I say no?"

Dr. Opps smiled slightly and tapped the silver ball. "You won't remember anything after the pizza arrived tonight, and your aunt will never have heard of my school. As I said, the existence of the school has to remain secret, for the protection of my students."

Fort nodded, still imagining the pained screams of the creature. "I'm in."

- SEVEN -

SORRY ABOUT HITTING YOU WITH MY magic missile, New Kid," Rachel said as they sat on the curb outside the house, waiting for Dr. Opps and his aunt to go over some paperwork. "Dr. Opps said you might freak out a bit, and I wasn't going to take any chances."

"That's what it's called, a magic missile?" Fort asked.

She shrugged. "That's what *I* call it. Stole it from Dungeons and Dragons and, like, every other role-playing game. Destruction spells are all named after whoever invented them, supposedly, but I'm not going to call it Backbinder's Bolt of Magical Energy."

"Sure," Fort said. "That makes sense." He went silent, picturing what could have been if he'd had a spell like Rachel's magic missile back in D.C.

Her foot began tapping impatiently at the silence. "So . . . which specialty are *you* hoping for?"

Her question yanked him back to the present. "Specialty?"

"Right, Dr. Opps didn't tell you," Rachel said. "Maybe I shouldn't say, then." She paused, then shrugged. "Eh, you'll find out soon enough. We've got two of the magic books at our school, Destruction and Healing. Destruction is just how it sounds: You've got your magic missiles, your whirlwinds, your fireballs, all the fun stuff. Basically, if it can destroy something, we've probably got it in our spell book. Healing, well, is pretty self-explanatory." She grinned. "Makes the sniffles go away, that kind of thing. And then there's a third book at a school in the UK, Clairvoyance. That's got spells that will tell the future and stuff."

Fort's eyes widened. "No way. Does it actually work?" And if so, why hadn't anyone seen the attack in D.C. coming?

"Barely." Rachel snorted. "It's not like Spider-Man's spider-sense or something, where you'd get warned before someone hit you. Clairvoyants can only use the magic to look ahead to a specific time and place, and the further into the future they go, the less accurate they get. Kind of useless, if you ask me. *And* it's messed with most of the kids' minds, from what I hear. We've got one clairvoyant at our school, and he's just barely holding on as it is."

Fort nodded, struggling to process everything she'd said. If they couldn't look ahead without knowing when and where an attack might be, there'd be no way to see something unexpected. *That* limited the magic quite a bit. "So Dr. Opps said that four books were found. Or he thought it, in his memory, I guess." Fort paused. "Which one could control a monster like the thing that killed my father?"

Rachel gave him a pitying look. "I'm sorry about what you went through, Fort. Everyone at the school knows about how your dad was the only casualty in the attack. I'm so sorry. But I honestly don't know what could have done that. I've only heard of three books so far: Destruction, Healing, and Clairvoyance. I guess the memory magic that Dr. Opps uses must have come from somewhere too, but he's never mentioned it, or any other book."

Fort frowned, sure he'd heard four. He went silent again, only to look up and find Rachel giving him a guilty look.

"Maybe I'm wrong?" she said. "I did hear once that when the books were first found, various countries shared them with each other, trying to figure out what they were. But as soon as someone realized they actually worked for kids born on Discovery Day or after, the sharing stopped, and everyone went all top secret."

"Discovery Day?" Fort asked.

She shrugged. "That's what the adults call it, 'cause they think they're being all clever, talking in code. But it's not like we *discovered* magic or something. It's more like we dug it up. But Dug-Up Day doesn't sound as important, I guess."

Fort nodded. He took a deep breath and let it out. "Then to answer your question, I'm going to study Destruction magic." If he couldn't learn to control one of those creatures and stop it from harming anyone, then he'd just have to destroy it. Hopefully in the most painful way possible.

"That's what everyone says," Rachel said, and put her hands up in front of him. She concentrated, and a small ball of fire jumped back and forth between her palms. "But you have no idea what you're getting into yet. Destruction is the most dangerous power, obviously. And until you learn how to control it, you're more dangerous than you are useful."

The fire died out, but Fort shrugged. "I don't care," he said. "I still choose Destruction."

"You don't choose, New Kid," Rachel said, rolling her eyes. "There's a test when you first get to the school. You cast the first spell in both books, Healing and Destruction, and they watch to see which one you're better at. It doesn't matter how much you want to destroy things if you're better at Healing. Of course, once they figured out the birthday thing, they realized most of us were going to be good at either one."

Fort raised an eyebrow. "Birthday thing?"

She sighed in annoyance. "Dr. Opps didn't even tell you that? Anyone born on Discovery Day is a *lot* more powerful at magic. I was born a year later, and I'm one of the most powerful destructives we have." Her tone made it sound like that was no big deal, but Fort could see from her smile that she was pretty proud of that fact. "Anyway, ever since they figured *that* out, they only took in kids born on May ninth." She looked closer at him. "How old are you, twelve? You must have been born the same day as me, then!"

Fort immediately stiffened. "Yeah, I'm twelve," he said, nodding much too obviously.

She looked at him strangely. "Don't lie, New Kid. If you're only eleven—"

"No," he said, clenching his fists so tightly his nails bit into his palms. "It's . . . it's not that. I *am* twelve. But, um, my birthday's in September."

Rachel's eyebrows shot up like rockets, and she leaned back, going silent again.

"Well," she said finally. "I don't know why Dr. Opps is bringing you in, but good luck, New Kid. You're already behind, and . . . wow. They brought in some kids with other birthdays a few months ago for testing, and, *yikes*. It wasn't pretty. Hopefully they don't fail you out your first day."

Fort turned to stare at the ground. "I don't care," he whispered. "I'll catch up, I'll work three times as hard as anyone else if I have to. I'm going to learn magic, no matter what it takes."

Rachel cringed, then patted him on the shoulder. "Uh, yeah, that's the spirit! Well, it was nice meeting you, and if nothing else, at least you probably won't have to bother unpacking. See? Silver linings!"

- EIGHT -

THE GOOD-BYES WITH AUNT CORA THE following day were awkward. Both of them knew this was the right decision, Fort leaving to go to the Oppenheimer School, but neither one could say that out loud. Cora hugged him and cried, promising she'd write to him. Fort said he'd do the same, but at that moment he couldn't wait to leave.

If nothing else, this new school wouldn't be filled with memories of his mom and dad. And if things went well, he'd be learning to destroy one of those monsters, to make it suffer like his father must have. The image that Dr. Opps had given him of the creature shrieking in pain propelled him now, keeping him going in spite of the fear of leaving his old life completely behind.

A black car had come the night before to take Rachel, and a

duplicate vehicle arrived to drive Fort and Dr. Opps to a military base a few hours away. Fort spent the trip staring out the window, lost in thought about what was to come. Dr. Opps didn't seem to want to talk either.

"Anything to do with the books will have to wait until we're there," he'd told Fort before they got in the car. "I've already shared more than I should have. This is all information that can't get out to the public, Forsythe. Even your aunt can never know. Keep that in mind when writing letters. Any mail in and out gets read and censored if necessary to keep the school's secrets safe. You won't have access to a cell phone or a computer, either. There can't be any trace of the school's location leaked, for the safety of everyone involved."

That made sense, but Fort did wonder what would happen if he *was* kicked out, like Rachel figured he'd be. What would it be like to have his memory wiped? Would he remember anything?

No. That wasn't even worth considering. He wouldn't fail, and he *would* learn magic. There was no other option. This was for his father, and Fort wasn't going to let him down.

Not again.

When they reached the military base, Dr. Opps got out of

the car to speak in very quiet tones to the guards at the gate. He gestured back at Fort a few times, and the guards checked three different IDs Dr. Opps gave them, then did the same for the driver. Finally Dr. Opps came back and the gate went up, allowing the car to drive across the base to a small airfield where a few helicopters waited.

"Have you ever flown in a helicopter, Fort?" Dr. Opps asked, as the driver opened the door for him. Fort shook his head. He tried to take his suitcase from the trunk, but the driver just smiled at him and waved him off.

"Has to go through security," the driver said, and left carrying the suitcase to a smaller building near the airfield. Fort watched it go, wondering if he was going to see his things again.

Not that he'd taken much. Too many of his favorite books reminded him of his father reading them out loud, reciting them like he was onstage on Broadway. Most of those he'd left behind with Aunt Cora, who said she'd put them in storage until he came back. Same with all his photos, except for one of his mother and father, which he had brought. The Gettysburg Address brochure was in his pocket, as usual. But nothing else seemed to matter anymore.

As Fort watched his suitcase disappear, Dr. Opps pushed a

helmet down over his head. Fort pushed up the visor, giving the doctor a questioning look. "Probably won't do much if we crash," Dr. Opps told him, putting his own helmet on. "But it never hurts to take precautions."

That wasn't *reassuring*, exactly, but fair enough.

Dr. Opps led Fort to the nearest helicopter, which was just starting up. As the rotors whirled faster, Fort ducked beneath them to enter the helicopter, even if he was much too short to worry about getting hit. He felt a bit less embarrassed when Dr. Opps did the same.

"This everyone?" the pilot asked, turning around from the seat in front as Dr. Opps closed the doors.

"We're it," Dr. Opps said, and Fort realized he'd been right about not seeing his suitcase again. Part of him felt relief, like he was leaving even more of his old life behind. But the rest of him wished he hadn't packed his most comfortable hoodie.

The pilot pulled back on a long stick in front of him, and the helicopter lifted into the air with a jarring jump. Fort quickly grabbed ahold of the handrail next to him tightly enough to turn his knuckles white. Dr. Opps just sat across from him, looking unconcerned. "Don't worry," he said. "The flight can get a bit rough, but we'll be fine."

"A bit rough" turned out to be incredibly bumpy, with abrupt drops out of nowhere every few minutes whenever they'd hit a pocket of rough air. They flew for a few hours, crossing land with almost no roads or houses. Trees spread out beneath them in every direction, missing only from some mountains they had to circle around. Fort wondered where they were, but decided the location of the school was probably something else he was better off not knowing, so he could never accidentally give it away.

By the time they reached their destination, Fort had gotten airsick, so had started focusing his gaze on the floor, hoping that'd help. That meant when the helicopter landed, he jumped in surprise. But Dr. Opps just smiled and opened the door as the rotors above them slowly began to wind down. Fort took a deep breath, trying to get his heart rate back under control before following the headmaster out.

No matter what else was to come, this was going to be his first glimpse of a real, live school for magic, and that alone was enough reason to be excited.

Unfortunately, his excitement quickly dropped when he found himself standing on a military base almost identical to the one they'd taken off from.

If his father were there, Fort knew exactly what he would

have said. He could almost see his dad, standing there with a disappointed look on his face. *They could have put a* little *effort into magical-ing it up, couldn't they?* he'd say. *Maybe some living portraits or moving stairs or something? But don't you worry, Fort. When you're the top student here, you'll make up for it all by being so amazing, people will come to the school just for a glimpse of* you*!*

Fort reached his hand into his pocket to grab the Gettysburg Address brochure, squeezing it between his fingers until the image of his father disappeared and he could breathe again.

It didn't matter what the school was like, as long as it taught him Destruction magic.

And besides, maybe this was just another stop on the way, and they'd take another helicopter or car to the real school.

"Here we are," Dr. Opps said, gesturing around the base. "Welcome to the Thaumaturgic Defense Agency, home to the Oppenheimer School."

"The . . . what Defense Agency?" Fort asked, vaguely remembering hearing that somewhere before.

"Thaumaturgic. It basically means magic, but doesn't embarrass the military when they have to ask our special congressional committee for more funding. Speaking of, don't worry about all the guards here." Dr. Opps gestured all around them, and for the first time Fort realized there were dozens of soldiers grouped around the airfield, each one holding some sort of assault rifle. "They're just here for your protection. Like I mentioned back at your aunt's house, we have the best protection available here at the TDA, and no one gets in that we don't let in, Fort. There's no safer place on earth than the Oppenheimer School."

Fort nodded, but as he glanced around, he saw that none of the soldiers seemed to be looking out toward the walls. Instead, they were all staring at Fort and had their fingers on the triggers of their weapons.

"This is the airfield, obviously," Dr. Opps said, waving a hand around them. "Boys' dormitory is over to your right. Soldier and officer barracks are those buildings past that, and off-limits to you." He pointed at a short, fat building straight in front of them. "That's the students' mess, where you'll be assigned specific times for breakfast, lunch, and dinner. And behind the mess is the Training Hall. That's where you'll be spending most of your time."

Fort stared up at the five-story brown building, and again, was completely taken aback by how boring it looked. Mostly it resembled an office building, like the headquarters of a bank. "The Training Hall is where I'll learn magic, then?"

"That's right. But first, we're going to get you a security ID. Then I'll show you the books, take you to the dorm, and get you settled."

Fort nodded, feeling a bit more excited now. The Training Hall might *look* boring, but if it had books of magic that could teach him a magic missile spell like Rachel's, then boring was worth it.

The soldiers around them waited as they passed. Then four on either side broke off and strode alongside them as they went, their guns still at the ready.

"What are they doing?" Fort asked Dr. Opps.

He patted Fort's shoulder. "Nothing to worry about. Just here for protection, remember?"

Right. But if the students were the ones being protected here, why did all the soldiers have their eyes on Fort?

- NINE -

THE TRAINING HALL ENTRANCE DOORS were guarded by two more soldiers, each holding their weapons in their hands, though aimed at the ground. Fort smiled at the one closest to him as they entered, but the guard just stared back without a hint of friendliness.

"New student," Dr. Opps murmured to the guards, and both of them nodded, still watching Fort carefully. Dr. Opps touched a badge to a small black box beside the door, and a small light clicked from red to green, unlocking the doors. He pulled one open and gestured for Fort to enter, which he did, followed by two of the soldiers accompanying them.

Inside, two more soldiers waited at a desk behind a large, incredibly thick pane of glass or maybe some kind of transparent plastic. On either side were metal turnstiles that rose all the way up to the ceiling.

The guards at the desk took Fort's fingerprints through a small opening in the plastic wall, then aimed a camera at him and took a quick photo. They handed over a badge that looked a lot like Dr. Opps's, only Fort's had the word STUDENT in large letters at the top and showed a photo of him looking completely unaware he was getting his picture taken.

"I could retake this photo if you want," Fort suggested to the guard, but the man ignored him.

Dr. Opps held his badge to another black box, this one by the turnstiles, and something clicked, allowing him to turn the metal teeth as he pushed through. Fort passed through the turnstiles as well, but the soldiers stayed behind.

"They're not coming with us?" he asked Dr. Opps as the soldiers turned and left the Training Hall.

"No, they're not needed here," the doctor said. "We've reinforced the Training Hall to withstand almost anything you students can throw at it. Remember when I showed you Rachel blowing up the wall? We've taken precautions so that's not possible anymore. We want you to be able to use the powers you gain in a safe place, after all. Just never against another student, outside certain parameters."

Fort stopped in place. "Wait, what? What do you mean, outside certain parameters?"

Dr. Opps didn't seem to hear the question. Instead, he kept moving, and eventually Fort had to jog to catch up, reaching the doctor at a bank of elevators. Instead of going up or down, Dr. Opps used his badge to pass through another set of doors just beyond the elevators. "I've arranged for your testing to happen immediately," he said, holding one of the doors for Fort. "We'll have to be a bit quicker than usual, as the classes will need the books back for training."

"Testing?" Fort asked, his heart beginning to race. "Is this when I find out which type of magic I'll be learning?"

Dr. Opps nodded. "There will be twenty or so, ah, school administrators watching, but don't let them bother you. Just concentrate on the words you see in the books, and you'll be fine."

There was going to be an audience? Of school "administrators," whatever that meant? Fort swallowed hard, now more nervous than excited. Rachel had mentioned something about him being watched, but he'd figured that meant Dr. Opps and maybe one or two others. But *twenty* people? Couldn't he just try a spell first in private for practice?

They passed several offices with the same thick transparent walls that had covered the front desk, allowing Fort to see in. Most of the offices were filled with soldiers in camouflage uniforms at desks, some on phones, other typing on computers. Many of them looked up and stared as he walked past, and more than one rose from their seats in surprise, one even letting his hand rest on his weapon.

At the end of the corridor, double doors opened into a large circular room. Stone benches ringed the room on each level, and a set of stairs led down to a center area with a wooden podium. Fort froze as he entered, recognizing the room as the same one where Rachel had blown up the wall. He glanced over to where the hole should have been and found it repaired, though a thin line still showed the outline of her attack.

Most of the room was empty, but various men and women sat on the lowest level of seats, the ones nearest the podium. These people weren't wearing camouflage like the soldiers, but instead had uniforms that looked very official and intimidating. Lots of stars and medals everywhere.

As the men and women turned to look at Fort, he heard them murmur comments to each other quietly.

"That's him? He won't last a day. Why are they even bothering?"

"This whole thing is pointless. We can't train one that we know can't handle the power."

"Why Charles and Oppenheimer want this kid here is beyond me."

"I apologize that we're late," Dr. Opps said, ignoring their comments. "This is Forsythe Fitzgerald, and you all know his unfortunate history. I know this isn't the way we usually do things, so I thank you for allowing me this experiment."

Uh, what? *Experiment?* That's what Fort was to them? Was this because his birthday wasn't on the day the books were discovered?

Dr. Opps turned to Fort as the others shifted uncomfortably in their seats. "Don't worry about anything but the magic," he whispered, guiding Fort to the podium. "It's really just a simple test. Pick up the books one by one and turn to the first page. The books will start you on the least powerful spell and won't let you read further in until you've mastered that one, so you won't have a choice anyway."

Fort nodded, since it seemed like the response Dr. Opps wanted, but the doctor had already turned to take a seat, leaving

Fort standing alone in front of everyone. His palms began to sweat, so he wiped them on his pants, feeling way too many eyes on him.

Strangely, the lights seemed to flicker as he stood at the podium, and several of the officers looked around curiously, so Fort knew this wasn't a usual problem. Maybe it was some kind of reaction to the magic he was about to perform?

Two books lay on the podium, both closed. Strange letters ran across each cover, but as he touched them, the letters seemed to blur, changing into words he could read, just like they had in Dr. Opps's memory. The one on the left said *The Magic of Destruction, and Its Many Uses*, while the one on the right was *The Magic of Recuperation, and Restoring What Has Been.*

Blowing things up, or healing paper cuts. There wasn't even a choice here. He *had* to learn Destruction magic. Healing would be useless against those monsters. To make them suffer, he needed powerful weapons on his side.

Fort picked up *The Magic of Destruction*.

The tome felt much heavier than it looked, and Fort almost fumbled it back to the podium. Someone behind him coughed, and Fort blushed as he heard someone else mumble, "He can't even lift it. This kid's useless."

His face burning, Fort quickly opened the Destruction book to the first page and set it back down on the podium. Whatever this spell was, he was going to make it the most powerful one these people had ever seen.

He leaned over and scanned the page. Only, it didn't look like a spell. It actually looked more like a poem.

One for the body, bones and skin,

One for the spirit, its spectral kin,

One for the mind, thoughts and dreams,

One for the world, from dirt to streams,

One for all space, wide and vast,

One for all time, future and past.

Seven from six, the rest unearthed.

One saves all, if proved their worth.

Fort's eyes widened as he read. What did *that* mean? Was it some sort of—

"Ah, Forsythe, I forgot," Dr. Opps said from his seat. "I'll explain that poem later, it's in all the books. Just turn one page further."

Fort nodded, despite facing away from the doctor, and turned to the next page, where the same unreadable language that had been on the cover of the book slowly morphed into something legible here, too.

Canterbury's Flash: Ignite the air before you, creating a dazzling light to momentarily blind your foes.

A small picture to the right of that showed what looked to be some sort of short goblinlike creature wandering around blind.

Below the description were two words not in English, and they didn't seem to be translating themselves: "gen rexelum." As he read them, a warm feeling spread over him, and the words disappeared from the page, but their afterimage seemed to burn into his brain.

Had . . . had he just learned his first magic spell?

Okay, Fort thought. *Make this the biggest flash they've ever seen.*

Fort turned back to the audience, then paused, not really sure how to cast the spell. Should he raise his hand? Did he need a wand? Or did he just say the words? And what happened if he pronounced them wrong?

"Gen . . . rexelum," Fort whispered, holding up his hands.

Immediately, power flowed through his body and out of his hands, setting them aglow.

Too late, he realized he should have closed his eyes against the blinding flash.

Unfortunately, there was no need.

The flash from his hands slightly brightened the room

momentarily, like there'd been a tiny power surge, then faded into nothing. Overall, there was even less of an effect than when the lights had flickered a moment earlier.

NO! he screamed in his mind. Why hadn't it worked better? He *needed* to learn Destruction magic. There was no other option!

"Even the Healing students do better with Destruction magic than that," someone said.

"We already knew kids not born on Discovery Day are basically useless," said someone else. "Why is Oppenheimer bothering with this one?"

"I can do better," Fort said, turning around to look at Dr. Opps. "Let me try again. I *know* I can do better!"

The doctor, though, was staring at the lights, looking lost in thought. He seemed to come out of it abruptly and turned back to Fort. "Move on to the other book, Forsythe."

All the hope he'd felt since meeting Dr. Opps faded away almost to nothing, and Fort moved numbly to the second book. As he opened it, he wondered why he was even bothering. What was the point? He was here to learn how to fight monsters like the one that had killed his father, not heal someone's stubbed toe. What use was this?

"Continue, please," Dr. Opps said from behind him.

Fort wiped his sweaty hands on his shirt and looked down at the open book, skipping past the same poem from the Destruction book.

Heal Minor Wounds and Scrapes, the text said. *Restore small cuts or shallow burns with a cooling touch.* The drawing next to it had a woman holding her hands over a man's arm with a cut that barely would have required a Band-Aid.

Great. Even more useless than he thought. But maybe if he could cast this spell, they'd give him another chance at Destruction?

Fort read over the words to the spell, "mon d'cor," and again, they faded away. But as he turned back to his audience, ready to cast it, he realized he'd need someone to heal. Turning even brighter red, he looked pathetically at Dr. Opps. "I . . . um, I need a minor scrape to heal."

Dr. Opps snapped his fingers like he'd forgotten. "*Right.* Anyone have an injury? If not, I can choose a volunteer."

The others chuckled politely, while Fort tried not to climb under the podium to hide.

"I cut myself during training yesterday," said someone next to Dr. Opps. Fort turned to look at the man, and his eyes widened. He'd seen this man before. On television, standing in front of a bunch of reporters. What had his name been? The one who'd introduced the Department of Tharm-whatever?

"I'm Colonel Charles, Forsythe," the man said, giving Fort a friendly smile and a small wave as he stood up. He pulled his uniform jacket off, then folded it up and left it on his chair before unrolling his shirt sleeve and presenting a small cut to Fort. "One of my students was a bit overzealous."

Fort nodded, not sure what else to say. He half wanted to apologize in case he made the cut worse, but instead, he put his hands over the wound and shut his eyes, just in case everything went horribly wrong. "Mon . . . d'cor," he whispered.

This time, Fort's hands seemed to lower in temperature, and he felt some weirdly cold energy leave his fingers and pass into the man's arm. Worried, he opened his eyes, expecting to have frozen the man's skin, but the cut had disappeared.

"I'd say that's a minor wound healed," Colonel Charles said, holding his arm up for the others to see. "Looks like we've got ourselves a Healing student!"

"Not much of one," someone said as the group all rose to their feet, collecting their belongings.

"Wait," Fort said, stepping around to face Colonel Charles.

"I'm *not* a healer. I need to learn Destruction magic! Let me try again. I swear I'll be better this time!"

The colonel smiled down at him gently. "That's the spirit. Work hard and do your best here, Forsythe, and maybe we'll see if we can't get you into the Destruction program after all. You look like you have the makings of a powerful warrior to me."

He tousled Fort's hair, then returned to his seat to grab his jacket and follow the others out.

When the room had emptied, Dr. Opps rose out of his seat and walked over to Fort, then patted him on the shoulder. "You did well," he said, turning to the podium and closing each book. "The next few days will be hard, but I have faith in you. You'll be a welcome new addition to the school."

Fort turned away. "That's not what the others were saying. They couldn't stop talking about how useless I was."

"That's just your imagination running away with you," Dr. Opps said as he walked Fort toward the door. "None of the other administrators said a word during the entire test."

- TEN -

FORT FOLLOWED DR. OPPS BACK through the facility, completely confused. He'd *definitely* heard the officers talking, and not just once. How could he have just imagined it? He'd never done anything like that before, even when he *was* nervous.

"Let's get you situated with a bunk and uniforms," Dr. Opps was saying, and Fort realized he hadn't heard much of anything else the doctor had said. "After that, I'll have a student take you to meet your new Healing teacher, and she'll explain what's to come over the next few days."

Fort nodded. "If I do well with Healing, maybe I could switch to Destruction? Honestly, I think that suits me better, and Colonel Charles said—"

"No, I'm afraid there won't be any switching," Dr. Opps said. "The test determined you have more of a facility for

Healing. It's a noble study, Forsythe. You should be proud."

Proud? Fort clenched his fists, wanting to shout that he didn't care about pride, that he had let his father down and wouldn't be able to make those monsters pay for what they'd done to him. But instead, he just took a deep breath, then slowly let it out. If he yelled at the school headmaster, he'd be gone as quickly as Rachel thought he'd be.

Prove to them you can learn magic first, he thought. *Then worry about showing them how powerful you'd be at Destruction.*

In order to change the subject, Fort offered up another question he'd had from the test. "So that poem at the beginning of both books—what exactly was that?"

Dr. Opps coughed. "We, uh, don't know. It seems to reference the books themselves, but we only know of four books, not seven. And the last line suggests some sort of savior type, but in my experience, that's seldom how life works." He gave Fort a side glance. "Every student here believes it's referring to them, Forsythe. Don't follow their bad example. Work hard, and you'll succeed. We don't need a hero. We need dedicated, reliable students working as a team."

"Don't worry," Fort said. "I couldn't care less about that." And he meant every word. Let the other students worry about saving the world. He'd be content just making those monsters suffer.

They left the facility, and soldiers joined back up around them as they walked across the grounds. Something sizzled behind them from one of the upper floors of the Training Hall, like a burst of electricity, and each of the guards around them froze, immediately turning their weapons on the building. But when nothing else happened, they seemed to relax slightly and resumed their walk.

"Don't worry," Dr. Opps said, noticing Fort's jumpiness. "You won't be training with the Destruction students. Healing students practice on a different floor, and interdisciplinary interaction is carefully moderated. You won't be getting electrocuted if we can help it."

That "if we can help it" sounded a bit more ominous than Fort would have liked, but there wasn't much time to question it, as he found they were almost to the building Dr. Opps had pointed out earlier as the boys' dormitory.

The building where he'd be living now was long and narrow and had windows running the length of it. It had only one floor and was painted the same dull brown color as the rest of the base. Fort glanced behind him and noticed an identical building on the opposite side of the base, which was probably the girls' dormitory.

"The dorm should be empty right now, but you can meet the other—" Dr. Opps stopped talking as they entered the dormitory and found a boy sitting on one of fifty or so bunks facing each other down the long building. "Cyrus?"

The boy looked up from a comic book he was reading. His hair was curly and bright white, almost glowing in the fluorescent lighting. The boy half smiled, his gaze a bit unsteady as he looked between Fort and the doctor, almost like he hadn't had enough sleep.

"Hello, Dr. Opps," Cyrus said with a British accent. Then he turned to Fort and grinned. "Fort! Nice to see you again!"

Dr. Opps just stared at him. "This is . . . uh, Forsythe, Cyrus. He just joined us *today* at the school. Would you mind showing him around the dormitory and helping introduce him to the students when they return?"

Cyrus hadn't stopped staring at Fort, who had *no* idea what was happening now. "Oh, that's right, we're meeting for the first time," the boy said, winking at Fort. "I can definitely give you a tour of the place. I can't believe you're finally here!"

Fort gave Dr. Opps a confused look, but the teacher just

smiled. "Cyrus is a student here as well, in a way, but not in either of the two areas of study we focus in. He transferred here from a facility just like ours in the UK, after some issues arose."

"I'm told everyone went quite insane except me," Cyrus said to Fort, then seemed to consider what he'd just said. "Though I added the 'except me' part myself, which makes me wonder if . . . ah well."

Dr. Opps sighed, but he clapped a hand on Fort's shoulder. "He's kidding," he said out loud, then more quietly, "but try not to take anything he prophesies too seriously. We haven't had access to clairvoyants long enough to truly know what they're capable of."

"Clairvoyants?" Fort whispered back, remembering what Rachel had said about a school in the UK, a school where the students—

"We see the future," Cyrus said, moving next to them so quietly that Fort jumped. "And what we see *always* comes true. Unless we change it, of course."

"We don't know that for sure, Cyrus," Dr. Opps said. "Certainly you've had some misreadings in the past."

"They were misinterpreted, that's all," Cyrus said to the doctor, then turned to Fort and grinned. "I can take a look at *your* future, if you'd like?" He leaned in closer, reaching for Fort's hand.

Dr. Opps pulled Fort just out of Cyrus's reach. "Let's let Fort get settled in first, Cyrus. He has plenty to get accustomed to without worrying about what's coming next."

"Of course, your bunk!" Cyrus said, and motioned for Fort to follow him. "Follow me. I'll show you which one is yours."

Fort just watched the other boy walk away, barely able to keep up with what was happening. "Are we . . . assigned beds?" he asked Dr. Opps.

The doctor shook his head. "Pick whichever one you want, assuming it's not occupied already."

"Here, it's this one," Cyrus said, pointing at a bed all the way at the end. "Next to mine."

"I think I'd prefer this one, near the door," Fort said, just to feel like he'd had a say in it. He patted the perfectly made bed closest to him with no signs of anyone's things. "Is this free?"

Cyrus shrugged, moving back toward them. "It is for now. But you're going to choose the one in the back later tonight. Why not save yourself the trouble of moving your things?"

"Cyrus, how about you take Fort over to get sized for uniforms before lunch," Dr. Opps said. "And I'm going to see about getting your training courses developed a bit faster. We can't have you sitting around unsupervised like this."

"They won't be ready for another week or so, but they're not going to be needed anyway," Cyrus told him. Then, to Fort's horror, Cyrus grabbed his wrist, and he braced himself to hear something awful coming in the future.

Fortunately, the boy didn't start spouting archaic language foretelling an ancient prophecy. Instead, he just yanked Fort toward the door. "Let's get you your uniform. You look so odd to me in regular clothes. I'm just used to you in the green, I suppose."

"We'll talk again at dinner, Fort," Dr. Opps said. "I'll answer any further questions you have at that time."

"But—" Fort started to say, then Cyrus pulled him out the door.

"It's not far," Cyrus told him, releasing his wrist as he led Fort across the yard. This time six soldiers fell in around them, most of them keeping their eyes on Cyrus, which actually made Fort *much* more nervous. Who was this kid? There was no way he could actually tell the future . . . right?

"So you're from the UK?" Fort asked.

"London," Cyrus answered. "But the school was in Carmarthen.

It's one of the oldest cities in Wales, and where Merlin was from, in legends." He winced. "When they found the Clairvoyance book, and you Americans found yours, there was a bit of talk about how if magic had come back, this must be some sort of return of Merlin, especially because he was meant to have lived backward in time, whatever that means. And if Merlin was returning, so must King Arthur be on his way, arriving with Excalibur to save all of Britain." He waved an imaginary sword around majestically.

Fort stopped in place. "Um, *did* he come back?"

Cyrus laughed. "Not that I noticed. I'm fairly sure that King Arthur was no more real than your magician Harry Houdini."

"Um—"

"Anyway, after the other students lost their minds, I think all the Merlin stuff suddenly looked like pure vanity, and the government got rightfully embarrassed about the whole thing. I got sent here because I think they wanted to forget it ever happened." He paused. "Are the others still there, though? It's hard to remember. I get confused sometimes between what I've seen to come, and what I've lived already, but I'm fairly certain I'll be seeing the school again in the months to come. . . ."

"Oh, so you're heading back?" Fort asked, feeling slightly less nervous if Cyrus was leaving.

"Not the way you're thinking," Cyrus told him.

Uh, okay? "So someone told me that you have to look at specific dates and times to see the future. That means you don't just automatically know what happens to random people, right?"

Cyrus grinned. "Are you asking me to look into your future? I'm happy to, if you'd like!" He closed his eyes for a moment, mumbling some words Fort couldn't hear. "Oh wow. That's just gruesome. How are you still able to stand—"

Fort's eyes widened, and he shook his head violently. "No, *not* mine, I just meant in general. I'd rather not know what's coming for me."

This seemed to confuse Cyrus. "But it's so helpful. Like your bunk. You end up choosing the one I pointed out for a good reason. And the table at lunch. If you knew ahead of time what's about to happen, you'd make different choices. Why wouldn't you want all the information?"

Fort just stared at the boy for a moment, not sure how to respond to that. If Cyrus knew every decision Fort was going to make, then was Fort really the one making the decisions? If his whole future was already mapped out, could he still change it? Could he—

"Oh yeah, you can *definitely* still change it," Cyrus told him. "It happens all the time."

This was too much for Fort to handle, and he started to wonder if *he* was the one going insane. "Did . . . did you just read my mind?"

"Oh no, I've never studied *that* magic," Cyrus said, laughing. "No, you were just going to ask me that question a minute from now, and I wanted to prove the point. See? Now you won't ask! Future changed. Come on, let's get you a uniform before lunch. I'm famished!"

- ELEVEN -

GETTING FITTED FOR A UNIFORM didn't take much time at all, and after talking to Cyrus, it was comfortingly normal. As he looked at himself in the mirror, thinking how boring an all-green uniform looked, Fort could hear his father again in the back of his mind.

Wow, you really make that color come alive, Fort! Watch out, because that uniform is going to be considered high fashion when you're done with it.

"What do you think?" Cyrus said, startling Fort out of his daydream.

"Oh, it's fine," he said, forcing a smile. "At least I won't stand out this way."

The mess hall wasn't too far, which was good, because though Fort's new shoes did seem to fit, they also rubbed his feet uncomfortably. Hopefully they just needed to be broken in.

But between the uniform and the constant presence of soldiers everywhere, Fort was starting to worry that this whole school of magic was going to involve less spellcasting and more boot camp. Hopefully they'd be too busy learning magic to run fourteen miles with a hundred-pound backpack.

When they entered the mess hall, Cyrus sped up, practically yanking Fort off his feet to pull him toward the food line at one side of the room. The rest of the cafeteria was empty, with long tables filling most of the room. "We're early," Cyrus said. "Enjoy it while you can. Healers are always late to lunch, and the mess usually runs out of everything good."

"Great," Fort said, surveying the choices as bored-looking soldiers slowly stuck spoons into large trays of what looked like brown glop. "Is that . . . the good stuff?"

Cyrus laughed. "That's the chili. You probably want to avoid that for a few days. You're going to have a hard enough time making friends without causing air pollution. The chicken fingers are always the first thing to go, so I'd grab at least a few now, since you'll never see them again."

Fort did as Cyrus suggested, taking some french fries as well, and then chose water over milk, the only two drink options. Cyrus did the same, then started to lead Fort to the table nearest the food line, only to stop abruptly and switch to the table closest to the door.

The choice made Fort even more nervous as he began to hear voices in the hallway. "Was something wrong with that first table?"

Cyrus took a bite of a chicken finger. "Not *wrong* necessarily. But you'll get hurt less at this one."

"Less?" Fort asked, almost choking on a fry. Before Cyrus could answer, though, a group of soldiers entered the cafeteria, all armed, and spread out along the walls. Behind them, the source of the voices appeared as a bunch of kids all around Fort's age came into the mess, some shoving each other, others chatting loudly, all seeming like they had way too much energy.

"Everyone gets lessons in the mornings," Cyrus whispered to him as each kid turned to stare at Fort as they walked past. "Since the Destruction students haven't had their combat drills yet, lunches can get a little loud."

Combat drills? But Dr. Opps had said they weren't going to do any fighting, just make weapons for actual soldiers to use.

A trio of blond boys all slowed down as they passed Fort's

table, then stopped to stare at him. "You're the new Band-Aid?" one of them asked.

"His name is Fort," Cyrus answered brightly, and Fort dropped his head into his hands.

"No one asked you, future turd," a second one said, placing his palm down on the metal table. His hand began to glow, and Cyrus immediately lifted his tray into the air, but Fort didn't realize what was happening until it was too late. His tray began to sizzle, turning white-hot with heat, and he yelped as it burned his hands. His food slowly blackened, and a burning smell wafted through the mess.

"Hey!" Fort shouted, leaping out of his seat. "What did you do *that* for?"

Behind him, the soldiers began to shift nervously, and a few of the soldiers across the way even raised their weapons. But the blond boy in front of Fort just smirked at the soldiers, then turned back to Fort. "I hear you weren't born on Discovery Day. Can you even cast a spell?"

Fort took a deep breath, not wanting to get kicked out of another school for fighting. "I can," he said slowly, deliberately unclenching his fists. "And I'm sure I'll get better at it . . . as I learn more."

The three boys looked at each other, then laughed.

"Great," a third blond boy said. "Just what we need, an underpowered nurse."

"Nurses actually do most of the work in hospitals," Cyrus pointed out. "Many of them know just as much about medicine as doctors do, and—"

"Do you ever say anything worthwhile?" the first blond boy said to Cyrus, then turned back to Fort. "What, you've got something to say?"

Fort could feel his heart beating in his ears and he took a step closer, clenching his teeth, before a hand nervously tapped his shoulder. "No altercations outside of training," said one of the soldiers, sounding more anxious than Fort felt.

The second blond boy looked up at the soldier with a slow smile, his hands starting to glow, and the soldier backed away. Apparently even the guards couldn't intimidate the Destruction kids.

"They won't stop us," the boy whispered to Fort as fire played over his fingers. "We're too important . . . and they're *afraid*. Why don't I show you why?"

- TWELVE -

"WELL, BAND-AID?" THE BLOND BOY said, his hands glowing red with heat that Fort could feel from across the table. "I hear you were in D.C. in the attack. Were you as scared then as you are now? How much did you cry?"

Fort could barely hear him over the ringing in his ears. His face contorted with rage, and he pulled back his fist—

"Wow, you guys are pathetic," said a voice from behind the three blond boys. They whirled around, revealing Rachel and two other girls, all staring in boredom at the boys. "Picking on the new kid. He doesn't even know any magic yet."

"So?" the second blond boy snarled. "Even if he's new, he's a healer, and they all suck. What do you care, anyway?"

Rachel flicked a finger, and a tiny magic missile slammed into the boy's stomach, sending him crashing across the table, taking Fort's burning-hot tray with him. He tumbled into the back wall as the soldiers nearby all leaped out of the way, their weapons now aimed at Rachel. She didn't seem to notice.

"Our job is to *protect* weaker people, like Fort," Rachel said as the two girls at her side pushed the remaining blond boys out of the way. "And I better not see you Chads or Blaines or whatever your names are messing with him again, or I'll set fire to you all in practice and make it look like an accident. You know Colonel Charles will believe me too."

The blond boy on the ground slowly picked himself up. "I'm *Bryce*, actually. And that's Trey. And you *know* he's the only one named Chad—" He pointed at the last boy.

"Quiet, Blaine," Rachel said, and flicked another finger at him. The boy flinched, but this time nothing happened, and Rachel's two friends laughed. "Now get me some lunch or something. I don't have all day here."

Bryce or Blaine slowly nodded, then moved quickly around the table, giving Fort one last death look before getting into line with the other two boys.

"See?" Cyrus whispered. "*He's* going to be the reason you switch beds tonight."

"I didn't need your help," Fort told Rachel, his heart still beating hard. "I could have handled him."

Rachel grinned as her friends rolled their eyes. "Nah, you couldn't. He's a Discovery Day boy, so he's more powerful. That's just how it is. Even if not, you're still just learning Healing magic, while he could electrocute you without a second thought. He won't touch you while I'm around, but I'd watch yourself in the dorm."

"Especially tonight," Cyrus whispered. "It's gonna be *bad*."

"How are *you* doing, Future Man?" Rachel said, throwing Cyrus an amused look. "Still see me saving the entire world?"

Cyrus nodded. "It's a bit hazy, but you definitely either save the world, or you buy a globe. I really do think it's the former, though."

"I'll be sure not to buy any globes, then," she said, grinning at Cyrus. She turned back to Fort and patted him on the shoulder. "You, try to stay alive. I like healers. You're all a lot nicer than the meatheads in my classes. Speaking of . . ." She turned toward the cafeteria line. "Hey, Blaine, hurry it up! We're hungry! And we better get chicken fingers!"

Bryce and the other boys threw her a disgusted look but pushed their way ahead in line, past several students who got annoyed, only to look back and catch a glimpse of Rachel. Immediately they all let Bryce and his friends pass.

Apparently being the best had some advantages. Or maybe they were all just terrified of her.

Cyrus and Fort sat back down at the table, Cyrus with his tray full of food, and Fort with nothing but the mess behind him and a group of boys ready to set him on fire later in the dormitory. "So you thought sitting at this table would be a *good* idea?" he asked Cyrus.

"Oh, definitely," Cyrus said, handing him a chicken finger. "If we'd sat any farther from the door, Rachel wouldn't have gotten here in time." He picked up another and took a bite. "You two are going to be friends, once she decides you're not here to destroy the school."

Destroy the school? What was . . . forget it. It didn't matter. And he didn't need anyone protecting him. He'd be just fine on his own, as soon as he learned a little magic. The last thing he needed was someone watching out for him, or making him run away when he was able to fight for himself. If he hadn't had to run back in D.C. . . .

"What about Blaine and those guys?" Fort said, trying to distract himself. "Are we going to be best friends too?"

Cyrus laughed, stopped for a moment to stare at Fort, then laughed again.

After a quick (and incident-free) remainder of their lunch, Cyrus led Fort out of the cafeteria, being careful to leave before the Destruction students finished eating. As they walked out, Fort noticed several new kids coming in, many of them looking sick to their stomachs. He stopped to watch as most of them glanced at the food line, then decided to just grab some water instead. Some didn't even do that and instead just sat down at a table, looking queasy.

"Who are they?" he whispered to Cyrus.

"Oh, those are your new classmates," Cyrus said. "The healers. I'm guessing they had some disgusting anatomy lesson in class. Something to look forward to tomorrow! I'll go introduce you to your teacher, then see you back in the dorm later."

Fort nodded, his eyes on the pale faces of the healers. Almost to a student, they looked like they'd never eat again. All but one, that was: A tall African American boy with buzzed hair had arrived with the rest of the healers but seemed to be the only one interested in lunch. Apparently, *he* hadn't had any problems with the lessons.

Cyrus led Fort from the cafeteria over to the Training Hall, the boring five-story office building where Fort had his test earlier. This time, once they got through security, Cyrus stopped him at the elevators instead of taking him back through the glass-walled offices to the auditorium where he'd first seen the books of magic.

Once the elevator arrived, Cyrus hit the button for the fourth floor, then stepped out. "Only healers allowed up there," he said as the doors banged against his shoulder, then reopened. "Just follow the signs for Dr. Ambrose. She's your new teacher."

Cyrus stepped out of the way of the doors before Fort could object, then let them close with one last wave. Fort sighed, alone for the first time since he'd arrived at the Oppenheimer School.

Well, this was going *great.* First, he'd completely failed at Destruction magic, the one thing he'd come here to learn. Then he'd made some enemies without even trying, only to be rescued out of pity. What was next, forgetting to wear pants tomorrow? Assuming he lived through the night to even *see* the next day?

The door opened on the fourth floor, and Fort stepped out, finding himself in an ordinary hallway lit with fluorescent lights overhead. Several plaques in front of the elevator had names and arrows, so he located the one for Dr. Ambrose and followed it down the hallway to the right.

As he walked through the mostly quiet hallway, he could just make out voices at the end from an open doorway. He slowed, realizing that one of the voices might belong to his new teacher, and he didn't want to interrupt her in their first meeting.

"This is *insane*, Oppenheimer," a woman's voice said. "Do you know how dangerous this is? You've seen the reports we've been getting from all around the world. They're *looking*—"

"I don't want him here any more than you do," Dr. Opps said. "But Colonel Charles insisted he come. He think there's a possibility that Forsythe—"

"Gets us all *killed*, maybe," the woman said. "I can't be a party to this. He needs to go home *now*, before more damage is done. I've seen the charts. Every minute he's been here, the activity has increased. And what do you think happens if we're discovered, Oppenheimer?"

Fort's heart began to pound in his chest. They were talking about *him*, but none of it made any sense. Dr. Opps didn't want him at the school? He'd only been invited because Colonel Charles wanted him here? What did *that* mean? Why would the colonel care about him?

And apparently his new teacher thought he might get everyone *killed*. But how? He wasn't even being allowed to learn Destruction magic!

"Give me the three days we agreed on," Dr. Opps said. "If I send Forsythe home early, Colonel Charles will just remove me from my position and keep him here anyway. The rest of the administrators think he's just here as an experiment, to see if kids not born on Discovery Day can effectively use magic. So lean into that. Test Forsythe. Give him the challenge we talked about and make sure he fails. Then we'll have a cover to send him home and keep the kids safe."

Fort's breathing quickened, and he had to reach out to steady himself against a nearby wall. Dr. Ambrose was going to make sure he failed? They were going to cheat to make sure he couldn't stay at the school!

"Do you *know* how crazy you sound?" the woman said. "This is beyond dangerous!"

"You think I have a choice here? Colonel Charles is looking for the slightest reason to fire me, and the moment I'm gone, he'll be prepping those kids for the front line of any future attack. This is the best idea I've got right now, the only way I know to keep the students safe for as long as I can."

"Remind me how safe you're keeping them when one of those things comes climbing up from beneath us."

Dr. Opps sighed. "Rebecca—"

"No, just go. The kid's supposed to be here any minute."

Fort couldn't breathe, and could barely even think. And after all of that, now he had to go meet Dr. Ambrose and look her in the eye, knowing she was going to make sure he failed out of the school. All because she thought he was dangerous somehow? That didn't even make sense.

And what reports had she seen from around the world? Someone was looking for . . . *something*. But what, or who? And what did that have to do with Fort?

Footsteps sounded from the office next door, and Fort panicked, then pushed into the darkened room next to Dr. Ambrose's office, just as Dr. Opps emerged. Fort went absolutely still, not daring to even breathe until he heard the headmaster pass. A moment later the elevator dinged, and the doors opened, then closed again, and Fort let out his breath.

This was too much to handle all at once. He'd left his old life behind to come to learn magic, but it'd all been a lie. Even the administrators at his testing earlier didn't know the real reason he was here.

But Colonel Charles wanted him here. The one person at the school who'd actually believed in him and thought he might switch into the Destruction school. Maybe that was why he wanted Fort there to begin with, because he knew how strongly Fort needed this, after the attacks. A soldier like Colonel Charles would know what going through an attack felt like.

The image of his spells hurting the creature, making it cry out in agony, filled his head again, and he clenched his fists.

If he let Dr. Ambrose and Dr. Opps fail him out of the school, he'd never make that monster feel the same pain he had when it'd taken his father. And that was *not* going to happen.

Completely lost in thought, Fort leaned back against the door of the office he'd been hiding in, only to have it loudly squeak as it pushed open farther.

"Who's there?" Dr. Ambrose shouted from the next room over.

"Uh, it's . . . it's Forsythe," Fort said slowly, his face burning with embarrassment.

"Congratulations," Dr. Ambrose yelled. "Do you want a medal? Get in here already. I swear, you kids these days."

- THIRTEEN -

DR. AMBROSE TURNED OUT TO BE A middle-aged woman wearing a lab coat and glasses, her dark hair tied up in a ponytail. She glared at him through the thin lenses, shaking her head.

"Do you always hang around outside doors without saying anything, kid?" she said. "Just because I knew you were coming doesn't make it not creepy."

"I'm, um, sorry," Fort said, his mind still reeling from the conversation he'd overheard.

"I'm Dr. Ambrose," she said, and Fort stuck out his hand. She stared at it for a moment, then rolled her eyes. "You can call me Dr. Ambrose. Sit down and pay attention. I'm too busy to get you fully caught up, so the less time we waste here, the better."

Fort quickly took a seat. "Thanks for, uh, allowing me to

join your Healing class." The one she was going to make sure he failed.

"Don't thank me," Dr. Ambrose said, turning away to glance at papers on her desk. "I don't want you here. I think you're going to distract my students who actually have potential, and as far as I'm concerned, that's reason enough to send you home right now. But unfortunately that's not up to me. So here's the deal: You have three days to master the first three Healing spells. If you fail, you're going home. If you succeed, pigs will be flying, which I imagine will make for some fun photos. Do we understand each other?"

"I don't . . . what?" Fort said, sitting up straighter, just trying to follow.

Dr. Ambrose sighed. "What did I say about paying attention? I swear, you kids will be the death of me. Three days, three spells. Heal Minor Wounds, Cure Disease, and Cause Disease." She half smiled. "And try not to follow the example of a truly stunning student who mastered Cause Disease first, only to end up with a case of walking pneumonia that he couldn't cure."

This was a *lot* of information at once, so Fort focused on the last thing she'd said, just to buy some time. "What, um, happened to him? Did someone use magic to cure him?"

"If antibiotics are magic, then sure," Dr. Ambrose said. "They're not, by the way. I shouldn't have to clarify that, but I never know with your generation. Now, most kids have taken a week or so to learn each spell, and you've got only a fraction of that time, not to mention barely any power, given your birthday. In order to make this vaguely less of a joke, I've agreed to allow my best student to tutor you. Of course, that's going to waste *her* time, but does Oppenheimer care about that? Nope."

Fort just nodded along, unsure what to say. He had to master these spells in three *days* when it had taken the other kids three *weeks*? And if he failed, that was it, he'd be sent back home to live with his aunt.

That was *not* going to happen, no matter what Dr. Opps and his new teacher wanted.

"I'll master them," Fort said, his anger rising. "Whatever it takes, I'll do it. I *won't* be going home."

Dr. Ambrose rolled her eyes. "Actually, you probably will, so you might want to get used to the idea. Just try not to monopolize all of Jia's time. Her bandages are the best we've got right now, and the way things are going, we'll probably need them soon."

"Bandages?" Fort blurted out.

Dr. Ambrose stared at him for a moment, then gestured at a clear plastic case behind Fort. "In spite of what Colonel Charles believes, we can't send kids out onto a battlefield. At least not until you're eighteen. So instead, my healers infuse bandages with their magic. Easy to apply, and you can stack them."

Fort turned to find a small number of what looked like large pads in clear bags lined up in rows inside the case. Each pad was labeled with a different injury, like BROKEN BONE, BULLET WOUND, BURNS, and more. There were easily three times the number of burn bandages as others, which didn't make Fort feel great about the Destruction students.

"Generic Healing spells are all well and good, but we've found that making spells specific to different injuries enhances their restorative properties," Dr. Ambrose said. "A generic spell might set a broken bone, but it'd still be fragile, while a bone-specific spell would heal it completely."

Fort stared at her in wonder. "So that bandage right there can heal a broken bone? Just by touching it to someone's arm or whatever?"

"Did Oppenheimer not tell you what happens here?" Dr. Ambrose said. "This is a school for *magic*, kid. Broken bones are the tip of the iceberg." She sighed, turning away from him.

"I could be pushing the field of medicine to new heights, but no, here I am explaining myself to a twelve-year-old."

"Sorry," Fort whispered, turning back around.

"Just . . . just don't talk," Dr. Ambrose said. "Jia will be here shortly, at which point you'll be wasting her time instead of mine. Until then, if you have any questions . . . don't."

Except he *did* have questions. Too many to even know where to begin. But if he asked about the conversation he'd overheard, she'd know he'd been listening, and might just send him home right then and there. But maybe he could do it subtly? "Um," he said, "I was wondering—"

"Nope," Dr. Ambrose said.

"But—"

"What does 'no questions' mean to you?"

"You're my teacher, though. Shouldn't you answer questions?"

"I'm sorry, are you telling me how to do my job?" Her eyebrows shot up.

"No, of course not!" Fort said quickly, his face flaming hot. "I'm just—"

"Dr. Ambrose?" said a voice from behind him, and Fort turned to find a girl with long braided black hair standing in the doorway uncomfortably. "You wanted to see me?"

Dr. Ambrose kept her narrowed eyes on Fort for another moment, then turned to wave the new girl in. "Jia Liang," she said. "Meet Forsythe . . . something. Doesn't matter. You're going to be tutoring him to the best of your abilities for the next three days, before he fails and is sent home. Try not to let him be too much of a distraction."

Jia glanced down at Fort like she wasn't sure what to make of him. "Tutoring? Is he a new student?"

"Yes, but he wasn't born on Discovery Day, so he won't be staying long," Dr. Ambrose said, then gestured for them both to leave. "Now get out. I have important things to do."

Fort stood up and followed Jia out. "I'm sorry about—"

"And close the door!" Dr. Ambrose shouted. Jia quickly did so, then turned to Fort, visibly relaxing.

"I'm sorry about that," she said, shaking her head. "She's like that to everyone. Don't let it bother you."

"I'm fine," Fort said, just trying to collect himself after everything that had just happened. "And my last name is Fitzgerald. Fort Fitzgerald."

"That sounds like a Civil War garrison or something," Jia said, smiling slightly. "I'm Jia, like Dr. Ambrose said. Nice to meet you."

"I'm sorry you have to help me, but honestly, it sounds like I'm for sure going home if you don't."

She frowned. "I was going to ask. What's in three days?"

"Dr. Ambrose said I needed to master the first three Healing spells by then," Fort said. "What does that mean, mastering the spells?"

Both Jia's eyebrows raised. "Three days? *Wow.* There's no way. To master a spell means you've internalized the magic inside your mind, so you don't need to use the words anymore. Before you master it, a spell disappears from your head as soon as you cast it, so you constantly have to go back and read it from the Healing book. To master it, you've got to cast it a few hundred times minimum. No one's ever mastered one faster than a few days before!"

That sounded about right. Dr. Opps needed an excuse to send him away, so this would be an easy one. "I have to," Fort told her quietly. "Please, I can do this. Just tell me whatever I need to know, and I'll learn, I promise. I just . . . I can't go back home."

Jia went quiet and looked away for a moment, then turned back to Fort. "Okay. I'll do whatever I can to help you, but I wouldn't get your hopes up. We'll start in training today, which begins in, like, a half hour. They're just working on broken bones anyway, which I've got down, so I can afford to miss it."

"Working on them?" Fort asked. "What does that mean?"

"You'll see when we get to training," Jia said, and started walking toward the elevator, making Fort hurry to catch up. "You're going to *love* the Boneyard."

- FOURTEEN -

THE BONEYARD TURNED OUT TO BE what the students called the healers' training center, a long room one floor below the lobby level in the Training Hall. The name fit, at least today, since half the Boneyard was filled with long metal tables covered in an assortment of bones.

Around each table was a curtain that could be pulled closed, which didn't bode well for Fort's stomach; that was bound to mean disgusting things happened frequently enough to need privacy. Not to mention that the far wall of the room was covered in half-sized metal doors, just like ones Fort had seen in morgues on television shows. That seemed even *more* ominous.

"Just be glad there are no actual organs out today," Jia said, confirming his fears. "We'll probably be back on those tomorrow, if you're still here." She half smiled. "Maybe that's a good excuse to fail out, huh?"

Fort didn't respond as he stared at the bones. They were all different sizes, each one broken in two, clean through. All in all, it looked like the tables were covered in a grotesque jigsaw puzzle.

"We have to put them all back together?" he said, his stomach dropping to his feet. For the first time, he was glad he hadn't eaten much at lunch.

"*You* don't," Jia told him, and brought him over to the other side of the room, where *The Magic of Recuperation, and Restoring What Has Been* sat on a podium much like the one in the room where he'd taken his test. "All you need to worry about for now is mastering Heal Minor Wounds, Cure Disease, and Cause Disease."

"Right," he said, secretly happy not to jump into bones right away. She opened the book to the first page, which now showed the Heal Minor Wounds spell again, though it had disappeared when he had last read it earlier that day. "I don't care if it's never been done before. I'm going to master all three. I *have* to."

"Whatever you say," Jia told him, looking doubtful. "To prove you've mastered them, Dr. Ambrose will ask you to cast each spell twice, usually by making you create a bandage of the spell on the second try. If you haven't mastered it, you won't be able to cast it twice, and that'll be that."

"How do you do that?" Fort asked. "How do you . . . add magic to something like a bandage?"

"We'll get to that, once you know the spells," Jia said. "No use wasting time with it unless you've got the spells permanently in your head. It won't work until then anyway. But don't worry about that part. It's pretty simple in comparison."

'Simple in comparison' was the first positive thing he'd heard all day. "Got it," he said, then thought of something. "Do you think Dr. Ambrose would be more impressed if I mastered one more powerful spell, rather than three weaker ones?" Anything that could give him a chance here was worth considering.

Jia waved him forward. "Be my guest."

Fort stepped past her and tried to flip forward to the more powerful magic, but the pages wouldn't move beyond the first few. It was as if the book was made from cement past the first spell, Heal Minor Wounds.

"These books were designed for teaching students," Jia told him, flipping the pages herself, though it stopped maybe a quarter of the way in for her. "They won't let you go past the range of your abilities. Basically it means the book doesn't trust you yet."

"Fine." Fort sighed as she turned back to the page with the Heal Minor Wounds spell. "So how do I practice it?"

"Welcome to the Boneyard," Jia said, dropping a sewing needle down on the podium next to the book. "You're going to be bleeding a lot."

Fort stared at the needle for a moment, not comprehending, then suddenly he almost choked on his own saliva. "Wait, what?" he said, his eyebrows shooting up. "I have to stick this through my finger?"

"I suppose, if that makes you happy," Jia told him, then picked up the needle and pricked his index finger until a drop of blood appeared. "*Or* you can go the less dramatic route. A minor wound is a minor wound, Forsythe."

"Fort," he said, beginning to feel slightly less terrified. "You can call me Fort."

"Right, Fort, sorry," Jia said, grinning at his roller coaster of emotions, though she didn't seem to be mocking him. "The spell will disappear from the book when you have it mastered, since you won't need it anymore. It's still there, of course, but you won't see it. And from there on, you won't need the spell words anymore, and you'll be able to cast those three spells silently."

"Perfect," Fort said, staring at the page with the Heal Minor Wounds spell, willing it to disappear already as he ran his eyes over the spell words. "So to master it, I just have to cast it a hundred times?"

She nodded. "Several hundred times, minimum. It's different for everyone, so it could take you over a thousand, for all I know."

The positive feeling of the last few seconds disappeared, and for a moment, Fort agreed with everyone else that there was no way he could do this. But then he pictured one of the creatures digging its way up through his aunt's apartment, and he forced himself to ignore the doubt. This had to happen, no matter what.

"Whatever it takes," Fort told her, and took the pin from her.

"After you've mastered that spell, I'll get you some cultures of bacteria from storage for the next two. They're pretty weak, but they'll qualify as a disease that you can cure. Then you can just use the Cause Disease spell to restore them, and repeat the process. That way you can work on both the disease spells at once." She shrugged. "That's how I did it anyway, and it went a lot faster than the way Dr. Ambrose teaches it."

"Thanks," he said, meaning it. "I really appreciate your help."

She stared at him for a moment, almost looking sad. Finally, she nodded. "No problem. And for what it's worth, I hope you succeed."

He smiled in return, then repeated the words from the spell book to heal his finger. "Mon d'cor," he whispered, holding his uninjured hand over his finger, and felt the same cold energy from before flow into the tip of his finger. The blood immediately absorbed back into his fingertip, and the tiny hole closed up.

"Nicely done," Jia said, showing him the spell again. "Since we've only got the one book, you're going to have to share it with me as you go. We'll just flip it back and forth."

And that was how they went, with Fort practicing healing his pinpricks, while Jia jumped forward to a variety of more powerful spells to practice. At least, that was what she said she was doing, but Fort had no way of proving it, since all the later pages just looked blank to him.

Even so, he was moving more slowly than she was, as she ended up waiting on him several times. While she waited, she'd share her thoughts about magic.

"It's not that you get more powerful as you progress," she said, slowly wiping away the remains of a sunburn on Fort's neck with a spell. "You just learn more complex magic. The more spells you learn, the more complicated healing you'll be able to do. You'll be reattaching broken bones months before getting anywhere close to curing a headache. I'm still working on migraines. Brains are the hardest part to heal, because they're so intricate."

"Why would a headache be harder than reattaching a bone?" Fort healed his finger, letting Jia turn forward to her spell again. "One takes aspirin, the other takes months to heal."

"You're thinking of it scientifically, and that's not how magic works," she said. "At least not Healing magic. Healing is restorative, meaning it restores something to an earlier state. If you think about it that way, reattaching a leg is just putting something back where it belongs. The magic just . . . encourages the leg to become what it used to be, one complete bone. But with something like a headache, you have to be much more careful. You might cure the headache, yes, but maybe by doing so, you restore the entire brain to a point two hours ago, and lose all the memories you made since then."

Fort's eyes widened, the needle inches from his finger. "Healing sounds kinda dangerous."

"That's what those Destruction kids don't get about it," she said, running a hand over her arm and slowly growing a protective armor made of toughened skin. "Healing isn't just about fixing cuts. While they're setting things on fire, we're learning how to build and rebuild living things." She brought her hand back over her arm, restoring it to normal.

"So it's a lot more complicated than it looks," Fort said.

"This is why Dr. Ambrose spends each morning teaching us so much about medicine and how our bodies work. Without that knowledge, we can't really perfect our magic. It's the basis for how we cast our spells."

By this time, other students were beginning to show up at the Boneyard too, followed by Dr. Ambrose.

"Ignore the new kid," their teacher said, standing between Fort and the rest of the class as the students assembled at the tables of bones. "Now, today's training is simple. You've all mastered bone mending, so I want to see every single bone in here healed before dinner. And just to give you added incentive, whichever table finishes last gets sent to Destruction training tomorrow."

Several of the kids actually gasped.

"Don't blame *me*," Dr. Ambrose said to them. "Colonel Charles says he needs healers working alongside his little soldiers, since his kids keep getting injured." She sighed loudly and theatrically. "I swear, if child services ever showed up here, it'd be a bloodbath."

Fort looked over at Jia, wanting to ask why Healing students would participate in Destruction training, but she was concentrating on a new spell, so he went back to practicing instead. That was the most important thing, anyway. Once he'd passed Dr. Ambrose's challenge, then he could ask all the questions he wanted.

Including why Colonel Charles wanted him here, but no one else did.

Behind him, the students sorted through the pile of bones, reattaching each pair they found that fit together. Dr. Ambrose wandered around, watching the work, but not saying much. It took Fort a few minutes to realize why: Dr. Ambrose was too old to use magic, so she wouldn't be able to cast even the first spell in the book.

That had to be odd for a teacher, Fort thought. Usually, someone like Dr. Ambrose would have been an expert at whatever subject she'd be teaching, but here, no one really knew much about magic, and the teachers themselves couldn't even see the spells.

That made her less of an actual teacher, and more of . . . maybe a trainer? Or just a related expert in the field, who could teach the students relevant information, but nothing about the actual magic? Did that make her feel a little powerless?

"What is this?" Dr. Ambrose said, picking up a random bone from the table. She stared at one of the students, then snapped the bone in half. "Mason, was this *your* doing?"

Mason nodded, looking nervous. Dr. Ambrose nodded as well. "If you'd healed a bone in a human being like that, it'd be too weak to hold the weight of your patient. The bone would need to be rebroken before being set again. Congratulations. You just won your whole table Destruction training."

"No," Mason whispered, glancing around at his tablemates, who seemed ready to badly heal *his* bones. One look from Dr. Ambrose sent them silently to the door instead. Once the door closed, they could all hear one of the boys begin to sob.

Dr. Ambrose sighed loudly, rubbing her temples. "Get used to this," she said, not looking at her students. "By next week, Colonel Charles wants you *all* cycling through Destruction training. I tried to . . . I really . . . oh, forget it. I'm not your mother. Get back to work."

- FIFTEEN -

LATER, AFTER TRAINING WAS OVER AND the other students filed out, Dr. Ambrose waved Fort and Jia over to her desk.

"You two can use the book in the Viewing Room until it's locked down tonight before dinner, Jia," she said, taking off her glasses and rubbing her eyes. "Just make sure he meets Dr. Oppenheimer for dinner in the officers' mess at 1900 hours. Don't bother killing yourself trying to help him, though. There's no way he's going to master one spell, let alone three."

Fort swallowed his protest as Jia nodded and picked up the book from the podium, then led Fort out. "See you tomorrow," Fort told his teacher, since it felt weird to just leave without a good-bye.

"Ugh, that sounds like a threat," Dr. Ambrose said with a sigh.

Jia brought him to the elevator, where they waited in silence.

Finally, the doors opened, and Fort almost leaped inside, anxiously shifting back and forth until the doors closed. Finally they did, and all the questions Fort had been holding in came flooding out like a dam breaking.

"What's Destruction training? Why is everyone so afraid of it? Do people get hurt? Why would they let that happen? I thought we were too young to actually fight, and that's why we were making bandages—"

Jia took a step back from his onslaught, holding up her hands. "Whoa. Okay. Wow. Slow down. One at a time."

The elevator opened again, letting them out on the first floor. Fort kept quiet as they walked through the offices to where he'd first had his testing earlier that morning, conscious of the soldiers' eyes on him. When they reached the testing room, what Dr. Ambrose had called the Viewing Room, it was empty, meaning Fort could get back to the questions.

"So, Destruction training?"

Jia sighed. She placed the book on the podium next to the Destruction magic book, then sat down in front of both. "We learn to heal by studying anatomy and practicing our spells. Destruction students practice through . . . well, combat. Once you know how to cast a magic missile, there's not much you need to learn in terms of specialization, like with Healing. So they learn to fight, usually against each other. It's pretty brutal."

"They don't *actually* attack each other, do they?" Fort asked.

"Well, do you know paintball?"

"Yeah," Fort said. "That's where you shoot paint pellets instead of bullets at each other?"

Jia nodded. "Imagine that, but with fireballs, or magic missiles, or lightning. The Destruction students either split into teams, or go every student for themselves, and try to hit each other with their spells. They have protective gear on, but someone's always getting injured. That's why Colonel Charles wants us there, for quick healing. Whenever someone gets hit in an unprotected area, a Healing student has to rush in and heal the player up. Only hits on protected areas count in their training, so we have to make sure whoever got hit can still train."

Fort paused, several thoughts passing through his mind at once. Their training was *that* dangerous? But of course it would be, if they were using real magic against each other. Rachel had thrown him across the room without even trying, when she thought he was attacking Dr. Opps.

But why would the teachers be forcing the Healing students

to do this? Or even allow it in the first place? What happened if a healer got hit while training was happening?

Right. Combat experience. Which made sense, if Colonel Charles was trying to teach his students how to fight for real. And if that was the case, all the more reason Destruction was where Fort needed to be.

"So, I'm guessing it's okay to hit the healers, too," he said.

Jia nodded. "The Destruction kids think it's funny to aim for us. Most of them are jerks, honestly. The teachers don't stop them either, 'cause they think it's better training."

"Maybe they should give *us* Destruction magic too," Fort said, his mind racing with possibilities. "That'd make it a bit more even."

"No one studies two books at once," Jia told him. "It'd be like learning two foreign languages at the same time. If you mixed up a spell somehow, combined Destruction and Healing . . ." She shuddered.

Just because no one had *yet* didn't mean it couldn't happen. "Sounds like I should get back to mastering these spells, then," Fort said, and walked over to where Jia was sitting. She didn't move as he opened the Healing book and took out his sewing needle.

For a few hours, he worked at mastering the Heal Minor Wounds spell in silence while Jia read a medical handbook she'd brought. Every so often he'd think of a new question to ask her, but held back, as he really needed to concentrate on learning the spells.

As for the Destruction training, it did sound intense and pretty dangerous, but if it could prepare him for what he needed to do, then he was happy to participate. Maybe if he volunteered to take another student's place, Dr. Ambrose would take pity on him and knock the spells he needed to master down to two?

Ha, right, like she'd care about her students at all.

"Why are you here, anyway?" Jia said out of nowhere, startling Fort from his thoughts. "I mean, I get it, the idea of learning magic is amazing. But I know what happened to you in D.C. Everyone here does. I'd think that'd make you want to get as far from this stuff as possible."

Fort bit his lip, not sure what to say. *I want to keep what happened to me from happening to anyone else, especially my aunt. I want justice for my father. And I want to watch that monster suffer. To make it feel like I felt. To make it* afraid.

"I don't really have a choice," he said finally. "I don't have much of a home to go back to. Both my parents are . . . gone. And my only family is my aunt, who can't afford to take care of me at all. I think this is it for me."

Jia nodded. "I don't think any of us really had a choice. My dad was from a small village in mainland China, near to where the Healing book was found, actually. He had left to study theoretical physics, and met my mother, who was becoming a chemist. But when the book was discovered, the government brought him in because they could send him to the site without bringing up too many questions with the locals. And then after a few years, we were sent here, with the Healing book, to combine research with the scientists here."

Wow. She'd left her entire country behind? "How old were you?" Fort asked.

"Only three," she said. "I hardly remember it anymore. We've never been back, because my father refuses to return until he figures out the mystery of the books." She flashed a small smile. "He doesn't believe there's any such thing as magic. He keeps quoting some science fiction writer, saying, 'Any sufficiently advanced technology is indistinguishable from magic,' so the books must be some kind of source code to the universe. He had Dr. Opps convinced for a while, but who knows now."

Fort shrugged. "I must have missed the lesson in school about how making fireballs was just a natural thing to do."

She raised a hand, and Fort watched as it began to glow with blue light. "All I know is that if this is science, then whoever wrote the books was thousands of years more advanced than we are."

Fort frowned. "Has Dr. Opps discovered anything about who did write the books?"

Jia shook her head. "Just that the books are only a few thousand years old. That's younger than the pyramids in Egypt, but no one had seen any historic evidence of them before Discovery Day. Which brings up all kinds of questions, like where did the books go for all that time? Why were they buried? Why did magic disappear at all? Why can't adults use it, but anyone born after that day can?" She smiled again, staring off into space. "All questions my father couldn't answer. He and my mother are off at one of the sites now, still digging for answers. Or at least, that's my guess. Even with their security clearances, all our letters to each other are heavily censored."

So in the past thirteen years, the government hadn't managed to find out much more about the books than Dr. Opps had known the day they were found. That was interesting. Was it because people were working in secret, so they couldn't be too obvious with their research? Or were the answers not to be found through science?

Unfortunately, Fort didn't know the answers any more than Dr. Opps did. "So how did *you* end up here?" he asked, changing the subject back to Jia.

"Since we were already here, and I was born on the right day, they pulled me in immediately," she said. "Helps when both your parents are already working on the project."

"Right," Fort said quietly. "Would you go back to China if you could?"

"I'd like to see it," Jia said. "I probably wouldn't remember anything, but it'd still be nice to visit. We just never traveled because my parents were so busy with the books. All I've known is our place outside D.C., and, well, now the school."

D.C.? Fort's whole body seemed to tighten, like a rubber band pulled tightly. "So you were close to the attack?"

Jia looked up in surprise. "I didn't . . . what?"

"You said you had a place outside D.C. Were you there during the attack?" He leaned forward, not sure why this was so important to him. Maybe it would help in some way if he wasn't the only one here who'd gone through that.

"No, I . . . I wasn't on the Mall," Jia said, shaking her head.

"Were you close?"

She seemed to be getting more tense with every question. "No. I was . . . I wasn't around. I don't really remember, okay?"

This set Fort back. "You don't remember? How could you not—"

"I know what happened!" she shouted, and her sudden anger made him take a step back. "Why do I have to remember every single detail about my day? Is it so wrong that I'd rather forget, maybe?"

"I'm sorry," Fort said quietly, not sure what had just happened. "It's not wrong at all. I would probably forget if I could. I was just curious."

"I wish we all could forget," she told him. "I wish this could all just go back to normal, and we'd never heard of magic to begin with." She stood up and motioned for him to follow. "C'mon. We have to get you to the officers' mess for dinner. Don't want to be late."

Fort watched as she walked out of the room, then checked his watch. Six p.m. If dinner was at 1900 hours, that was military time for seven o'clock. They still had an hour.

I always knew you were great at making friends, his father said in his mind. *Winning hearts left and right, that's my Forsythe!*

- SIXTEEN -

"SO HOW HAS YOUR FIRST DAY BEEN?" Dr. Opps asked Fort as they ate together in the officers' mess hall. While several of the assembled military personnel gave them odd looks, at least no one was heating up Fort's tray to molten-hot levels or making quiet snarky comments that only he could hear, so that was at least a step up from earlier. Also, the soldiers guarding them seemed noticeably more comfortable than the ones in the student mess.

On the other hand, he was having dinner with a man who'd lied to him from the very first moment they met, and was looking for any excuse to send him back home to his aunt.

Fort took a moment to think about Dr. Opps's question, running through all the things he wanted to say but couldn't, before finally settling on something that might not get him in trouble. "I like Colonel Charles. Do you think he's happy I came to the school?"

Dr. Opps's fork froze midway to his mouth, then finished the journey. "We all are. Why did you ask about him in particular?"

"He was just really nice during the testing earlier," Fort said. "He told me that if I worked hard, I might be able to switch to Destruction."

"Dr. Ambrose told you about mastering the first three Healing spells, I take it?"

"She did," Fort said. "It sounds like it's pretty challenging to do, though." *Almost like you're giving me an impossible task so I'll have to go home.*

"Are you not up for a challenge?" Dr. Opps asked, giving him a side glance. "I thought you wanted to be here."

"No, I'm definitely up for it," Fort said, trying to casually eat his own food, only to have some potatoes drop off his fork. "Three days or not, I'll master those spells. I'm not leaving, even if I have to work ten times as hard as anyone else. I guess I don't understand why I have to learn them so quickly, when the other students take a week just to master one spell. That's what Jia said, anyway."

"Maybe that's why," Dr. Opps said, taking another bite. "Maybe we need more hard workers around here."

"That doesn't really answer the question," Fort said, his annoyance starting to outweigh his caution.

Dr. Opps gave him a look. "I'm the headmaster here, Forsythe. I don't answer any question I don't want to. Now, how are you and Jia getting along?"

Given that she'd dropped him off at the officers' mess almost an hour early, then walked off in silence, probably not great. "Really good," Fort said. "She's incredibly helpful."

"Good," Dr. Opps said. "Stick with your studies, and do whatever Jia tells you to do. She's one of the best healers we have, way ahead of the rest of the class." He paused. "And while this certainly is going to be a difficult challenge for you, I intend to show the rest of the school that a birthday means nothing. I refuse to believe that you can't be just as powerful as the other students. And you working hard and mastering the first three spells in a third of the time will prove that."

"I'll catch up to them," Fort said, not even paying attention to his food as he tried a different tactic. "Maybe if I do, I could join Colonel Charles's class. I think he sees something in me—"

Dr. Opps's fork dropped to the plate loudly. "What did I just say? You'll be in the Healing course, or you'll be heading home. I don't care if you master the entire book in twenty-four hours."

Anger rose in Fort's chest, and he had to fight not to shout at the headmaster. "But you *showed* me that I could fight those creatures using Destruction magic, back at my aunt's house," he said quietly, trying to stay calm. "Why would you do that and then not let me learn how?"

"You would never be allowed within ten miles of an attack, even if you did master Destruction," Dr. Opps told him, turning back to his plate. "None of you students will be involved in any combat operations until you're at least eighteen. Not as long as I have anything to say about it, at least."

Fort clenched his fists below the table. "But that's not *fair*," he snarled. "Don't I deserve justice for what happened?"

"You don't want justice," Dr. Opps told him, setting down his silverware. "You want revenge."

"Fine!" Fort said, his voice rising now. "Maybe I do! But don't I deserve it? That thing killed my father!"

Other uniformed officers started turning to look at him again, but Fort didn't care. Dr. Opps didn't seem to notice either. "Whether you deserve it or not," the headmaster said, "it would only lead to further pain on your part, even if you *were* powerful enough to face one of those things, which you wouldn't be. Given how little we know about the creatures, I'm not sure anyone here is."

"I could be!" Fort hissed, leaning in close. "Just give me the chance. My father is *dead—*"

Dr. Opps dropped his head into his hands and sighed.

"And you would be too, if not for Sierra."

Fort immediately went silent, staring with wide eyes at the headmaster, who glanced at him once, then turned back to his food. "What did you just say?" Fort whispered.

Dr. Opps looked back up, then reached to take a bite. "I said, I'm not sure anyone here would be able to face one of those things."

"No," Fort said, his voice low as he leaned in close. "After that. You said that I would be dead too, if not for Sierra."

Dr. Opps slowly put down his fork, staring at Fort. "No, I didn't."

"Yes you *did*," Fort said, not sure why Dr. Opps was lying again. "I heard you! What did you mean by that? Who's Sierra?"

"I didn't say that," Dr. Opps said, looking just as surprised as Fort felt. "I *never* said it. How could you have heard that?"

"I know you said it. I heard it!" Fort shouted.

This time, he was staring straight at the headmaster when he heard Dr. Opps's voice again.

The boy heard my thoughts. It has to be her. There's no way he could do this. Sierra must be connected to him more than we even suspected. But how can she still use her magic?

And the whole time, Dr. Opps's lips never moved.

- SEVENTEEN -

FORT PUSHED BACKWARD IN ALARM, his chair tumbling to the floor. "How did I . . . what . . . I just heard you *thinking*. . . ."

Dr. Opps leaped forward, grabbing for Fort's uniform. *"What did you hear?"* he hissed, his face a mix of anger and fear. "What is she—"

But other voices around the room were now rising, and not because of them. The silverware on the tables began to clink against the plates, and the temperature in the officers' mess plummeted until Fort could see his own breath. The lights flickered just like they had in the Viewing Room during Fort's test, and several of the officers started crying out in alarm. A few of the soldiers even raised their weapons, but they had nowhere to point them.

What was going on? For some reason, even surrounded

by armed guards, Fort suddenly felt very exposed and totally vulnerable.

"Oppenheimer, what's happening?" Colonel Charles said, rising from a nearby table and pulling Dr. Opps away from Fort.

"I told you those worldwide reports were true," Dr. Opps said, shouting over the general noise. "What did you *think* would happen if you brought the boy here?"

Colonel Charles turned around to yell into his phone, something about increased activity of some kind, while Dr. Opps turned back toward Fort. "Get him back to the dorm," he yelled at a soldier just behind Fort. "Charles, come with me!"

Colonel Charles threw Dr. Opps an annoyed look but started to follow him out, even as the soldier dragged Fort toward a different door. "Wait!" Fort shouted. "What is this? What's happening?"

Before Dr. Opps could answer, someone screamed in the middle of the mess, and the rest of the room went deathly silent. The tables stopped shaking, and the lights stopped flickering, though they stayed low.

And somehow, though he couldn't have explained why, Fort knew that something had changed. Something was in the room with them.

Something . . . *inhuman.*

A high-pitched, wet squealing came from the center of the room, and terror passed through Fort's veins like ice water. He wanted to yell or run or just close his eyes and curl up into a ball, anything to not see whatever it was that had just appeared out of nowhere. But his body refused to move, and he could only struggle to breathe in the freezing air.

The soldier holding Fort was tall enough to see over the assembled crowd, and whatever he saw made his eyes widen and his mouth open and close without any words coming out. His hands went limp, dropping Fort's arm.

"Shoo-shoot it," a man covered in medals whispered from Fort's side. "For the love of all that's holy, *shoot it*!"

Fort heard the click of a gun safety being turned off and saw a soldier nearby raising his weapon toward whatever it was. But as he aimed, the soldier started to softly weep, and the gun soon tumbled to the ground, with the man right behind it. He curled into a ball there, slowly rocking and crying to himself.

Through the assembled bodies, Fort caught a glimpse of something *floating* in midair, and his heart stopped. Whatever it was shimmered transparently, like a ghost or even a holographic projection. It wore some kind of opaque crystal armor, but beneath the armor, where a human being's feet would have been, a multitude of tentacles squealed as they dragged across the floor. Behind each one, some sort of black goo singed the tile floor.

Fort's entire body screamed for him to run, to hide, anything. But even as he struggled just to breathe, part of him wondered if this thing *was* a ghost, how was it touching the ground?

"It's looking for the boy!" Fort heard Dr. Opps hiss at Colonel Charles, both of their faces deathly white. "I've got the medallion Sierra made. It might be our only chance of getting out of here alive"

"Is it—" Colonel Charles whispered.

"Yes," Dr. Opps replied. "And you know what these things can do!"

"Get Forsythe out of here," Colonel Charles snapped at another soldier, who nodded, trying his best not to look at the thing in the center of the room. The man grabbed Fort and dragged him toward the door. Still too afraid to even take a step on his own, Fort couldn't do anything but stare in the direction of the horror, not wanting to see it, but unable to look away, either.

And then the creature turned to *follow him.*

YOU USE THE THOUGHT MAGIC, said a voice ancient and all-powerful inside Fort's head. The strength of the voice made his skull ache, and he cried out as he grabbed the sides of his head, trying frantically to keep himself together.

"Oppenheimer?" Colonel Charles shouted, raising a shaking gun toward the creature. "Whatever you're going to do, do it *now*!"

The inhuman creature shuffled another step and was just about to appear fully in Fort's line of sight when Dr. Opps stepped between them, holding the same medallion he'd used on Fort's aunt in her apartment. He raised it up for the creature to see, and it began to glow brightly. "GO BACK TO WHERE YOU CAME FROM," Dr. Opps shouted, and light shot out from the medallion, some sort of magical burst.

Fort saw another mass of tentacles rise, this time where its hand should have been, and the beam of light froze in midair. THIS ITEM WAS THE SOURCE OF THE THOUGHT MAGIC? came the voice in Fort's head, and he shrieked in pain again. Several people around Fort grabbed their heads, so he knew he wasn't the only one to hear it this time.

"I command you!" Dr. Opps shouted, though he seemed to be in great pain as well. "Leave this place, and never return!"

But the monster gestured with one of its tentacles and the medallion shattered into pieces, the light that had emerged from it disappearing into nothingness. IF THAT WAS THE SOURCE, WE HAVE BEEN MISLED. PRAY THAT WE DO NOT RETURN TO THIS PLACE.

And with that, the inhuman horror disappeared, and Fort began to sob in relief, surprised to still be alive. What *was* that creature? He'd at least been able to move during the attack in D.C. But here, now, he couldn't even face the thing!

Dr. Opps fell to his knees in front of Fort, cradling his hand that had been holding the medallion. Colonel Charles came swiftly to check him over. "Get Jia here to heal him," he ordered a nearby soldier, his voice still shaking. He turned to Fort and glared at the soldier still gripping him. "And what did I say about the boy? Get him *out* of here—now!"

The temperature had now returned to normal, and the lights brightened to their usual setting as the soldier holding Fort resumed dragging him toward the door. For once, Fort was happy to let him. It had come here looking for *him*. Even just speaking, the thing had almost ruptured his mind.

If that was how it communicated, what could it do if it wanted to hurt them?

"Happy, Charles?" Fort heard Dr. Opps say. "Is this what you wanted? That thing could have killed us all if it wanted, and that was just a shadow of its power!"

Colonel Charles glanced over at Fort. "This just proves the need for all of this. We must have the boy's power. If this is what it takes to awaken it, then so be it."

"We need to see if Sierra . . . ," Dr. Opps started, but Fort missed whatever else he said as the door to the mess hall slammed shut behind him, and he found himself out in the evening air.

"What . . . what was that thing?" the soldier asked.

Fort just stared at him in silence, no idea how to answer.

The soldier waited for a moment, then shook his head. "We should have set fire to those books when they first appeared. What we're doing here, it's *wrong*. You kids are messing with something we've got no business touching. And that thing is the result."

Fort wanted to argue but couldn't honestly think of a thing to say in their defense, so he just followed along quietly back to the boys' dorm.

- EIGHTEEN -

THE SOLDIER HURRIED FORT TO THE dorm, then shoved him inside and slammed the door behind him. All the boys turned to look at Fort, but for once, he didn't feel embarrassed by all the attention. Almost dying seemed to have put his priorities in order.

"There was . . . something in the officers' mess," he said quietly. "Something from . . . I don't know, another dimension or something. It wasn't human, whatever it was. I think the school was just attacked."

"What are you talking about?" a boy Fort didn't recognize asked. "There wasn't an attack. There are alarms all over the base that would have gone off."

"I don't know what it was," Fort said, trying and failing to slow his heart back to a normal speed. "It was wearing some kind of armor, I think, but it had tentacles, and it spoke in our heads."

Someone snorted nearby, and Fort turned to find Bryce sitting on the bed next to his. Or was it Blaine? He couldn't even begin to remember at this moment which was correct.

"Is this what you're going to do for attention?" Blaine asked. "Since you're done getting pitied for the D.C. attack, now it's time to make up another one?"

Anger coursed through Fort, and he slowly turned to face the Destruction student, just now noticing that Chad and Trey had moved to surround Fort. "I'm *not* making this up. I was just in the officers' mess, and—"

"The officers' mess? That's where I usually have dinner too," Chad said. "What did the tentacle monster do, order the steak?"

His two friends snickered, while the rest of the boys went back to whatever they were doing before Fort entered. Were they serious? Something supernatural had just appeared out of nowhere, and none of the boys even cared? Or did they really just not believe him?

"Must have been a really *bad* attack," Trey said. "You know, considering how none of us heard anything, and no one's outside bringing in the tanks. By the way, Band-Aid, who said you could take this cot?"

"Who cares about the *bed*?" Fort shouted. "I'm *telling* you—"

"This is *our* bunk," Blaine said, sitting down on it and shoving Fort's clothes off. "We use it as a spare. Pick another one, or we'll see how long it takes to burn that uniform of yours."

"The one you're *wearing*," said Trey.

"I think that was implied," Blaine said, giving the other boy a dirty look.

Trey shrugged. "I could see it going either way. But it's not very threatening if we're just talking about lighting his extra ones on fire."

Blaine sighed. "Did *you* get my point, Band-Aid? That we're going to burn you and the uniform at the same—"

Fort plowed into the boy, crashing them both to the ground. Blaine landed hard, still surprised by the attack, and Fort punched him in the stomach, once, twice, a third time, rage overwhelming his mind. All the anxiety and betrayals and terror of the past day bubbled up inside him, and he let it out on the boy beneath him.

Someone yanked him backward, and he lashed out wildly but missed as Blaine rose unsteadily to his feet, one of his hands burning with a deep red flame.

"Hold him," Blaine said to the other two, and strong hands grabbed Fort's arms, pulling them behind his back painfully.

"Of course you'd fight like some kind of . . . *normal*, without any magic."

"At least I fight one-on-one!" Fort shouted, kicking out at Blaine, though his foot came up short.

The two boys behind him laughed, and Fort began to smell smoke. They dropped his arms, releasing him, and he quickly pulled his now-flaming shirt off and beat it on the ground to put the fire out. Trey and Chad now both had flames in their hands too, and all three surrounded him, leaving him nowhere to go.

"You chose that bed, Band-Aid," Blaine said. "Now sleep in it."

Even with the threat of being burned, part of Fort was still thrilled to have an excuse to fight again, to let his anger out. And it wasn't like these boys didn't deserve it. But a voice that sounded a bit like Jia's broke through his fury, reminding him that if he got caught fighting, he was probably going to get sent home even earlier then Dr. Opps already wanted.

"No," Fort said finally, taking a deep breath and lowering his hands. "I'm done with this."

"Lie down on your bed or we *burn you*," Chad said.

"If I lie down, then you'll just burn the bed," Fort said, his eyes flicking from Blaine to Chad to Trey.

The other three boys just looked at each other. "And?" Chad said.

"So if you're going to burn me either way, I'm not doing what you say."

Someone groaned loudly from farther in the dorm. "All right, I've had enough of this."

All four of them turned to find the tall boy Fort had seen in the cafeteria earlier, the only healer to actually still have his appetite. The boy strode toward them from his bed at the far side of the room, and the three Destruction students actually seemed to shrink in response.

"This is none of your business, Sebastian," Chad said, but Fort saw him back away a bit.

"It is if you're annoying me," Sebastian told him, his hands glowing a strange color of blue. Fort could feel the cold coming off them from a distance, and he realized with a start that these Destruction students were actually afraid of a *healer*.

"We were just having some fun with the new Band-Aid," Blaine said, holding his hands up defensively as Sebastian grew closer.

"Cool, let me join in," Sebastian said, and lunged forward, grabbing Blaine's flaming hand. The fire was immediately extinguished, and the boy started to yell in pain as some sort of pustules began to grow on his hand.

"Stop that!" Chad yelled, and launched a yellow bolt of energy at Sebastian. The healer just sidestepped the magic missile, letting it slam into an innocent Destruction student behind him as his hand stayed locked on Blaine's.

"I'm never quite sure what I'm going to get with Cause Disease," Sebastian said, then reached out his free hand toward the other two. "Apparently Bryce has had the chicken pox in the past, so that's what came up for him. It's pretty rare now, actually! Want to see if you two are that lucky?"

Both the other boys immediately put up their hands in surrender, their flames going out, as Blaine—no, Bryce—fell to his knees, tears streaming down his face. "They *itch*," he whimpered as the rash spread over his face and the rest of his body. "They itch *so bad*!"

"I wouldn't scratch," Sebastian said, releasing him. "Not unless you want permanent scars."

Bryce angrily pushed to his feet, his hands on fire once more, but Sebastian just threw him a look. "Apologize, or I leave you like this."

The flames on Bryce's hand gradually went out, and he sniffled loudly. "I'm . . . I'm *sorry*. Would you please fix this?"

"Apologize to the new kid," Sebastian said, nodding toward Fort without looking at him.

Bryce wiped his nose, then turned to Fort. "I'm sorry. You can have this bed."

Fort grabbed his extra uniforms. "That's okay. I think I'll take one in the back."

Sebastian waved a hand over Bryce, and his chicken pox immediately cleared up. The Destruction boy laughed almost hysterically in relief as Trey and Chad pulled him away. Sebastian, meanwhile, just turned and strode back to his bed. Fort followed quickly behind him, noticing Cyrus was waiting in the bed next to the one he'd pointed out that Fort would chose earlier that day.

"You didn't have to do that," Fort told Sebastian, as he moved to match the other boy's pace. "I don't need people protecting me here. I can handle myself."

Sebastian gave him an ice-cold smile. "Did I ask? They were bugging me. If they'd set fire to you outside, I'd have been fine with it."

Fort paused, not sure if he was kidding. "I'm . . . I'm Fort. I'm a healer too, and—"

Sebastian's hand locked on Fort's wrist, and he felt his head grow cloudy as his whole body started to ache. "You were the one distracting Jia in class. She usually covers for Mason. I had to heal, like, half a dozen of his wounds when he got back from Destruction training."

Fort began to shiver violently, suddenly feeling like the room had dropped ten degrees, but he refused to look away. "Maybe he should have been better at bone mending, then."

Sebastian's eyes widened a bit, but he smiled wider. "Welcome to the Oppenheimer School, new kid. Let's hope you survive the experience."

And with that, he climbed onto his bunk, leaving Fort to collapse into his new bunk with a full-blown case of the flu.

- NINETEEN -

APPARENTLY A FLU VIRUS WASN'T considered a minor wound in terms of magical spells. That would have been helpful to know before Fort cast his only spell on himself, since using it made it disappear from his head, and nothing much happened other than some temporary relief from the aches and fever, like he'd taken some aspirin.

"Don't worry, I've already seen Jia fixing that for you tomorrow," Cyrus told him as they faced each other from their beds. The lights had gone out a few minutes ago, and most of the boys were either reading or playing video games. "I'm sorry that you're not going to get much sleep tonight, though."

Tomorrow—when he'd be down to just *one* full day before the test. And here he hadn't even mastered one spell yet. Fort sighed, shivering under his blanket. Even without the flu, he couldn't imagine getting much sleep, not after everything that had happened today.

But even so, getting a prophecy of insomnia was something he could have done without.

"Something really did appear in the middle of the officers' mess, Cyrus," Fort whispered to his only friend, and filled him in about everything that he'd found out since he'd last seen Cyrus, from hearing Dr. Ambrose and Dr. Opps's conversation about how both wanted him gone, to somehow hearing Dr. Opps's thoughts at dinner about someone named Sierra, to the fact that the creature had been looking for Telepathy magic, which somehow it had felt Fort using. Or this Sierra girl was using it *on* him, from what he'd heard in Dr. Opps's head.

Having finally caught up to the present, Fort pulled his blankets up closer to his face, trying to glean every last ounce of warmth out of them as his teeth chattered. "You believe me, right?"

"Of course!" Cyrus said, smiling supportively.

For the first time all day, Fort actually felt a bit better. "And you can use your powers to see all of it, and tell everyone else I'm not crazy?"

Cyrus's smile didn't fade. "Nope, not even a little bit. I can only see the future, not the past. And since you were just going to dinner, I didn't bother looking to see what might happen there. Seemed like it'd be a fairly dull affair, to be honest."

Fort groaned and rolled over on his back. What use was being able to see the future if you had to know ahead of time where to look? "Of course you didn't. Tell me you at least know who Sierra is?"

"Never heard of her," Cyrus said. "I can try looking in the future for her, but without knowing more about her, I'd have almost no hope of finding her."

Fort scrunched his eyes closed as he shivered. "Is there *anything* you can tell me? Like, am I going to get sent home?"

The other boy paused, closing his eyes. "Tonight . . . *no*." His eyes reopened and he grinned. "See, that's good news! Do you want me to look ahead to the next few days?"

Fort sighed softly. "*Nope.* How about we just look up lottery numbers and call it a night."

Cyrus shrugged. "The future isn't good or bad news, it just is. Life is less about what happens and more about how you deal with those events. For some people, winning the lottery might end up ruining their life. And look at you, learning magic. You're only seeing the obstacles, but lots of people, including most of the adults here, would kill for the chance to cast even one spell."

"I get that," Fort said, flopping back to face Cyrus in irritation, now sweating from the warmth of the room. What was wrong with the heating here? "But I'm not here for the magic. I'm here for what it can *do* for me. But now I don't even know what's going on. How could I hear Dr. Opps's thoughts? And why did that thing show up, right after I did? It had to be connected, right?" His eyes widened. "Wait a second. Earlier today, I heard all the school administrators saying stuff during my test, but Dr. Opps said no one said a word. The lights flickered then, too. Maybe I was hearing their thoughts, and that thing was tracking me down somehow?" He shivered, and this time not from the chill. "What if it comes back, Cyrus? I don't even know how I'm doing this! What if I do it again, and it hears me?"

"Could you two shut up?" Sebastian said from a few beds down. "If I hear one more word, I'm going to heal both your mouths closed."

At least *that* had been out loud. Cyrus gave him an apologetic look, patted his shoulder, then settled into his bed. Fort sighed and flipped over, far too worried and apprehensive and flu-ish to sleep.

Minutes ticked by, and Fort got cold again, though he somehow still seemed to be sweating. The rest of the boys had turned out their personal lights now, and next to him, Cyrus quietly snored away. For a moment, Fort wondered what it would be like, knowing the future. Would it be comforting, since you'd always know ahead of time if something bad was going to happen? Or would you just be dreading all the worst things you knew were coming?

At least he'd know if that creature was coming back. Who could have sent it? Had it come from the same place as the creature who'd attacked D.C.? But that monster hadn't seemed intelligent, while the horror in the mess hall clearly could think for itself.

Wait a second. All this time, he and everyone else had assumed that some foreign country had sent the creatures to attack D.C. But what if it wasn't some other human being? What if there were creatures out there, creatures like the one in the mess hall, that were to blame? None of the adults in the room had been able to stop the thing tonight, and Fort doubted many of the students would have had any better luck.

If that thing wanted humanity dead, was there any way to

even stop it? Colonel Charles had said something about awakening a power within him, which probably just meant Fort learning Destruction magic. But what if it didn't? What if there was some other form of magic that he could learn, that might actually let him face these things?

Speaking of other magic, there was the Sierra problem.

You would be too, if not for Sierra, he'd heard Dr. Opps think. Meaning he'd have been dead in the attack in D.C. if not for this girl. But who was she? He *had* heard a girl's voice in his head, both during the attack, and in his nightmares ever since. Was that what Dr. Opps meant, that her voice telling him to run was what saved him? But who was she?

More importantly, if she *could* take over people's minds—which explained all the silent tourists fleeing in single-file lines during the attack—then she was the one who'd stopped him from saving his father. And that was something he couldn't forgive.

Sierra, if you're out there, we need to talk *about some things,* he thought about yelling out into the void, just to see if she heard him. But wait, what if that creature sensed her using her Telepathy and came back to the base? The last thing he wanted was to hear any more thoughts!

Sighing, Fort pulled his blankets up again, wondering miserably if sleep would ever come. At least if he stayed up all night, he'd avoid any of those really crazy fever dreams he always got when he was sick. . . .

- TWENTY -

"OKAY, TELL ME WHAT YOU CAN SEE," A FAMILIAR girl's voice said as Fort watched through her eyes, his mind in a dreamy haze.

"Whoa!" said a red-haired boy with closed eyes who stood in front of the girl. He quickly raised his arms and began to flap them. "I'm flying! How are you doing this? I'm really flying! It feels completely real!"

The girl laughed gently. "That's because it *is* real, as far as your mind knows. Think about it: Your senses tell your brain what exists outside your body. If I fool your brain with a little magic, how would you know my illusions *aren't* real?"

The boy broke into a wide grin as he swung his arms around in place, like he was gliding. "This is *amazing*," he said. "Can you see what I'm seeing?"

The girl grinned, and Fort could feel how much fun she was having. "Of course. I'm the one creating the scene in your head. You're just seeing what I'm imagining, Michael." She turned to a dark-haired boy off to the side, who was paging through one of the books of magic, ignoring the rest of them. "You want to try next, Damian?"

"No thanks," he said quietly, not looking up. "I don't have time to play."

The girl felt a pang of annoyance at this but wasn't exactly surprised. Damian avoided the other three whenever he could. She couldn't tell if he didn't like them, or just really was that intent on studying his magic, but whichever it was, she was torn between wanting to help him and punching him in the face.

"I wouldn't exactly call it playing," said another familiar voice. Fort looked up through the girl's eyes to find Dr. Opps smiling down at her and Damian. "Think of the uses for something like this. There'd be no need for anesthetic in surgery, not if the patient had no idea they were being operated on. We could send someone to space, and the rest of the world could witness it through their eyes."

"You could also sneak into places pretty easily," the girl

said, and Michael laughed. Damian threw her a look that she couldn't read, and for some reason, it made her feel guilty for joking. Ugh. The punching side was winning now.

"That's not why we're here, Sierra," Dr. Opps said, and Fort gasped silently. This was Sierra's memory he was seeing? "These books are a gift, and we have to use them for the betterment of humanity, not to break into banks."

"I never *specifically* said banks," Sierra said, grinning at Michael. "It's not like I'd need the money, not if I could trick someone into thinking I'd paid them in their mind."

"Could you be serious for one minute?" Damian asked her, his look even darker this time. "Dr. Oppenheimer is trying to make a point."

"Well, how exactly is Destruction magic supposed to help humanity?" Michael asked, creating a sword of fire in one hand and swinging it around the room. "I mean, sure, I can protect people with my powers, I guess, but—"

"Is that what you call what you did to my office, Michael?" Dr. Opps asked, smiling gently. "Protection?"

Michael blushed, and the fire sword disappeared. "That was an *accident*."

"And a good lesson for why we train," Dr. Opps said. "Sierra, I think it's time we move on to mind reading, shall we?"

Michael's eyes widened, and he slowly moved toward the door. "I really should go, um, study or something," he said quietly.

Sierra gave him an innocent look. "What's wrong, Michael? Got things in your head you don't want me to see?"

"Well, yes?"

"You won't be reading their minds, of course," Dr. Opps said. "As usual, I'll be thinking of random numbers, and I want you to confirm that you can see them."

Sierra sighed, hating this lesson. Of all the things she could do with the spell, why did mind reading have to have the most tedious training? Dr. Opps closed his eyes, and she concentrated on him, already feeling bored. There were so many possibilities, and here she was, reading out numbers like a stage magician.

1829228, Dr. Opps thought, holding a finger to his forehead unnecessarily. Sierra threw a glance at Michael, and they both hid their smiles. Damian just rolled his eyes.

"1829228," she said out loud.

99783112723232.

"997 and a lot more numbers," Sierra said, feeling even more restless.

"Sierra, please," Dr. Opps said. "This is important. We have to determine the limits of your Telepathy when you use the magic. Now concentrate, and tell me my full thought this time."

"Yes, Dr. Opps," she said, and glanced over his mind again. "39808901821 21, and then something about how Michael needs to stop picking his nose, because frankly, it's disgusting."

"Hey!" Michael shouted. "I didn't have my finger anywhere near it!"

"Maybe Dr. Opps is reading the future," Sierra said. "Like those kids in the UK?"

"That will be quite enough," Dr. Opps said. "Michael, Damian, you're both dismissed. Try not to burn anything down, Michael. And, Damian, please keep practicing the spell we talked about."

"Yes, Dr. Opps," Michael said, while Damian just nodded and left the room right after Michael.

Dr. Opps sat down on the table a few feet from Sierra

in his classic lecturing pose, and she sighed internally. This would go a lot faster if she just read his mind instead of waiting for him to yell at her.

This is important work, and I need you to take it seriously, she saw in his mind. *Think of the miracles we could accomplish with the power we've found. And maybe just as important is the potential for great evil, and that must be avoided at all costs.*

"Sierra, this is important work," Dr. Opps started, but she held up a hand.

"I know, I've heard the entire speech already," she said, then flashed him an apologetic smile. "I get it, I really do. And I want to get better at it, to learn more powerful spells, if just so I can actually stop Michael from all the nose picking."

Dr. Opps gently smiled at this. "He really does seem to have a problem."

"Wait till he sets fire to it," Sierra said, giving him a terrified look. "But I just don't get why we have to go over the spells I've already mastered again and again. Can't we try something new? Damian's, like, ten Telepathy spells ahead of me, and he doesn't have to practice."

"Damian's a special case," Dr. Opps said. "He's obviously talented, but his usefulness will be in his flexibility, not in his depth. We need you to be our master of mental magic, Sierra." He patted her shoulder. "If nothing else, I want to see you control Damian's mind in your next one-on-one challenge. The boy could stand a little humility, I think."

She snorted. "Done and done."

"Good," Dr. Opps said. "Now, since you asked so nicely, let's change things up a bit. Why don't you tell me what the boys are up to, along with our resident Healing queen? Don't think I didn't notice she didn't show up today."

Sierra winced. "I, um, don't see her right now." That wasn't exactly true, but Sierra *had* promised to cover for her. "But Michael is setting fire to things in the Destruction training room, and Damian . . ." She paused, then gasped.

"What do you see?" Dr. Opps asked her as he jumped to his feet.

Sierra just looked at him. "There's something in the room with Damian. Something . . . not *human*."

- TWENTY-ONE -

THE SOUND OF A TRUMPET JOLTED Fort straight up in bed, only for the aches and chills to knock him right back down. Right, the flu. Why was someone evil playing music so loudly? He looked around frantically for the source and noticed Cyrus sitting on his already made bed, smiling.

"That's the reveille," he said. "Think of it as an alarm. Welcome to your last full day before the test!"

The thought of having so little time left woke Fort up more than the trumpet had. Then the events of yesterday and the feverish dream came flooding back to Fort, and he groaned loudly.

"You don't seem thrilled," Cyrus said. "Was it because you didn't sleep well?"

"Nope. But I think I know who Sierra is now."

Cyrus closed his eyes for a moment, then popped them back

open. "Ah, she's a Telepathy student? I didn't know that we had a book of mental magic here."

Fort just stared at him. "How did . . . did *you* read my mind?"

"No, I just looked ahead to when you told me about things and saw the conversation happening at breakfast," Cyrus said. "And now you don't have to tell me. So efficient!"

This hurt Fort's brain almost as much as the fever. "But . . . doesn't that mean you won't find out, because I *won't* tell you at breakfast? And then you won't see it, so you wouldn't know now? Aren't you changing the future?"

"Of course," Cyrus said with a shrug, standing up as the other boys around him groaned and began to rise as well. "The future's *always* changing. That's one of the tough parts about this magic. But it's not like I'd forget what I already saw, just because you're not going to tell me then. You *will* have told me if I hadn't seen it, so in one sense, you already did."

". . . No," Fort said. "Just *no*, to all of that." He pulled his covers over his head and reveled in the warmth for one last minute.

"Let's go find Jia before breakfast," Cyrus said, patting his shoulder through the blankets. "She'll get you cured. I've already seen it."

With the promise of good health as motivation, Fort quickly

got dressed, then followed Cyrus out as the rest of the boys got ready more slowly. Bryce, Chad, and Trey all grinned at the sight of Fort's miserable, sickly face, and for a moment he considered coughing all over them, but that would take effort, and he barely had the energy to walk.

Outside, there were noticeably more soldiers around, after the events of the night before in the officers' mess. They all seemed much more on edge than before, and they hadn't exactly been calm to begin with.

Fortunately, Cyrus turned out to be very handy at finding people, considering he could look into the future and see where they'd be in five minutes. With that knowledge, they timed their arrival at the cafeteria just as Jia showed up. She took one look at Fort's face and sighed.

"I shouldn't be surprised," she said, her hands already glowing blue. She ran them over his head and chest, and the energy passed into his body, immediately curing him of the flu. "Sebastian, I take it?"

"Yeah," Fort said, sighing in relief, both from the healing and from the fact that she seemed to have forgotten whatever he'd done to annoy her yesterday. Maybe the flu had helped him out after all. *"Thank you."*

"I'd stay away from him," Jia said. "His mother is on the congressional committee that the TDA has to answer to. He's the only one at this entire school who definitely will never get sent home. But she wouldn't let him learn Destruction magic, and I doubt he'll ever get over that, so he's perpetually annoyed with everyone."

"How is Dr. Opps's hand?" he asked her. "I heard Colonel Charles yell for someone to get you to heal him."

Her eyes widened. "How did you know about that?"

"Let's get some food, and I'll explain," he told her. "I'm starving!"

She raised her eyebrows but went quiet as other students began coming into the mess. After grabbing some scrambled eggs and pancakes, they sat down at a table that Cyrus promised would stay otherwise empty, and Fort filled Jia in on what had happened the night before in the officers' mess, as well as his dream (which also negated any paradox of Cyrus not officially hearing it too).

Jia didn't seem to take it as calmly as Cyrus did, though. "They wouldn't tell me what happened," she said quietly, looking away. "This is bad. This is *so* bad."

"Do you have any idea where this Sierra girl is?" Fort asked her. "She definitely seems like a student here, but I didn't recognize the room I saw in her memory."

Jia swallowed hard and wouldn't look at him. "She's . . . she's gone. She's no longer a student. They sent her home."

"You know her?" Fort asked. "What about those other two, Michael and Damian?"

Jia seemed to flinch at the names, and she pushed her tray away. "I didn't know them. I'm not really hungry anymore. Can we stop talking about this?"

Fort gave Cyrus a confused look, and the other boy returned it with a shrug. "This is pretty important, Jia!" Fort said. "If you do know them—"

"None of them are here, okay?" she said, standing up abruptly and grabbing her tray. "Now *let this go*. You said yourself that thing was looking for Telepathy magic. The last thing we need is for you to lead it back here. You have no idea what you're messing with, Fort."

"I don't, you're right," he said, even more confused now. "That's why I'm trying to find out more—"

"Just let it go, for all of our sakes!" With that, she walked over to the garbage and dumped her uneaten food, and then, with a quick look back at them, left the cafeteria.

"What was *that* all about?" Fort asked Cyrus. "Did I offend her somehow?"

His friend just stared off into space for a moment. "Seems like she knows more than she's saying, doesn't it?" Cyrus said finally. "At times like this, I feel like it'd be kind of useful if I could see the past, too." He frowned. "I wonder if there are spells for that, later in the Clairvoyance book."

"Wait," Fort said, realizing something. "Why don't you look ahead in my future, and see if we get answers out of Jia?"

Cyrus smiled. "And then we wouldn't need to even have the conversation. You're right!" He closed his eyes, so he missed Fort's wincing at his words. "Hmm," Cyrus said after a moment, his eyes still closed. "Today is . . . not really going to be your day. Ouch."

"Great," Fort said. "What about tomorrow?"

Cyrus furrowed his brow. "Tomorrow . . . looks really fuzzy for some reason." He opened his eyes back up. "That's weird. Usually the future's only fuddled up when the person is near the books of magic. I don't know if the books cause it, or if the chaos of pure magic messes up my sight somehow, but I've never been able to see anything around them, or even closely related to them. The teachers tried having me search the globe for the rest of the books already, and it's like there's just a hole in that part of my vision."

"Perfect, so maybe we never find out what Jia knows," Fort said, dropping his head into his hands.

"Too bad you can't use the Telepathy magic yourself," Cyrus pointed out. "That'd make this a lot easier."

Fort shook his head violently. "Even if I could, I'd never use it. What if that thing from the officers' mess heard it and came looking for me again? There's no way I'd take a chance. You didn't see it, Cyrus." Even the thought of it made Fort's blood go cold.

The other boy gave him a supportive look as Fort turned back to his breakfast, his appetite now gone. First Dr. Opps and Dr. Ambrose, now Jia. Why did everyone at this school have something to hide, a secret to keep? How was Sierra sending him thoughts if she wasn't even at the school? And why him to begin with?

"So on the bright side," Cyrus said, having no problem eating his own breakfast, "you *will* be seeing Jia later today. You won't get any answers out of her, but at least she's not still mad."

"Oh yeah?" Fort said. "Last time she only forgave me because I had the flu. What happens this time, a hospital visit?"

"Whoa!" Cyrus said. "See, now you must be reading my mind, because that's *exactly* why!"

- TWENTY-TWO -

AFTER BREAKFAST AND CYRUS'S prophecy about what was to come later that day (if that was what it really was), Fort found himself in a surprisingly normal situation: math class.

Before he and the rest of the healers went to Dr. Ambrose's medical training, they had two classes of regular school, taught by a very nervous-looking soldier. That probably shouldn't have surprised Fort as much as it did; there was no way even a secret government agency would let kids get away with skipping school.

Fort quickly figured out where the class was in their lessons and felt confident he could keep up without worrying too much about it. And that was good, because he found it pretty impossible to pay attention, considering everything that had happened in the last twenty-four hours, not to mention that his test to remain at the school was *tomorrow*, and if he failed that, he was getting his memories wiped before being sent home.

The regular school classes were small, and the students from both magic disciplines were mixed in together. Cyrus and Jia weren't in Fort's class, nor were Bryce, Trey, or Chad. Sebastian and Rachel were, though neither seemed to be paying much attention to him, which was probably for the best. He didn't need another case of the flu, or someone protecting him like he was a little kid, either.

Though between the two, at least Rachel didn't involve aches and chills.

When it came time for Dr. Ambrose's class, Fort prepared himself to confront Jia, ready to demand answers about Sierra and the other two boys he'd seen in his dream. But when he arrived with the rest of the healers, Jia was nowhere to be found.

Instead, Fort got thrown into what turned out to be the most graphically disgusting lesson he'd ever seen as Dr. Ambrose walked her students through the workings of an arm muscle, showing on a screen exactly how various injuries looked, and how they could be fixed.

"Now *this* is a torn muscle," she said, flipping to a new picture of an *actual* muscle with an *actual* tear in it, making someone next to Fort dry heave. "See how the muscle strands are all literally ripped? Someone didn't stretch before working out, am I right? So which spell would you use on this? Mason?"

"Would it be . . . Heal Heavy Wounds?" Mason asked.

Dr. Ambrose sighed. "If you think *this* is a heavy wound, wait until we get to pictures from the ER. No, Mason. Please try to keep up, as I'm not actually teaching these classes for *my* benefit."

Sebastian raised his hand, then started speaking before Dr. Ambrose even called on him. "The spell to use is Restore Body, the same as rebuilding bones," he said.

"Right, as usual," Dr. Ambrose said, shaking her head. "How is it that the only one of you who *doesn't* need to study to stay in this school actually knows the answers?"

In spite of Dr. Ambrose wanting him to fail out of the school, Fort actually found himself fascinated by the lesson. It did help to know what sort of magic he'd need to use on various injuries, given how little his Heal Minor Wounds spell had worked on his flu symptoms. Besides, who knew what might help him with his first three spells?

The lessons continued, getting more and more disgusting,

until even Fort ran out of the room after Dr. Ambrose showed a slide of severed toes, then demanded Mason answer whether *that* was a major wound. Fort wasn't the only one to excuse himself either, and there ended up being a line for the restroom.

After the class finished, Dr. Ambrose stopped Fort on the way out. "Only one day after today until your test, Forsythe," she said as the other kids left, looking various levels of nauseated. "Jia told me you don't need her help anymore, which I think we both know is a lie. But given that Oppenheimer confirmed to me that she's off the case, that tells me you did something to annoy her, or him." She narrowed her eyes. "But while I'm glad to have Jia back, I'd like to know why."

"Wait, what?" Fort said, his eyes widening. "No, I *definitely* still need her help. Where is she?"

"What am I, her daily schedule?" Dr. Ambrose said. "Clearly you know less about this than I do, so further conversation won't help. Not that it ever does. Off you go."

She shoved him out of the classroom, then slammed the door behind him as he stood in the hallway, shocked.

Jia wouldn't help him anymore? And somehow she'd gotten Dr. Opps's permission to stop? What could she know about Sierra that they wouldn't let Fort find out? This was maddening!

"Argh!" he shouted, and slammed his fist into the door.

"Take your angst somewhere else, please!" Dr. Ambrose shouted from inside the classroom, and Fort blushed, then quickly headed for the elevator.

As he left the Training Hall, he caught sight of Dr. Opps walking toward the officers' mess, presumably for lunch. Fort sprinted to catch up and stopped the headmaster before he could go in. "Dr. Opps! I need to talk to you."

The doctor turned and visibly flinched when he saw it was Fort. That was never a good sign. "Forsythe, *stop* there."

Fort did, several feet away. "But I have questions—"

"I have too much classified information in my mind for you to get anywhere near me again," Dr. Opps said, shaking his head. "It's for your own good. And there's nothing I can tell you about what happened last night anyway. The TDA is running an investigation, and Colonel Charles isn't in a sharing mood today." He seemed annoyed at this, so maybe Fort wasn't the only one getting left in the dark.

"It's not about that, though I do have a lot of questions," Fort said. "Like where is Sierra, and why is she—"

"All you need to know is that she's no longer a student, and we *will* find a way to stop her using her power on you," Dr. Opps said. "Now if you'll excuse me, I'm rather hungry. I spent all night using one of our mental items to hide the school from that thing, in case you have any more telepathic experiences out of nowhere. It won't last more than a day or two, but we shouldn't need it much longer anyway." He gave Fort a long look.

"If you won't tell me about Sierra, then why isn't Jia tutoring me anymore? Dr. Ambrose's test is *tomorrow*, and there's no way I'm going to pass it without her."

"I can't imagine you will, no," Dr. Opps said, no longer even hiding the fact he wanted Fort gone. "I've given her permission to get back to her studies, so if I find out that you're keeping her from them in *any way*, I'll have no choice but to send you home, Forsythe. Do you understand me?"

Fort's eyes narrowed, but he nodded.

"Good day, then, Forsythe," Dr. Opps said, and made his way into the officers' mess. The doors closed behind him, and two soldiers guarding the entrance gave Fort a close look. Fort backed away with his hands up, then turned and made his way back to the Training Hall.

There was no way he was going home now, not before he found out what was actually happening at this school.

If only he didn't have to master three spells by tomorrow in order to do that.

- TWENTY-THREE -

FORT HELD *THE MAGIC OF RECUPERATION, and Restoring What Has Been* on his lap as he sat on the floor of the Viewing Room. Just twenty-four hours earlier in the same room, a bunch of military officers had mocked and criticized him—at least in their heads. Fort didn't want to think about how close they'd all come to that horror showing up even earlier in the day, considering how the lights had flickered then, too.

"Thanks for that, Sierra," he whispered to himself before pricking his finger, then healing it. Drop of blood, cool healing energy, over and over, so many times he'd lost track long ago. And still he hadn't mastered the first spell.

Did it matter, though, considering how much Dr. Opps and Dr. Ambrose both wanted him gone? He might not make it to the test, at the rate things were going. Not to mention that

Cyrus saw him in a hospital bed later that day too, which was just *great* news. Even if it wasn't true, Fort didn't exactly need another thing to worry about.

Why did there have to be so many secrets at the Oppenheimer School? Why couldn't people just be up front? Dr. Opps had even lied about never lying!

"Why is everyone *hiding* things?" he shouted into the empty room, then slammed the book of Healing down onto the floor next to him.

"You know, they don't really like it when you mistreat the books," a voice said behind him, and Fort felt a cold, sinking feeling. He whirled around to find Rachel watching him with a curious expression on her face.

He immediately blushed and turned away. "Sorry, I didn't know anyone was there."

"So you just beat up on books in private, then?"

His blush got deeper. "No . . . no! I just meant, um, about what I said."

Rachel walked around to face him. "You seem upset, New Kid. Did those Chads all steal your uniforms? Is that what you mean by 'everyone hiding things'?"

Fort opened his mouth to tell Rachel what was happening,

then reconsidered. Every time he shared, he lost another friend. Maybe it was time to just keep his mouth shut for once. "It's nothing. What are you doing here?"

"I'm *always* here," Rachel said, coming over to grab *The Magic of Destruction, and Its Many Uses*, before sitting down next to him. "Whenever I'm not in class or training, I'm here. Colonel Charles gave me special permission." She stopped and then raised an eyebrow. "How exactly did *you* get in? Your badge shouldn't have worked. Only a few of us have permission to come in here."

Fort turned even brighter red, not wanting to reveal that when he'd been turned away, he'd had to track Cyrus down to badge him in. "Oh, you know, I've got my ways."

"Oh, so *you're* hiding things now too?" She flipped open the book of Destruction and paged about a fifth of the way in. "Being mysterious is a lot less cute than people think, New Kid. And I know you had Cyrus get you in. I saw him do it. That was a test, and you failed at not being lame."

"Call me Fort, okay?" he said. "New Kid just reminds me of Bryce and his friends."

"Right, the Chads," Rachel said. "If you stay long enough, Fort, you're going to see there are two types of students here:

the ones who work hard, and the ones whose parents got them in. Like that Sebastian guy in your classes, his mom's a congresswoman. And the Chads' parents are all rich, and donated to Sebastian's mom and the other members of the congressional committee that really runs this place."

"You seem more like a hard worker, if you're always here," Fort said, pricking his finger again. "Where did you come from?"

"Army brat, my whole life," Rachel said. "My mother and father both worked their way up to sergeant major from private. Could have gone further, but they enlisted and never got a chance to go to officer school." She half smiled as she formed a small icicle in the palm of her hand. "It's the way the world is for enlisted folk. Most never get a chance to go any higher. Even if you work as hard as you can, there'll always be someone who gets a head start."

"Yet here you are, training after class," Fort said.

"Gotta make Mom and Dad proud, don't I?" she said, making a dancing flame in her other hand. She brought her palms together, and the flame melted the ice. "And what better way to do that than be the best?"

Fort nodded. He healed his finger, then read the words to

the spell again. "If you're the best, have you figured out any faster way to master a spell?"

"Most people do it in a week," she told him, glancing at his book. "I've got it down to, like, three days at this point. Why?"

Fort snorted. "Dr. Ambrose gave me three days to master my first *three* spells. The test is tomorrow, and I haven't mastered one yet."

Rachel gasped. "No way! That's completely impossible, even for me."

Fort nodded. "That's the general opinion. Doesn't matter. I'm going to do it anyway."

"You can try, but trust me, I know how this works. You'd have to stay up all night practicing, even if you had three full days left."

"I don't care." He tried to hold back, but for some reason, the words just kept coming. "All I know is I *can't* go home, Rachel. There's too much here that I . . . I need to find out. And there's nothing waiting for me back there, other than just being a burden to my aunt. Not to mention, who knows if it's even safe, considering . . . anyway. I can't go home. I *can't*." He realized he'd clenched his fists at some point, and the needle was poking into his palm.

"Whoa, okay," she said, putting a hand out to calm him down. "Don't hurt the book again. I get it. Well, I can't help you master a spell faster, but there is one thing I *could* do."

He cast his spell over his bleeding palm, letting the cool energy heal the wound. "Convince Dr. Opps to give me three weeks instead? I'll take it."

Rachel snorted. "No, but I can meet you here after class, before dinner, and let you in. If Cyrus does it again, someone's going to ask questions, but they see me here every night. It'd only be for, like, an hour before they lock the whole thing down at dinnertime, but at least you'd have more study time."

Fort gave her a confused look. "You'd do that? Why?"

Rachel laughed. "Wow, you really *have* had a tough couple of days if you question someone being nice. Remind me to talk to the Chads again. I'll make sure they don't bother you anymore."

Fort felt his shoulders tighten up, and he shook his head. "That's . . . thanks, but it's okay. I can handle myself."

"Not really. Not without magic to back you up."

He felt the frustration begin to rise, and not wanting to turn it on her, he took a deep breath instead, then let it out slowly. "Listen. The whole reason I'm even here is to learn to fight back. I couldn't do anything against that creature in D.C., and it makes me crazy every time I think about how . . . about my father. So whenever someone comes along and saves me, protects me, it just . . . I don't know, reminds me of how *useless* I am."

She gave him a sympathetic look, then patted him on the shoulder. "That makes zero sense," she said. "Is this a boy thing, like you can't have a girl show you up? Because trust me, I've humiliated every guy here, and I'm going to do it again tonight in training."

"No," Fort said. "I was just as annoyed when Sebastian protected me from the Chads too."

"Oh, that would've been fun to see!"

"I just . . . I want to be able to stand up for myself, okay? I don't know how to explain it any better."

"Fair enough," she said, standing up. "I promise that if I see you getting ganged up on, I'll just keep walking. *Happy* to do it."

Fort groaned, dropping his head into his hands. Why did he have to make enemies of everyone who was trying to help him? Why did it have to be so hard to explain what he was thinking? "I'm sorry, I think that all came out wrong."

"Yeah, you could use some work, but that's no different from anyone else here. Don't worry, Fort. Just be glad I'm a great person and am *still* going to let you in here later. But be here before dinner, or you're out of luck."

She rubbed his head, messing up his hair, then left, laughing to herself. Fort sighed deeply, then turned back to the book of Healing, ready to learn Heal Minor Wounds again.

This wasn't going to work. If someone as talented as Rachel took three days for one spell, what hope did he have? He ground his teeth together in frustration. *Why can't I even just learn the pathetic Heal Minor Wounds spell?!* he screamed silently in his head.

But screaming wasn't going to help anything. He picked up the book and started to open it to the first spell, only to stop.

The page was blank. But he'd just cast the spell a minute or two ago, so it should have reappeared already.

Just for kicks, he looked into his mind to see if the words were—

Mon d'cor. He still had the spell in his head.

"Are you kidding me?" he whispered, slowly pricking his finger, then concentrating on his other hand. A familiar cool energy flowed out from his palm, making the drop of blood on his finger disappear completely.

Almost too scared to try again, he pricked his finger one more time, and again, the words were there in his head. He'd actually mastered a spell, and faster than anyone else.

Maybe this wasn't as impossible as they all thought! Could it be that things were beginning to go his way for once?

- TWENTY-FOUR -

AFTER HIS SMALL VICTORY IN MASTERing the first Healing spell, Fort strode across the base feeling hopeful for once.

Look at my boy! his father would have said. *Mastering spells in one day when it takes other people a week? Make him King Wizard already, people. Otherwise you're just wasting all of our time!*

The sadness flowed over him, just like it always did when he thought about his father, but with it now came determination. Even if it was just Healing, at least Fort was learning magic, and that was the first step to getting justice for his father. And while it might . . . not . . .

Fort stopped in place, noticing for the first time that the various guards nearby were all staring at him nervously. What was going on?

A shadow appeared on his left, and almost without thinking

about it, Fort jumped out of the way, right before a ball of fire struck the ground where he'd been standing.

"Whoops!" Trey said, snickering as he, Bryce, and Chad came up behind Fort. "Sorry about that. My fireball got away from me."

Fort looked around to see if there were any teachers or school officials to notice what was happening, but of course the Destruction boys had checked first. "No Sebastian or Rachel to save you this time," Chad whispered, his hand glowing too.

Bryce's hands pulsed with red energy, and Fort's feet froze in place, ice forming on the ground around his boots. He struggled to pull them free, but the ice was too thick. "Don't worry," Bryce said quietly. "You can just blame whatever happens on another monster attack."

The other boys laughed as anger filled Fort's mind. He swung his fist out wildly but only succeeded in almost falling over his stuck boots. "Let me *go*," he hissed.

"Was it a big monster this time?" Chad said, and set the edge of Fort's shirt on fire.

"Were you scared?" Trey asked, sending a magic missile slamming into Fort's shoulder even as Fort tried to slap out the fire.

"Did you cry?" Bryce whispered, shaking his hands back

and forth, sending tremors through the ground below Fort's feet.

"I wasn't lying about what I saw!" Fort shouted, and swung for the nearest boy again, this time missing only by inches. The shaking increased below his feet, and the ice around his boots cracked enough for him to kick his way free. He straightened up to face the three boys, then fell to his knees as the earth began to quake more violently.

"Are you doing this?" he shouted up at Bryce.

But the three boys just laughed at him. "He can't even stand up!" Trey said. "This must be the worst monster attack yet!"

Fort tried to stand, but the tremors were so intense, he just fell back to the ground. This just made the boys laugh even harder, which was all the more frustrating since they seemed to have no trouble standing.

"What are you three doing to him?" a soldier asked, striding over toward them.

"They're shaking the ground so hard I can't stand up!" Fort shouted.

The soldier just looked at him in confusion. "Try to get to your feet, kid. It's okay."

Fort slowly pushed himself to his knees again, making the

three boys laugh hysterically. Then a massive jolt sent him flat onto the tiled floor, where he braced himself as items on tables began to shake all around him.

"What is *happening*?" he heard someone shout, a familiar voice. Sierra's voice.

This was another dream? Another memory?

And then Dr. Opps was there, looking terrified but still in control, and suddenly Fort wasn't so sure. "We need to get out of the building!" the headmaster shouted, and moved toward Fort to help him to his feet. But the shaking was so intense, it knocked Dr. Opps against a nearby wall before he could reach Fort.

"It's another attack!" Fort shouted as loudly as he could, but somehow couldn't hear himself over the rumbling. Even as terror filled his body, he realized that this couldn't be real: A moment before, he'd been outside getting bullied by Bryce, Chad, and Trey, not inside some strange room with Dr. Opps. So the shaking hadn't been real either, just the beginnings of this . . . this daydream?

"You need to send it back!" Dr. Opps shouted from across the room as parts of the ceiling began to collapse, sending showers of dust and materials down all around them. "Close the portal and send it back to wherever it came from!"

"What?" Fort shouted, still not hearing himself, and definitely not understanding. What portal? Who was Dr. Opps talking to?

"He can't hear you!" Sierra shouted, and now it made sense why she sounded so close: He was seeing everything from inside her mind, her memory of what had happened. "Damian's completely gone!"

And that was when Fort saw Damian and almost stopped breathing completely. The creature from the officers' mess had Damian's head in its tentacle hands, grabbing him through a glowing green portal. Damian was shuddering beneath the creature's touch, and opaque armor was growing over his chest.

"Jia!" Dr. Opps shouted. "See if you can use your magic to revert his mind to a past version!"

"On it!" Jia shouted, and Fort was surprised to see her in the room with them. She slid toward Damian on the ground and threw a hand out to grab his ankle. Blue light began to glow from her hand, and the creature in the portal pulled back abruptly from Damian.

And then the room shook so hard they all lost their footing, and a massive clawed finger burst through the floor right below him, sending Fort flying against the wall. He landed hard, and the room began to spin, this time not from the quaking.

"It's *here!*" Dr. Opps shouted. "Jia, you need to free his mind *now!*"

"I'm trying!" Jia shouted from just on the other side of the creature's massive claw. "But whatever that thing is, it's fighting back, negating my spells. I don't know what to . . . wait, I can feel it . . . NO!" She screamed then, loud and terrified, pulling her hands away from Damian and holding her head like it was going to fly apart.

Then her scream cut off abruptly, and a much deeper voice emerged from her mouth. "YOU WILL NOT DEFY ME FURTHER, HUMAN."

Fort felt his blood go even colder at her words, and he looked over to see the same terror on Dr Opps's face.

"This can't be happening," the headmaster whispered, only to turn to Fort, or really, Sierra. "It's up to you. It's taken over her mind. You need to free them both!"

Before Sierra could respond, though, another scaled

finger broke through the floor, and Fort found himself frantically rolling away before a third claw exploded through the floor below him.

"Free their minds, *now!*" Dr. Opps shouted, his voice filled with panic. "If you don't, we're all going to die here!"

"I'll try!" Sierra shouted, and a strange feeling overtook Fort. Somehow, he felt his consciousness reaching up out of his body and floating through the air to enter Jia's mind. Instantly Fort cringed at the absolute darkness he found within, completely repulsed by the awful, oily feeling of whatever it was that had taken over Jia's consciousness. He felt himself slowly pushing his own mind through hers, yanking the other creature off Jia's brain like ivy from a wall.

Then Fort/Sierra floated back across the room and collapsed against the wall.

"Jia's free," Sierra said. "But I . . . I saw something in the Old One's mind. . . ."

An image played through Fort's perceptions, one that he'd had nightmares about for the past six months.

The National Mall, and a monster just like the one below them attacking the Washington Monument and the Lincoln Memorial.

"It summoned a second monster," Sierra whispered. "Using Damian's powers. It sent it to the Mall. There are people there!"

"The priority is Damian!" Dr. Opps shouted. "We need his power to send these things back!"

"I know," Sierra said out loud, but inside, Fort felt his mind soar away, out of a large windowed office building and over highways filled with cars, down through a city with no skyscrapers to where the ground shook around the Washington Monument, and people were realizing that something was wrong.

RUN! Sierra commanded in their minds, using every ounce of her strength. *GO NOW, IN AN ORDERLY FASHION!*

No. NO. Fort couldn't watch what was to about to happen, not again. Not again!

Let me go! he shouted as loudly as he could, hoping she could hear him wherever she was, pushing this dream, this memory onto him. *Don't make me watch this. Please don't make me watch this!*

The scene around him began to waver, like the air in intense heat. He shouted again and again in his mind, hoping to push Sierra out of his head, or at least stop the memory.

Blue sky began to filter in from above, where previously office lights had been. All around him, he could just make out several soldiers holding their weapons aimed at him, interspersed with the attack in Sierra's memory. "No!" he shouted, holding up his hands. "I'm okay!"

"No you're not," Dr. Ambrose said from his side, her image appearing and disappearing inside the memory. "I'm going to sedate him. Someone be ready to grab him!"

"No!" Fort shouted again, but then felt something prick his shoulder, and both memory and reality faded away into nothingness.

- TWENTY-FIVE -

FORT WOKE UP IN A SHADOWY ROOM, and it took him a moment to recognize the steel table he was lying on. A day earlier, it had been covered in various bones, but now it was draped in a white sheet, with another sheet covering him.

"Hello?" he said, not sure if anyone else was there in the dark. He sat up and gently touched his chest and back, expecting to feel bruises or soreness from where he'd fallen through the floor. But wait, no, that had been in Sierra's memory. Still, Trey had hit his shoulder with a magic missile before he'd slipped into Sierra's past, and the shoulder was also totally healed. Not only was there no pain, but as far as he could tell, there wasn't even a bruise. How long had he been out?

"You're awake," said a voice, and the light flipped on. Dr. Ambrose stood up from a chair across the room and rubbed her eyes, then walked over to the table and gently felt for his pulse. "You might feel a bit groggy from the sedative, but otherwise you'll be fine."

"But my shoulder," Fort said, more confused than anything. "Did you—"

"Heal you?" Dr. Ambrose momentarily looked annoyed. "Do I look like I'm twelve? No, I just diagnosed the injuries, so Jia could target her spells better." She rolled her eyes. "Twenty-five years as a doctor, and I'm assisting a teenager. The universe hates me, kid."

Jia had been there? Apparently Cyrus was right, it *had* taken a trip to the hospital for her to see him again. But something else bothered him about Jia. She'd been in Sierra's memory too. Did that mean the two knew each other? Did that have something to do with why Jia wouldn't talk about Sierra?

And how much time had passed in Sierra's life between those two memories? The last time he'd seen Sierra, she'd been training with Dr. Opps. But this one had been a full-blown attack. Could that have been the attack at the NSA? It certainly wasn't the one on the National Mall.

But what were the students doing at the NSA? And were they the reason it had been attacked? There were so many questions, so many secrets that Dr. Opps was keeping from him.

Right now, though, Dr. Ambrose was staring at him like she was waiting for something. "I'm sorry about what happened out there," Fort said to Dr. Ambrose. "I don't know what—"

"Sounded like you were living out an attack by one of those monsters again," Dr. Ambrose said, sitting gently on the edge of the table.

The memory of the Chads doubting him came rushing back, and he quickly sat up. "I know it wasn't real, but I wasn't making it up, either. I don't know how to explain it, but I really did see another attack."

Dr. Ambrose sighed, then nodded. "I know you did, kid. And that's why you need to go home. Leave this stuff behind. There's only going to be more to come if you stay."

"You believe me?" Fort asked, almost too surprised to even hope.

She shrugged. "Let's just say I've got corroborating evidence in this case. But you're not listening to me. Whatever reason you're here, that's not why the school wants you. For your own safety, you should quit and just go back to your normal life."

"I can't," Fort said quietly. "I don't have a choice."

"Yes, you *do*."

"You don't get it," Fort said. "There's someone . . . she's in my head somehow, and—"

"Kid, who do you think you're talking to?" Dr. Ambrose said, looking insulted. "I know about Sierra and whatever weird connection you two have. That's *why* you have to go. None of us know what she's going to do next, and that means not only is *your* life in danger, but the rest of ours are as well."

Fort's eyes widened. "You know about Sierra? Tell me where she is! Why is she in my head? How can I stop this?"

"I can't . . . I can't tell you more," Dr. Ambrose said, turning away. "And not because it's top secret or something idiotic like that, though it is. But if I tell you what I know, you might use that information to do something even more dangerous, and that's not a risk I'm going to take."

Fort started to growl in frustration, only to stop and take a deep breath. "That thing in the officers' mess, the horrible tentacle thing," he said slowly. "It could sense Sierra's magic in my head, and it was looking for me. Don't I deserve to know why?"

"If you get far enough away from here, you should be okay," Dr. Ambrose said, still not looking at him.

"What if I'm not? What if this connection doesn't go away, and that thing comes after me at my aunt's house? I can't leave now. I could be putting *her* in danger too!"

"You're talking to the wrong person, kid. I'm just giving you the best advice I've got. Go home, and go tonight. You were never going to pass my test anyway, we both knew that. There's no shame in quitting when something just isn't possible, and the quicker you leave, the better off we'll all be. Or do you want those memories to keep happening for who knows how many more days until she either wipes your mind, or you lose your sanity like those poor clairvoyants in the UK?"

Fort started to protest, then just closed his mouth. What could he say that would change her mind anyway? She was obviously not going to tell him anything else, and she did make some good points.

But there was no way he was leaving, and *especially* not by quitting.

"Maybe you're right," he told Dr. Ambrose. "I'll think about it tonight, and then we'll see how the test goes."

Dr. Ambrose snorted. "It's your call, I suppose. Yours, and Colonel Charles's. If you change your mind, let me know before the test, and we'll save you some embarrassment. Otherwise, you're free to go. You should be good to walk back to the dorm without a wheelchair, so get your things, and I'll take you over."

Fort thanked her, then slid off the table, a little embarrassed to just be wearing his underwear. He padded on the freezing-cold floor over to where his clothes were, piled up next to the seat Dr. Ambrose had been sitting in. As he grabbed his shirt, he noticed her cell phone and security badge on the table next to him.

"I mastered one of the spells, you know," he told her, dropping his pants over her badge, then pulling his singed shirt over his head. "Who knows, maybe I'll even pass the test tomorrow."

"You won't," Dr. Ambrose said, not looking at him. "I don't know how you mastered the one so quickly, but it's impossible that you'd cover two more in one night, especially without access to the book." She turned to find him buttoning his pants. "And don't even *think* about sneaking into the Viewing Room for more practice unless you do want to head home tonight. Getting caught there after hours is an immediate expulsion."

"Don't worry, I'm going straight to bed," he said, bending over to tie his boots. "Thanks for helping heal me, by the way. And not letting those soldiers shoot me."

"You're welcome, Forsythe," Dr. Ambrose told him, moving to

grab her cell phone before pausing. "Wait a second. Where's my badge?" She turned to give him a suspicious look. "Get over here."

He stepped closer, and she frisked his uniform's arms and legs, then stopped, looking puzzled. "If *you* didn't take it, then I must have left it somewhere. I really hate these things. I've lost more than I care to admit, and the military always puts me through so much headache just to get a new one."

"I'll be sure to keep mine safe," Fort told her, showing her his STUDENT badge clipped to his shirt.

"Hopefully you won't need it past tomorrow morning," she said. "Now come on, let's get you back."

The dormitory was quiet, and the rest of the boys were asleep when Fort entered. Two guards waited outside the front door as Dr. Ambrose dropped him off, so Fort made his way back to the bathrooms, where he knew a few small windows would give him a way out without being seen.

What he didn't count on, though, was Cyrus sitting on the bathroom counter, waiting for him.

"Right on time," Cyrus said, checking his watchless wrist.

"What are you doing here?" Fort asked him.

"Sneaking out to help you study. What does it look like? This is your last night to master the spells, so I'm here to help!"

Fort shook his head. "If they catch us, we'll both get kicked out. This isn't like earlier, when the Viewing Room was still open to students. I appreciate that you want to help—"

"Oh, they won't kick me out," Cyrus said, flashing a grin. "I'm the only one in the world who can use Clairvoyance magic right now. They can't just send me home. Besides, I'm pretty sure my government wouldn't be thrilled if they tried, and they're the ones with the book."

"Fair enough," Fort said. "But this is something I don't need help with." He leaned down and untied his boot, then pulled it off and shook out Dr. Ambrose's badge. "This should open the security turnstiles, assuming I can get there without being seen."

"See, there's where you're wrong," Cyrus said. "Not about the badge, but you're definitely going to need my help. I already looked into your future, and you get caught in your first thirty seconds outside alone. But with me helping, you'll make it to the books without any trouble."

Fort paused. "Thirty seconds?"

"Fifteen, actually," Cyrus said, giving him a pitying look. "I was trying to be nice."

Fort rolled his eyes, but couldn't help grinning. "Okay, and *thank* you, Cyrus. So what do we do first?"

"Uh, first we go out the windows," Cyrus said, looking confused. "Why, were you just coming in here to use the bathroom?"

Fort helped Cyrus climb through the small window nearest the sink, then grabbed ahold of the sill and pulled himself through next. Cyrus stopped him as soon as he landed, pushing them both back into the shadows against the dormitory wall as two soldiers marched past on patrol. As soon as they'd turned the corner, Cyrus grabbed Fort's hand, and they were off.

The distance to the Training Hall wasn't actually that long, but the need to dodge security cameras turned the trip into a strange sort of maze, with Cyrus stopping and starting their movement every few feet at times. The soldier patrols ended up being pretty easy to hide from, but the cameras were everywhere, requiring careful timing to avoid being caught as the cameras slowly turned.

As they passed the fifth camera, then backtracked to avoid a sixth, Fort wondered how he ever thought he'd have made it to the Training Hall, let alone to the Viewing Room. Even with Cyrus's help, he got so nervous and sweaty as they moved underneath a seventh camera that his hand almost slipped out of Cyrus's.

Finally, they made it to the Training Hall, where Cyrus had them wait for almost five minutes, crouched next to the door. By the time two soldiers left the hall, opening the doors for them, Fort's leg muscles had almost cramped up completely, and it was all he could do not to groan in pain as they slipped inside before the doors closed.

They crawled through the lobby, just under the view of the soldier at the desk, then waited for the soldier to stand up to use the restroom, which Cyrus had promised wouldn't be too long. As soon as the soldier left, Fort swiped Dr. Ambrose's badge over the pad at the security door, and the door slid open, giving them plenty of time to scurry half-bent over through the offices toward the testing chamber before the man came back to the desk.

The office area was thankfully empty, but there were still cameras, and crawling wasn't exactly quick. Finally, they reached the door to the Viewing Room, and Fort shook his head, amazed they'd made it. "I can't thank you enough for this," he whispered to Cyrus.

"Oh, you're not quite done yet," his friend told him, rising to his knees to open the door. "Good luck with her!"

"Her?" Fort said, then looked up in shock at Rachel, who stood blocking the doorway with her hands glowing a deep red.

"I thought you might show up here," she said in a low, threatening voice. She leaned forward and grabbed Fort by the shirt, dragged him inside, then threw him down the stairs toward the podium with the books.

Each step sent pain rocketing through Fort's back and shoulders until he came to a merciful stop at the bottom, right below the podium. He groaned, then slowly pushed himself up to stare at Rachel. "What are you *doing*?" he asked, completely confused. Hadn't they been friends the last time he'd seen her? What had he done now?

"Dr. Opps says you're a danger to the school, but he can't send you home for some reason," Rachel told him. "I don't have that problem." She held up Dr. Ambrose's security badge, and Fort gasped—when had she taken it from him? When she'd grabbed his shirt? "Still, I wouldn't want you thinking I'm not a nice, sweet angel, so you have thirty seconds to give me a reason I shouldn't call the guards on you and get you expelled."

- TWENTY-SIX -

I'M NOT A DANGER TO THE SCHOOL!" FORT shouted as Rachel looked at a watch on her wrist.

"Twenty-five seconds," she said, raising one of her glowing hands. "Time's running out. . . ."

"I can't explain everything in just twenty-five seconds!"

"That's good, 'cause you only have fifteen now." She aimed her hand at the floor next to him, and a fireball formed. "This should send the guards running in here."

"They'll send you home too," Fort said. "Neither of us are allowed to be here."

"Maybe," Rachel said. "And if that happens, I'll just have to live with the fact that I saved everyone here from you." She glanced down. "Whoops, time's up!"

"No!" Fort shouted as she unleashed her fireball. Without thinking, he leaped into its path and took the spell right in his chest. Fire exploded all over his torso and face, and he quickly dropped to the ground, rolling around to put it out, trying his best not to shriek in pain in spite of the agony he felt.

"What did you do?!" Rachel shouted, running down toward him. "I didn't want to *hit* you!"

"I can't go home," Fort hissed, gritting his teeth to keep from crying. He quickly raised his hand over himself and cast Heal Minor Wounds over and over until the pain subsided enough to think. His uniform now had a hole in the chest, but at least his skin had stopped blistering. He touched his face, a little scared to check to see if he still had eyebrows.

"You're *insane*," Rachel said, her eyes wide.

"Probably," Fort said, slowly pushing himself to a sitting position. His eyebrows somehow had survived, which was good. That would have been a lot harder to hide than a singed uniform. "But I swear to you, I'm no danger to the school. There's a lot going on here that I don't understand—"

"Start with what you *do* know," Rachel said. Her hands still glowed, but at least she wasn't aiming them at him.

"Okay, but don't blame me if any of this sounds unbelievable," he said. "Here's what I know: There was a student here named Sierra, who studied Telepathy magic."

"There's no Telepathy book here," Rachel said.

"There was at some point," Fort said with a shrug, which sent pain through the burns on his chest. He winced and continued on. "I think Sierra used her Telepathy during the attack in D.C. to save all the civilians by making them flee the scene. She tried it with me, but I fought back. I couldn't just leave my father behind."

Saying it out loud somehow seemed less painful than it had in the past. Maybe because he felt like he knew more about what had happened now?

"How'd you fight back?" Rachel asked. "You wouldn't have had anything to use against her."

"Oh, I just resisted," Fort said. "Hard. I can be a little stubborn."

"I'm noticing."

"Something happened then," he continued. "I heard her scream, and then I blacked out and woke up in the hospital. Ever since, she's . . . been in my mind somehow. I see her memories in dreams, and even sometimes when I'm awake, like earlier today."

"Yeah, I saw that," Rachel said. "I noticed the Chads beating up on you, but I promised I wouldn't interfere again. But then you started screaming random things about an attack, and all the soldiers rushed in, and I wasn't sure what was happening." She looked away. "Dr. Ambrose sedated you, and that's when I heard Dr. Opps talking to her about how you're a danger to the whole school."

"He thinks so," Fort said. "But Colonel Charles won't let him expel me, because I have this connection with Sierra. Whatever it is. Somehow she's been using her magic to let me read other people's thoughts. But I don't understand why she's doing it, and I have no idea where she is. Dr. Opps says she's no longer enrolled in the school, but that's all he'll tell me. Jia knows more too . . . I saw Jia with Sierra earlier in that memory. But she won't talk about it, and Dr. Opps said he'd send me home if I bothered her anymore."

"None of this says danger to me," Rachel said. "Weird, yes. Unbelievable, obviously. But not dangerous. Well, not dangerous for anyone but you, I should say."

Now it was Fort's turn to look away. "There's something out there. Something that I think wants Sierra's power. It felt it when she allowed me to read Dr. Opps's thoughts, and it appeared in the middle of the officers' mess. Dr. Opps used some item that he said would keep us safe for now, but he didn't think it would last very long. So that's what he's afraid of, that the longer I stay, the more likely it is that this horrific thing comes back." He shuddered at the thought of it.

"Seems like you'd want to go home, that being the case," she said. "Explain to me why you're not on the first helicopter back to your aunt's, then?"

"What if it tracks me down there?" Fort said, his voice cracking. "I wasn't hearing thoughts before, but I've dreamed about Sierra ever since the attack. I heard her voice in my dreams, Rachel. What if that thing can sense that, too? I can't put my aunt in that kind of danger. But there's more."

"And what's that?"

"Colonel Charles wants me here," he said, staring at the ground. "I don't know why yet, but he said something about awakening a power that could hurt this thing. And if that's a possibility, then I *need* to stay, to learn how to fight back. You should have seen the officers' mess, Rachel. A whole room full of soldiers, and they were powerless to stop it. It even destroyed Dr. Opps's medallion thing."

Rachel frowned and sat down on one of the steps. "I did hear Dr. Opps say that Colonel Charles wouldn't let you go until you failed a test tomorrow."

"That's why I'm here, to make sure I don't," he said. "I already mastered one spell—"

"What? There's no way! Not in two days."

"So I just need to learn the other two tonight," he finished. "Because if I fail, I *will* get sent home. None of the other administrators know why I'm here, so Dr. Ambrose's test gives Dr. Opps the excuse he's waiting for. They'll just say I couldn't hack it here."

Rachel nodded slowly, then went silent for a moment. "I'm not saying I believe you," she said finally. "But I know Colonel Charles, and he wouldn't let you be here if there wasn't a really good reason. Not that Dr. Opps doesn't know what he's talking about too, though." She sighed. "I'll make you a deal. If you fail your test tomorrow, you go home."

"That's . . . already the deal I have."

"But if you pass," she said, glaring at him, "you and I are going to track down this Sierra girl, wherever she's hiding, and find out what this is all about."

Fort just stared at her in surprise. "You're going to . . . help me?"

"No, it's more like I'm not letting you out of my sight until I'm sure you're telling the truth," she said. "And we won't know that until we find this telepathic girl. If she's even here."

"You've got a deal," Fort said. He pushed to his feet, wincing at the pain in his chest again. "Now if you don't mind, I really need to practice. When do you want to meet tomorrow after the test?"

"What did I just say?" Rachel asked, settling in. "I'm not letting you out of my sight. That doesn't mean let's make plans to meet up tomorrow."

He raised an eyebrow. "I'm going to keep practicing until I master the last two spells, so you might be here for a while."

She crossed her arms and snorted. "Oh, bring it, little man."

- TWENTY-SEVEN -

BY THE FOURTH FLU VIRUS HE'D GIVEN himself, then cured, Fort was starting to hate Healing magic. "Utri cor," he whispered, casting Cause Disease on himself, then read over its twin, Cure Disease, as quickly as he could, before the fever set in again. Both spells appeared on the page, so apparently they were meant to be learned together.

From the benches, Rachel sighed dramatically. "Why does Healing have to be so boring? You should see *me* practicing." She pointed her fingers like guns and made little *pew pew pew* noises. "It's awesome."

"I got a personal viewing of that earlier," he said, wincing at the pain in his chest before casting Cure Disease. "Nenutri cor," he whispered, and the chills he was starting to feel disappeared. "And if you're bored, no one's forcing you to stay."

"I leave when you leave, New Kid," she told him, but she didn't seem as sure as she had been earlier. "I'm still waiting for you to acknowledge how I kept my promise and didn't protect you when the Chads were bullying you, by the way. You're welcome for that."

"You definitely kept your promise, yes," Fort said, giving himself the flu again. "I can't tell you how much that helped."

"That's the problem with Destruction magic, anyway," she said, ignoring him. "There's no real good way to defend against it. That means if you want to beat someone, you always have to be on the attack."

Is that why you threw me down the stairs earlier? Fort thought, before considering what she'd said. "There's no way to shield yourself, or, like, take control of someone else's magic missile and send it back at them?"

Rachel snorted. "Destruction at its core is about tearing things down, not a battle of wills. If someone shoots a magic missile at you, you jump out of the way, then shoot three back at them."

Fort cured his flu and read over the page again. "That doesn't make any sense. You can hold fire in the palm of your hand, which means you're controlling it. Why couldn't you do the same thing to someone else's fire?"

"Is one of those diseases making you deaf? Did you not hear what I just said?"

"I heard it, it just doesn't make sense!" Fort said, giving himself another case of the flu. "This might go faster if you were quiet, you know."

"Talk to me about what makes sense when you've been here longer than two days," Rachel growled at him, then turned away to mutter quietly to herself.

For the next few cycles of his spellcasting, there was silence, until Rachel leaned backward to lie down on the bench, putting her feet up on the next higher one. "Look," she said. "I'm just saying that every kind of magic is different. You've only learned Healing so far—"

"And had Telepathy used on me."

"Ugh, fine, whatever. But you don't get it. Each type of magic is thematic, you know? Healing rebuilds, Destruction tears down. That's why we've got those two books here, so we can practice both of them in the same place. The cool students break some bones, and you boring guys fix them."

"If Healing rebuilds, then why am I learning how to give people diseases?" Fort asked, wishing every time the chills set in that his shirt didn't have a hole in it.

"I always figured that was so you could practice the curing spell."

"No, I mean why would it be in the Healing book to begin with? We're not just learning how to cure things, we're learning how to cause them too." He paused, ignoring the fever for a moment. "You know, I bet there's an opposite spell in the Healing book for, well, healing, too. Like a Cause Harm spell."

Rachel laughed. "Uh-huh. Or it could just be that Healing's completely lame, and you have no idea what you're talking about."

Fort rolled his eyes, then looked back at the book. "We'll never find out for sure unless someone learns every spell in the book. And that takes way too long." He ran his eyes over the spell words for Cure Disease, "nenutri cor," then raised his hand over his arm, only to pause.

"Cor." The second part of the spell. He'd seen that word before. And since the spell words disappeared from his head as soon as he cast them, it could only be in one other spell.

Heal Minor Wounds. Those spell words were "mon d'cor."

That had to mean something, didn't it?

"Have you ever looked at the spell words?" Fort asked, turning to look at Rachel, who was staring at the ceiling.

"Maybe I could make, like, a shield of fire," she said, ignoring him. "That might stop a fireball. Or would it? Maybe the ball would just plow right through."

Fort picked up the Healing book, then dropped it, letting it hit the podium with a bang. Rachel immediately looked at him upside down. "What did I say about hurting the books?"

"Have you ever thought about what the spell words mean?" Fort said again. "I'm seeing the same word pop up in the first two spells. That has to mean something."

She shook her head. "You can't exactly study them that easily, since they disappear. And once you have the spell mastered, you can't write them down, either. Same thing happens. Only the books will hold the spell words, for whatever reason. Makes learning whatever language it is a bit harder."

"Okay, but they're all in your head," Fort said, feeling a bit dizzy now. "Like this same word, 'cor.'"

She looked at him weirdly. "What word?"

"Cor."

She paused again, like she was still waiting.

"You really can't hear me say it?"

"*Have* you said it?"

"Fine," he said. "There's a word that appears in both Heal Minor Wounds and Cure Disease." He paused, then turned back to the third spell, "Utri cor." "*And* in Cause Disease! What do they all have in common?"

"That you're not going to have mastered *any* of them at this rate?"

He stuck out his tongue at her. "I guess they're all about the body in some way. That would make sense, right?" He ran over the next two spells in his head, noticing another repeated set of letters that wasn't in Heal Minor Wounds, "utri." "If we figure out the language, we could come up with our own spells," Fort said, feeling weirdly excited about this, though the fever might be to thank for that. "Do you know what we could do if we knew the language of magic?"

"Get sent home for failing your test tomorrow?"

"My dad gave me something," Fort said, then braced for the wave of sadness he expected to feel upon mentioning his father. Weirdly, though, it wasn't as bad as usual. "This brochure, from the Lincoln Memorial. It listed the Gettysburg Address in a bunch of different languages, and my dad thought that'd be a fun way to learn foreign words, you know? Like pick out which ones fell in the same places as the English words, or repeated in the same way. You could do that with magic words, too."

"Do you have any idea what you're even talking about?"

Fort couldn't exactly say yes, not yet. But if that "utri" word was in both of the disease spells, Cure and Cause, then maybe that was what it stood for? "Disease," or something like it? And if Cure Disease was "nenutri cor," then that "nen" had to mean "cure," maybe.

Unless "nen" didn't mean anything, and was just like a "not"-type word. *Don't* cause disease. Or *reverse* cause disease, maybe? "I think I might be onto something," he said, his mind whirling with ideas, as well as soaring in temperature.

"Is this what you're going to tell Dr. Ambrose tomorrow instead of casting your spells?"

"Okay, *fine*," Fort said, annoyance derailing his train of thought. He quickly cured himself of the flu, feeling less excited even as his body healed. "Enjoy destroying everything, if you want. Once I pass this test—"

"*If* you pass, which you won't—"

"Then I'm going to figure this all out," Fort said. "Think about it. We could make up our own spells, if we knew what the words meant. We wouldn't need to wait to master the smaller stuff, and we could jump to the more powerful magic!"

"Are you almost done?" Rachel said, closing her eyes. "I'm getting kind of sleepy, and I don't have all night."

"I'm not even a *little* tired," Fort said, giving himself the flu again. "I'll be wide awake all night, just watch!"

- TWENTY-EIGHT -

THROUGH A DREAMLIKE HAZE, FORT FOUND himself running next to Dr. Opps through a door. Damian stood in the middle of a room, his eyes wide, his mouth hanging open, as a creature out of horror books floated in the air above him, its transparent and vaguely humanoid body covered in crystal armor, its tentacle fingers locked on Damian's head. A helmet in the shape of a screaming skull topped the body, and another mass of tentacles splayed out from the face hole grotesquely.

Whatever it was, Fort knew he'd seen it somewhere before, or one just like it. Through his daze, he barely recalled the officers' mess from the day before, and a similar set of armor, with tentacles for hands and feet. "It's back, Dr. Opps!" he tried to shout, but nothing came out of his mouth, and he cursed silently at his own powerlessness.

And that was when he realized where he was. Another memory of Sierra's, another dream he couldn't escape.

"Get away from him!" Dr. Opps shouted, pulling a gun from his waist and firing at the creature several times.

Each of the bullets passed through it harmlessly, and Damian slowly raised a hand.

"THERE IS NO NEED to hurt it, Dr. Opps," Damian said, his human voice flickering in and out with something darker, and much more ancient. "It found me. It can GUIDE US IN OUR USE OF THE BOOKS."

"Let the child go free *now*," Dr. Opps said, not lowering his weapon, even though it was useless.

"THE HUMAN IS NOT UNDER its control," Damian said. "It joined with me, so that YOU MIGHT UNDERSTAND US. SPEAK FOR US."

"Sierra, look inside and tell me if Damian's okay," Dr. Opps whispered. Louder, he said, "What do you want?"

"It just told you," Damian said. "It really is here to TEACH HUMANITY TO USE THE POWER THAT'S BEEN REDISCOVERED."

Sierra slowly reached her mind out toward Damian's, gently searching around the edges of his consciousness to see if he actually was under the creature's control. Though she could feel the creature inside his brain, hovering like a terrible coming storm, Damian did seem aware of what was happening and in control of himself still.

Unless the monster was somehow deceiving both of them.

"How do you know about us? Who are you?" Dr. Opps asked, slowly lowering his gun.

"It once lived here, OUR FORMER HOME," Damian said. "HUMANS LIVED ALONGSIDE US. WE DISCOVERED MAGIC, AND TAUGHT IT TO YOU. BUT YOU WERE NOT READY, so the magic went away, and WE LEFT. BUT YOU ARE NOW CAPABLE, SO THE MAGIC HAS RETURNED. AS HAVE WE."

Something lit up inside Damian's head, catching Sierra's attention. In a human being, she would have thought that she'd just heard someone lying to her. But this creature was so alien, it could have meant anything.

"Why did you leave?" Dr. Opps asked, his fear dropping away in the face of curiosity and excitement. "Where did you go? What should we call you?"

"We apparently used to CALL US THE OLD ONES," Damian said. "AS WE WERE ANCIENT WHEN

HUMANITY FIRST LEARNED TO CRAWL. WE HAVE JOURNEYED FAR TO return to their former home. But they need THE HELP OF THOSE WHO CAN USE MAGIC TO FULLY COME BACK."

"Why?" Dr. Opps asked. "What use could that be to you?"

"A DOORWAY," Damian said, and inside his head, the creature seemed to be expanding its reach, like it was searching for something. "OUR FORMER WORLD HAS BEEN LOCKED TO US. OUR POWER ENABLES US TO PROJECT A SHADOW OF OUR FULL PRESENCE, BUT ONLY THAT. WE NEED YOUR MAGIC TO OPEN A DOORWAY SO THAT WE MIGHT RETURN. DO THIS AND YOUR REWARD SHALL BE BEYOND YOUR UNDERSTANDING."

Damian's voice had disappeared, and inside his mind, Sierra could hear him begin to scream. "Dr. Opps," Sierra hissed softly. "We need to get that thing out of Damian now."

The doctor immediately glanced at her, then turned back to the Old One. "Please leave this child for now, and we'll consider your offer."

But the monster didn't listen, and its hold on Damian's

mind grew stronger. "It's not leaving," Sierra whispered. "Should I push it out?"

Dr. Opps swallowed hard. "Please. Give us time to speak about this. But you need to release the boy."

Sierra readied a Mind Blast spell and prepared to cast it at the creature, but right before she did, it removed its tentacles from Damian's head and slowly disappeared into nothingness. Damian toppled to the floor with a groan and went still as Dr. Opps leaped to his side.

"His body is okay," the doctor said, checking Damian's pulse. "How is his mind?"

Damian? Sierra called out inside his head. *Are you okay?*

I think so, came his reply. *I feel like my brain just ran a marathon. The Old One's presence was beyond anything you could imagine.*

"He's okay," Sierra said as Damian opened his eyes, groaning softly.

"Damian, listen to me," Dr. Opps told him. "If that thing returns, do not speak to it. Alert me immediately. I don't know if it's telling the truth or not, but we can't take the chance either way. Before we communicate with it again,

I want to be prepared. And that means finding a way to send it away if need be."

"What?" Damian said, giving Dr. Opps an incredulous look. "Are you serious? It offered to help us. It can tell us more about magic than we'll find out studying those books for centuries."

"*If* we open a door so it can come through completely," Sierra pointed out. "Am I the only person here who just saw a tentacle nightmare beast? Anyone else in favor of burning it with fire?" She raised her hand.

Damian glared at her. "Of course it feels unknowable to us. When it was last here, we barely had written language. Those things discovered magic, Sierra. We could reshape the entire world with their help."

"Unless it was lying about that," Sierra said. "And if they're so all-powerful, why does it need us to open a door for it?"

"I don't know what the right answer is yet, Damian," Dr. Opps said. "But we need the power to send it away if it turns out to be misleading us."

"It's *not*—"

"That's not a chance I'm willing to take," Dr. Opps told

him. "Do *not* seek it out, Damian. If it returns, call for me at once. You are *not* to speak to it alone, not ever again. And you certainly shall not use any magic at its request or command. Do you understand me?"

Damian started to say something, then looked up at Dr. Opps's stern glance and just nodded instead.

"Good," the doctor said. "Now you rest for a bit, Damian, and try to remember if there's anything you saw in your mind that you haven't told us yet. Sierra, come with me."

She nodded and walked with Dr. Opps outside Damian's room. The doctor gently shut Damian's door, then paused and turned to Sierra.

"I want the power to *destroy* that thing," he told her. "Just in case. What spells do you have that might work?"

She grinned. "I'll make a list."

- TWENTY-NINE -

"WAKE UP!" SOMEONE SHOUTED, and Fort bolted up.

Jia stared down at him in horror from the entrance to the Viewing Room, and the night before came crashing back in on him.

"I fell asleep?" Fort said, his eyes widening. "Rachel, you let me fall asleep?"

"Shh, five more minutes," Rachel said from the other side of the room, her eyes still closed.

"What time is it?" Fort asked, panic flooding his fevered body. "Did I miss the test? Am I too late?"

"I'm here to get the book," Jia told him. "But what did you do? Do you know what would have happened if Dr. Ambrose had come down here instead of sending me? Or if *Colonel Charles* had come for the Destruction book?"

"This is terrible," Fort said, jumping up. "I can't believe I did this!"

Jia stared at him for a moment, then sighed. "It's fine, I won't tell on you or anything. I mean, you're already probably in trouble for not returning to the dorm last night. Just hurry, because—"

"No, I mean I can't believe I fell asleep!" he shouted at her. "I needed to master the second two spells, and I . . . I don't even remember if I did!" He paused, staring at her, then leaned in close. "But I do remember that you *lied* to me, Jia. You *did* know Sierra. Why wouldn't you tell me?"

Jia flinched. "I don't know what you think you know—"

"I *saw* it, in her memory!" Fort shouted. "I don't *think* I know anything, I watched it happen!"

"You don't know what you saw," she said softly. "Now I have to go."

"Why did you lie to me?" Fort said as she pushed past him to grab the Healing book. "What did I ever do to you?"

Jia stopped in place, then turned to stare at him. "Maybe it's not all about *you*, Forsythe." With that, she walked past him, only to pause at the door. "If I were you, I'd get to class immediately. Dr. Ambrose will be there any minute."

Fort watched her go, not sure how he'd suddenly lost the high ground in that argument. Jia had been the one to lie to *him*. How had *she* gotten to leave indignantly?

Sighing, he turned back around and noticed the Destruction student still lazing on the bench. "Don't you have to get up too, Rachel?"

She yawned, then slowly sat up, cracking her neck. "I guess I've done my job here, protecting the school by watching you carefully."

"Really? That's what you call sleeping the entire time?"

"You're just cranky 'cause you were up all night," she told him, stretching. "Don't take it out on me. Wow, these benches are *not* comfortable, huh?"

"How'd it go?" said a voice from the door, and Fort looked up to find Cyrus standing there, holding a new uniform for Fort.

"How did it go?" Fort shouted. "I fell *asleep*! I don't even know if I mastered the spells. If only you'd seen this coming, I might have found a way to set an alarm or something. . . ."

Cyrus slowly turned red. "Um, honestly? I sort of did see it, back when I went through all the different ways of getting us here last night."

"What?"

"I didn't want to tell you," Cyrus continued as Fort changed his burned shirt. "But if you'd tried to get back to the dorm last night, you were going to get caught. Sleeping here was basically the only future where you made it to your test on time."

"What use is being on time if I slept through all my studying?"

"Think positively!" Cyrus said, pushing him toward the door. "Maybe your unconscious picked up something by osmosis!"

Fort growled in frustration but hurried after Jia.

"The least you could do is wait for *me*, after I helped you study all night!" Rachel shouted from behind him. "And don't forget our *deal*!"

The soldiers behind the glass walls all gave Fort a confused look as he and Cyrus passed by, jogging for the elevators, probably wondering if they'd seen him enter earlier or not, but that was the least of Fort's concerns now. Chances were that he was about to fail out of the school. And that couldn't happen.

Cyrus left Fort at the elevator, giving him a thumbs-up as the doors closed. Thankfully, there weren't any other students in the elevator with him, so Fort collapsed against the wall, trying to calm down. The last thing he needed to do was panic; it wouldn't exactly help anything.

Even if panicking felt really, *really* tempting.

Bursting into the Boneyard, Fort found Jia placing the Healing book on the podium at the front of the room as other students began filing in. Today the steel tables were all bare, except for the one that still had sheets on it from where Fort had been healed.

The sight of the sheets reminded him of something, and he quickly slipped Dr. Ambrose's badge back onto the table she'd left it on the night before, hoping no one saw him. He thought he escaped notice, only to turn and find Jia glaring at him, definitely having caught him in the act. He shrugged, not willing to get lectured by her on *anything*, and she just shook her head.

"So I *did* leave it here," Dr. Ambrose said from behind Fort, grabbing for her badge. "How did I not see it last night?" She gave Fort a suspicious look, then moved up to the front of the classroom.

"Dr. Ambrose?" Mason said, quickly walking up to her from his table as the other students arrived. "I'm having a weird problem. For some reason, I can't cast Heal Minor Wounds. I mastered it months ago, but I tried to use it on a blister this morning and couldn't think of the words."

"Oh, Mason," Dr. Ambrose said. "Maybe another round of

Destruction training will jog your memory." She surveyed the room as Mason gasped, then dejectedly walked back to his table. "Everyone here? I got a report of someone missing from a class earlier." Again, she gave Fort a long look.

Fort just gave her a nervous smile, which she rolled her eyes at.

"Fine, then," Dr. Ambrose continued. "Class, we have a special treat today. Forsythe, get up here."

Fort stood up and slowly moved to the front of the room as the other students all watched him intently. He couldn't tell if they were on his side or hoping he'd leave, especially given how many had laughed at him in the boys' dorm two nights ago. The girls didn't look much friendlier either, though that could have been confusion over what was happening.

"Forsythe will be taking a quick test," Dr. Ambrose said, taking three bandage pads out of her pocket and placing them in Fort's hands. "It's really quite simple. You'll cast each of the first three Healing spells once, then a second time, at which point you'll infuse these bandages with your magic. If you can't create three separate bandages, then out you go." She nodded at the door, then lowered her voice so only Fort could hear. "At which point everyone here will be much safer."

For the first time, it dawned on Fort that there were no school administrators or military officers around this time. "Is it just us?" he whispered to Dr. Ambrose. "Dr. Opps and Colonel Charles aren't coming?"

"No, they and the other administrators are watching on the security cams," she whispered back, giving him a look. "For some reason, none of them wanted to be in the same room with you. Any idea why?"

Fort swallowed hard. "Can't think of a reason."

She narrowed her eyes but nodded. Louder, she asked, "Are you ready?"

"I am," Fort said, hoping he was telling the truth. At least there'd be fewer people around to watch him fail, if nothing else.

"The process of creating a bandage isn't difficult," Dr. Ambrose told him. "Begin your spell like you intend to heal someone, but instead of releasing the energy altogether, just let it flow slowly into the bandage, like it's a sponge for your magic. Don't let go of the spell until the bandage is full, though, or the magic won't stick, and you'll fail the test."

Fort swallowed hard. That actually *did* sound pretty difficult, at least without knowing exactly what he was doing. "How did you learn how to do this, if you can't use magic?" he whispered.

"We had the students experiment early on," Dr. Ambrose said. "Stop stalling. You have one minute to cast Heal Minor Wounds, then create a bandage."

Fort closed his eyes, trying not to let the panic derail him before he even started. He pulled his sewing needle out of his pocket and pricked his finger, then quickly healed it, showing it off to Dr. Ambrose.

"Right, right," she told him, waving for him to continue.

He nodded, feeling nervous even though he knew he'd mastered *this* spell at least. He grasped the bandage in his hand ("It's not a stress ball, don't crush it," Dr. Ambrose told him), and slowly repeated the spell words.

He felt the familiar cold energy in his hand, but as Dr. Ambrose had advised him, he didn't release it, and instead just let it seep into the bandage as slowly as he could. The bandage began to glow with a dull blue light, surprising Fort to the point that he almost released the magic by accident. He quickly concentrated on reining it in, though, and the glow faded slightly at first, then brightened even more as the rest of the magic filled the bandage. Finally, the last of the magical energy left his hand, and the bandage lit the room in an eerie light before fading away completely, leaving the bandage looking ordinary once more.

"Hey, you really did master a spell!" Dr. Ambrose said, looking surprised. "That's one more than I would have thought you could. But the odds get pretty long from here. Next one, please. Cause Disease, if you don't mind."

Fort slowly raised a trembling hand and took another bandage from her. Here it was, the *real* test. Had he mastered the spell last night, or just passed out from lack of sleep? Would he be going home to a life of never knowing what he'd left behind at the Oppenheimer School, from answers about his father to the power to destroy the creatures that might have killed him?

Please, he thought. *Please. I* have *to know the spell.*

And then he tried to cast Cause Disease.

But there were no words to use. The spell wasn't there.

Not only hadn't he mastered the spell, but he must have forgotten to read the spell words again so couldn't even cast it once.

- THIRTY -

"WELL, FORSYTHE?" DR. AMBROSE said. "Let's see a disease. If you're not able to do the spell, just say the word and we'll end this right now."

Sweat rolled down Fort's neck, and he swallowed hard. He glanced quickly at Jia, not sure what help she could be, but she just looked away. The rest of the class had no problem staring, though, and Fort could feel their eyes burning into him as he tried to think of what to say next.

"Just give me . . . one minute," he said instead, not even sure why. What was the point of delaying things if he hadn't mastered the spell?

Dr. Ambrose sighed, but she crossed her arms and waited. Jia turned back to look at him almost curiously, like she wanted to see what he was stalling for. If only he knew. But he couldn't just give up! He *wouldn't.* Why couldn't he have mastered the spells last night—

Something slammed into Fort's mind with the force of a hammer, almost knocking him back.

The Cause Disease and Cure Disease spells were now in his mind, front and center.

So were four others.

Fort's eyes widened in surprise. Without any idea how, he now had the spells Heal Heavy Wounds, Paralyze, Ethereal Spirit, and Protective Armor all swirling around in his head, in spite of never having *heard* of half of them before, let alone seen them in the book.

He almost dropped the bandage, completely confused. Where had the spells come from? It was like someone had just downloaded them right into his head. Had Sierra done this somehow? But if she'd used her Telepathy magic on him, wouldn't she have had to copy the spells from someone else's brain? If so, then whose?

Looking around the room, his eyes fell on Jia, who was now staring at him with horror, her mouth hanging open. She reached up to touch her forehead, then mouthed, *What did you do?*

She did *not* look happy.

"Forsythe," Dr. Ambrose said, and Fort nodded, closing his eyes again. He quickly cast Cause Disease on himself, and the fever and aches began almost immediately. He coughed once, then cast the same spell on the bandage, and opened his eyes to watch as it glowed brightly only to fade away just as the last one had.

"This can't be," Dr. Ambrose said, her eyes widening. "How did you *do* that?"

"I . . . I practiced," Fort said, feeling miserable. "Now Cure Disease?"

"It shouldn't be possible," she said, still shocked. She took his arms and pulled up his sleeves. "Did you write the spells down? No, that doesn't work. How could you—"

The class seemed to realize things were getting uncomfortable, as they began to shift and whisper to each other. "Um, should I do the next spell?" Fort asked again.

Dr. Ambrose just nodded silently, still looking utterly baffled. Fort quickly cured his flu, then concentrated on the third bandage and cast Cure Disease a second time, letting the magic seep in until the spell was complete.

"No," Dr. Ambrose whispered so that only Fort could hear

her. "You were supposed to go home. To be safe! How could you do this? It simply isn't conceivable that anyone—"

Fort flashed a look at Jia, who looked like she wanted to strangle him. "I had . . . help," he said, just as quietly.

Dr. Ambrose went silent for a moment, then fell onto her stool next to him, almost deflating before his eyes. "Well, do you want a medal?" she said, her voice returning to its normal tone, though she still looked haunted by the results. "Take your seat, *student*. You more than anyone need to hear today's lesson if you're going to earn your place in the Oppenheimer School."

Fort slowly walked back to the tables, choosing an empty seat behind Sebastian, who glared at him as Fort passed him. Fort fell into the chair, still in a daze about what had just happened. He'd actually managed to pass the impossible test, which meant he wasn't going to get kicked out of the school!

Except he hadn't done it himself. Somehow, he'd stolen Jia's spells and definitely didn't deserve to have passed. Granted, the whole test had been a sham, but still. It was hard to feel victorious when he'd passed by cheating, even if he had no idea it was happening.

Would Jia's spells just disappear now, and hopefully reappear back in her head? Or had he taken them for good? And if that was the case, what did that mean for Jia?

As Dr. Ambrose began talking about the various sections of a human heart, showing far too graphic slides of each part, Fort laid one hand over the other and gave himself the flu. As the chills began, he quickly cured himself, then concentrated and repeated both spells again.

Cause and Cure Disease weren't disappearing from his head. He really had mastered them.

"No magic during lectures!" Dr. Ambrose shouted, not even turning around. "That's rule number one. I don't care if you just passed a test or not, one more time and we're having a pop quiz on healing bedsores!"

The other kids all turned to stare at Fort, and he quickly placed both hands up in surrender, then dropped them to his desk.

Was Telepathy magic really powerful enough to copy, even *steal* someone else's spells for good? That could mean anyone who knew mental magic could learn . . . well, any *other* spell from someone who'd mastered it. That kind of power was terrifying—

Something smacked him in the back of his head. He

turned to find Jia glaring at him with her teeth clenched, and he slowly reached to the floor to find whatever she'd just whipped at his head.

It turned out to be a piece of paper folded into a triangle. As quietly as he could, Fort unfolded the paper and laid it on his lap to read.

You IDIOT. You stole *those spells from me. I had mastered them, and now they're* gone. *GIVE THEM BACK* NOW.

He looked up at her again, and for a second he thought she might attack him then and there, she looked so furious. He tried to give her an apologetic look, but she just gave him a death stare, her knuckles white as she grasped the edge of her desk.

"And of course the pulmonary arteries carry blood from your heart to your lungs," Dr. Ambrose said, advancing a slide to show a pair of lungs on a table. "Now, if the heart stops and there's a Destruction student nearby, a burst of lightning might get it going again. . . ."

Fort pulled a pen from his pocket and quickly wrote down his reply on the note.

You of all people know I didn't have anything to do with this. It was Sierra. Why don't you *tell me where she is, and maybe we can fix this!*

With that, he folded the note back up, and as soon as Dr. Ambrose wasn't looking, he tossed the note to Jia.

A few moments later the note hit him in the head again, this time even harder. He groaned a bit, and Dr. Ambrose turned around. "Was there a question?" she asked.

"What if . . . um, there's protective armor around someone's body?" Fort asked, using the name of one of his new spells. "What would we do then? Would a spell like Ethereal Spirit work?"

"Ethereal Spirit?" Dr. Ambrose said, raising both eyebrows. "How did you hear about that? Wait, no, I don't care. That spell is forbidden to learn anyway. Theoretically, since Ethereal Spirit turns your body ghostlike, you *could* pass a hand through the protective armor, but you'd be useless to the patient since you couldn't touch the heart without solidifying again, which would kill them. Now, if I could return to something *practical*?" She turned back to her slide show.

Fort quickly reached down to grab the note, then unfolded it.

Meet me outside the girls' dorm at lunch. We will *get my spells back!*

Fort turned and nodded at her, agreeing to her terms.

Between Rachel and Jia, it sounded like he'd have plenty of company in his search for Sierra.

- THIRTY-ONE -

CLASS ENDED, AND JIA WAS THE FIRST one out. Fort moved much more slowly but was stopped by Dr. Ambrose as he reached the door.

"One moment, Forsythe," the doctor said, holding Fort's shoulder as the other kids pushed past. When the classroom had emptied, the doctor sat down on one of the tables and began cleaning her glasses. "How exactly did you do that?" she said, not looking at him.

"I cast the spells just like you told me to," Fort said, starting to get nervous. "I followed your instructions—"

"No. I mean, how did you master three spells that fast? Even if you spent all last night studying . . ." She paused, giving Fort a suspicious look. "You still shouldn't have been able to learn them so quickly. In my experience, it takes even the more gifted students at least three days per spell."

"I guess I'm just a quick learner," Fort said.

"Mhm," Dr. Ambrose said. "Or you've got a weird connection with a telepathic girl. I noticed that Mason couldn't cast Heal Minor Wounds today. I wonder if there are any other students missing their spells?"

Fort fought to keep his face calm. Had Sierra really given him the first spell as well? He hadn't even mastered *one*? "I don't know what you're talking about," he said finally.

"I'm sure you don't," she said. "Everything I said last night still stands. Whatever's happening to you and her, it's just going to get worse the longer you're here. And soon, Dr. Oppenheimer's stopgap safety measures won't be able to prevent that thing from finding us again. Is that what you want?"

"Of course not!" Fort said, louder than he intended to. "Why don't you take me to Sierra right now, so I can talk to her and get rid of whatever this connection is? Wouldn't *that* make everyone safe too?"

"Kid, believe me, you and her in the same room is on my list of worst-case scenarios," Dr. Ambrose said. "Trust me. Colonel Charles might think you're doing good here, but I don't see it. Right now, all you're doing is picking at some stitches, and they're all that's keeping you from bleeding out."

That was a graphic metaphor. Fort nodded. "I should get to lunch," he said, hoping she'd let him go.

Dr. Ambrose stared at him for a moment, then nodded. "Just, please, be careful?" she said as he exited. As soon as he was out and inside the elevator with the door closed behind him, he let out a huge sigh of relief.

He wasn't going to get kicked out of the Oppenheimer School. And that meant he could finally get some real answers.

The girls' dormitory was opposite the boys' dorm on the base, so it wasn't too hard to find. From the outside, the buildings looked exactly the same, and Fort figured the insides probably matched as well. Nothing about this army base seemed to suggest that uniqueness was a positive trait.

Jia was waiting next to the door to the dormitory, casually reading a book. She didn't look up as he approached, but instead just nodded her head to the corner of the building. He walked past her and around the corner, then waited in the shadows created by the small alley between the girls' dorm and the soldiers' barracks.

He didn't have to wait long.

"What were you *thinking*?" Jia hissed, her voice low but threatening as she rounded the corner. She shoved him hard, knocking him back several feet. "I was *helping* you! And this is how you repay me, by stealing my spells? Do you know how long it took me to master those?"

"You know I didn't do it," Fort told her. "I'm not the one with psychic powers. That'd be your friend Sierra, who you knew all along but lied and told me she was just some student who got sent home."

"I couldn't tell you the truth, you jerk!" she hissed at him. "Dr. Opps said I'd get expelled if I told anyone about what happened with her and the others."

"So what *did* happen?"

"What did I just say?" Jia growled in frustration. "Look. This doesn't feel like something that the Sierra I know would be doing. She wouldn't be messing with you like this just for fun. There has to be some reason."

"So take me to her, and we'll ask," Fort said, crossing his arms.

"I don't know if she's here or not," Jia said, glaring at him. "Dr. Opps told me she was sent home the day after the attack in D.C. So if she *is* here, he's hiding her, and probably for a good reason."

"She *has* to be here. Colonel Charles wanted me to come just to see what would happen. I never had her memories appearing out of nowhere before I came to the school. And I certainly never heard anyone else's thoughts."

"Fine," Jia said, throwing up her hands in surrender. "If he's keeping her somewhere, there's only so many places it could be. I think I might have an idea where to look."

"Where?" Fort asked, leaning forward.

She shook her head. "We're all going to get kicked out. The amount of security alone will make this impossible."

"Not if we don't get caught," Fort said. "What if we use the magic I got from you, that Ethereal Spirit spell? From what Dr. Ambrose said, that'd turn us into ghosts. We'd be able to go anywhere in the base, right?"

Her anger reignited at the mention of her lost spells, and she looked like she had to hold herself back from punching him. "I can't *believe* you brought that up. I wasn't even supposed to learn it! It's completely forbidden for that exact reason. What if Dr. Ambrose finds out I know it?"

"You'll get it back if we find Sierra," he said. "I'm sorry, I really am. But if that's a way in, then we should use it."

"*Fine.* Meet me back here tonight after lights-out. You'll cast *my* Ethereal Spirit spell, and then we'll go see if Sierra actually is here, so she can give me back my magic." She stabbed his chest with a finger. "I shouldn't be doing this. There are so many ways it could go wrong! At least it'll just be the two of us. If anyone else found out, this whole thing would blow up in our faces."

"Yup, just the two of us," Fort said slowly, trying to figure out a way to bring up Rachel. "About that . . ."

"You guys should really learn to keep your voices down if you don't want people listening," said a voice above him.

Fort whirled around in surprise to find Rachel leaning out one of the girls' dormitory windows, grinning at him.

"How much did you hear?" Jia asked her, completely freezing in panic.

"Oh, everything," Rachel said with a grin. "Don't worry, Jia. Fort and I already had a plan to do this, so we'll just add you in. See you here at lights-out!"

- THIRTY-TWO -

FORT DIDN'T FEEL MUCH LIKE EATING, not with his mind racing about what was to come later that night, so he didn't mind missing lunch. Smelling whatever odor came from the Boneyard as he got off the elevator made him even less interested in food.

"What died?" Sebastian asked, looking more curious than horrified as he entered the room just in front of Fort.

"You'll find out in a minute," Dr. Ambrose said from the front of the room. "Come on in, everyone grab a table. Well, not you, Forsythe. Your three spells are pretty much useless still, so you get to keep studying."

"What are *we* doing?" asked a girl named Janna.

Dr. Ambrose strode to the nearest table, where a tray lay covered by a white cloth. "You, my little healers, are going to be bringing the dead back to life!" She theatrically whipped the cloth off, revealing a wet, red, disgusting mass.

A chorus of groans filled the room.

"Had these hearts flown in with the rest of today's meat, all nice and fresh from the cow," Dr. Ambrose said, breathing in deeply. "Ah, doesn't that just reinforce your vegetarianism?"

Someone gagged, but Fort was too busy keeping down his own bile to see who.

"What . . . what are we doing with them?" Sebastian asked, and even he seemed a bit put off by this.

"Like I said, you'll be bringing them back to life," Dr. Ambrose told them. "Your Restoration spell should get these hearts beating again, so today's exercise is designed to focus your energy on that alone. As we talked about this morning, there'll always be a need for this sort of bandage on the battlefield." She grinned. "Plus, it's just good, clean fun."

Fort swallowed hard, incredibly happy not to be participating. "What should I do, Dr. Ambrose?"

The doctor gave him a long look, then waved at the Healing book. "Just go to the next spell in the book, Forsythe. It's Heal Heavy Wounds. You won't get to choose which spell to learn for a few more weeks yet, assuming you make it that far." She walked behind the nearest student, Moira, who was tentatively placing her hand over the heart. Dr. Ambrose pushed her own hand down onto Moira's, mushing them both into the muscle. "*Really* get in there, kids. If any of these hearts aren't beating by the end of class, I'll tell Colonel Charles you want Destruction training."

Another round of groans went up, and Fort watched as several hearts began to glow, though none started beating. He quickly turned around, trying to breathe through his mouth instead of his nose, and thankfully took hold of the Healing book.

He grabbed a chunk of pages and flipped it open, expecting to only be able to see through to the fourth spell, Heal Heavy Wounds, just like when the book had only opened to the first page in the past.

This time, a good third of the book clunked down on the left side of the podium. And spreading out before his surprised eyes were dozens, maybe even *hundreds* of spells.

Quickly throwing a glance behind him to make sure Dr. Ambrose wasn't watching, Fort paged through his options as quietly as he could.

Remove Fear: Take away the emotion of terror from any living thing for a period of one hour.

Restoration: Return a target to a previous state of health, including mending broken bones or undoing the ravages of disease.

Animate: Grant the power of movement to an inanimate object. Newly animated objects will operate under the spellcaster's control.

Whoa. He could learn any of these spells? Was this because he had Jia's spells in his head? Had he tricked the book? There were so many to choose from!

He took in Remove Fear and Restoration as fast as he could, then turned back to the Heal Heavy Wounds page, just in case Dr. Ambrose planned on checking on him.

"That's a start, Kevin," Dr. Ambrose was saying to another of the students, whose heart was now hopping all over the table. "Except you've overclocked it. That'd probably burst the victim's chest open. Can we at least *attempt* to think practically here when restarting dead hearts?"

Fort turned back to the book, and this time flipped as far forward as it let him. If he was going to be of any use to the world, he needed powerful magic, not just healing random wounds.

Farther in, the pages felt heavier, like they were made of a different kind of paper. As he watched, the words seemed to shift on the page before finally settling into place, and his eyes widened.

Create Zombie: Revive any deceased creature into an undead servant under the spellcaster's control.

Distort Body: Change the physical dimensions of any living being at the spellcaster's discretion.

Cause Heavy Wounds: Cause physical damage to any living being—

The book slammed shut on Fort's hand, and he bit his lip to keep from shouting in pain.

"What are you *doing*?" Jia whispered at him, leaning in close so Dr. Ambrose couldn't hear. "You are *not* ready for those!"

Fort slowly pulled his hand out of the pages and cast Heal Minor Wounds over it, relieving the pain. "First of all, that *hurt*."

"Good!"

"Second of all, this is exactly the kind of magic we need," Fort whispered to her. "Have you seen what those spells can do? Create zombies? Tie a body in knots, literally? These are *fighting* spells!"

"And we're *healers*," Jia hissed. "You're a year away at minimum from ever seeing these spells, let alone mastering them!"

"A year?" Fort blinked in confusion. "But *you're* already there, or it wouldn't have let me see them. How long have you been studying magic, anyway?" He looked closer at her. "When exactly did you start at this school? I thought it didn't open until after the attacks."

She started to say something, then shook her head. "Doesn't matter. *Don't* look ahead today. Practice the Heal Heavy Wounds spell. After tonight, you won't have mine to use anymore, and you're going to need to have it mastered soon enough anyway. Once I get my spells back, you'll be locked out of the rest of those spells, and hopefully everything can go back to normal."

She stepped away before he could say another word, and he rolled his eyes, opening the book back to the second page again.

Heal Heavy Wounds. Not at all what he was here to do. Healing was all well and good, but he needed magic to take down a monster like the one that had attacked D.C. and killed his father. And the magic was there for the taking, right in the book! Why would he ever just stay with the restorative spells?

He was here to learn to protect those who couldn't protect themselves. That was all that mattered. And for that, he needed powerful attack magic, no matter what Jia thought. Fort glanced around to make sure he wasn't being watched, then slid his fingers between two of the later pages.

He had just enough time to read over Cause Heavy Wounds before Jia slammed the book down hard enough to require a *Heal* Heavy Wounds spell.

- THIRTY-THREE -

FORT FOUND JIA WAITING IN THE ALLEY between the girls' dorm and the soldiers' barracks that night, an hour after the dorm's lights had been turned out. He'd waited until he heard snores around the boys' dorm just to be safe, only to have Sebastian pass his bed for a bathroom visit right before he was about to go. Fortunately, the other boy finished quickly and was back to sleeping soundly soon after, letting Fort finally sneak out of the building.

Well, letting *them* finally sneak out.

"What's *he* doing here?" Jia said, pointing at Cyrus with a horrified expression.

"Hey, Jia!" Cyrus said, waving happily. "Don't worry, I won't give us away." He turned to Fort. "By the way, did you notice Sebastian—"

"It's a party!" said another voice, and they turned to find Rachel slipping out of the girls' dorm. "Hey, Future Man!"

"He already knew it was happening," Fort told Jia, who looked about ready to explode. Even if it made her angry, he was secretly happy that Cyrus had been awake and waiting when Fort had gotten up to leave. He hadn't planned on telling Cyrus about the plan, not wanting to get the boy into trouble, but his friend had insisted on coming anyway. "And he can help us stay undetected."

"And her job is?" Jia said, nodding at Rachel.

"Hey, I'm just here to save the school and everyone else," Rachel said, grinning. "You won't even know I'm here."

"*Fine,*" Jia fumed. "Anyone else coming? Maybe some teachers, or a soldier or two?"

They waited for a moment, looking all around, but no one else seemed to be there. "Looks like we're all set," Fort said.

"Follow me," Jia said, shaking her head in disgust. "And stay close. If any of us get caught, we'll *all* get thrown out."

She started to leave the alley, but Cyrus grabbed her shoulder and yanked her backward. She looked at him in shock until two soldiers marched past the alley entrance.

"Okay, follow *Cyrus*," she said, waving the boy forward. "Stay close to him."

Cyrus smiled and shrugged, then strode out of the alley confidently. The others hurried to follow, then slammed to a halt as Cyrus turned back around. "Nope, we'll get caught fifteen minutes from now if we go that way," he said, gesturing toward the other end of the alley. "This path, we'll get there with only three close calls."

Twenty minutes later, they reached the side of the Training Hall, Fort's heart beating a mile a minute. What Cyrus called a close call, Fort would have termed oh-no-WE'RE-ALL-CAUGHT-whoa-okay-wow-we-just-got-incredibly-lucky instead. There were either more soldiers out tonight, making getting around the security cameras even tougher, or it turned out to be a lot harder to hide four of them than just Fort and Cyrus alone.

"From here, Fort is going to use *my* Ethereal Spirit spell on us all," Jia said, glaring at him. "With that, we'll be able to walk through walls, and even float through the floor, though it takes some getting used to. You just keep in mind that gravity no longer affects you, and you shouldn't have any problems."

"I thought that spell was banned," Rachel said. Jia blushed, looking guilty, but Rachel just grinned and slapped her on the shoulder. "No, don't feel bad. I like you better knowing you break the rules every so often."

"The rules are there for a reason!" Jia hissed. "I learned that when . . . it doesn't matter. The spell looked useful, so I studied it. Case closed."

"And now we're using it to break into the Training Hall, so it's *definitely* useful," Rachel said.

Fort ignored them and concentrated on the spell. He ran through the words in his head, then held his hands out over the three of them and slowly let the cold energy flow from his hands and into the others, saving some for his own body. As the spell finished, Fort felt a bit weaker, depleted, like he'd just run a long race. Did more powerful magic take more energy from you?

At first, the magic made each of them glow a bit, which wasn't exactly the best for sneaking around. But gradually each of them grew more transparent until he could see right through the others, and the glow disappeared. Glancing down, Fort realized he could also see the ground through his hands, which was a new experience.

"Cool," he said, his voice sounding less solid, almost ghostly.

"It's even cooler to master it *yourself* instead of stealing it," Jia said, her voice also just an echo of its former self. "Now be careful with this. I've practiced this a lot, and even *I'm* not used to floating up or down through floors. The magic defaults to keeping you on the level you start at, but you can still rise or fall at will, if you work at it."

Rachel poked her head through the side of the Training Hall, then gave them a thumbs-up. "We're by the offices," she said, pulling back out. "No one's there, so we should be good to enter."

"Any cameras?" Fort asked Cyrus.

His friend tilted his hand back and forth, as if to say, sort of. "Not right here, but if we move much farther in, we'll get caught for sure."

"There are floors below the Viewing Room that only Dr. Opps and Colonel Charles have access to," Jia said. "If Sierra's anywhere here, it'd be down there. I've explored a little on my own but never went too far down."

Cyrus closed his eyes, then frowned. "If we find the girl down there, I'm not seeing it. Everything starts getting weirdly fuzzy in a bit."

Fort gave him a worried look. That didn't exactly sound promising.

"Guess we'll have to just jump in and hope for the best," Rachel said with a grin. "Should I go first, or . . . ?"

Jia groaned at this but led the way inside, and the rest followed after her.

Moving through a solid object was a strange experience, and not one that Fort particularly enjoyed. It wasn't just like walking through air; instead, he could feel the wall within him as he moved, and it wasn't a comfortable sensation by any measure. Not that it hurt . . . but this was *not* the normal way one got past walls. From now on, Fort would take the door.

Jia held up a hand as they all made it inside, then nodded silently at a security camera aimed at the ground just past them. She pointed down at the floor, then closed her eyes and slowly began to sink right through the tiles. As her head disappeared, she waved her hand at them to follow, right before that sank through as well.

Not waiting for Fort or Cyrus, Rachel dove forward into the floor like a dolphin into a wave, a huge grin on her face. Cyrus shrugged, then sank at the same rate as Jia had, waving for Fort to follow him.

Fort closed his eyes and concentrated hard, willing himself to sink into the floor as well. After what felt like plenty of time to descend, he opened his eyes to see where he was.

Unfortunately, he was still standing in the offices on the ground floor.

Gritting his teeth, Fort tried again, squeezing his eyes shut, imagining himself descending through the floor, picturing it as clearly as he could in his mind. But when he opened his eyes again, he hadn't moved.

Why wasn't this working? He pushed his foot down through the tiles, and there was no resistance: It was as insubstantial as the outer wall had been. So why couldn't he sink through like the others had?

Cyrus's face appeared out of the floor. "You're too used to floors holding you up. Let go of that as a concept. Right now, you could sink right through the whole planet if you wanted."

Fort's eyes widened. "That actually doesn't help," he whispered.

"Oh, come on," Jia said as her face and arms appeared. "We don't have time for this."

She grabbed his legs (apparently ethereal people could touch each other?) and pulled down, yanking him out of the concept of floating and right into the floor before he could even object.

- THIRTY-FOUR -

AS THE FLOOR ROSE UP TOWARD HIM, Fort instinctively held his breath, like he was about to dunk himself underwater. His chest passed through the tile, and he decided to let the air out to experiment with something.

When his face reached the floor, he opened his mouth to breathe in, to see if it was possible while passing through a solid object. Unfortunately, there was no air inside the floor, and for a moment he began to panic as his body decided it must be drowning.

Thankfully, he emerged from the other side a moment later and took in a nice, deep breath. Jia pulled him down to the ground, and he found himself standing in Dr. Ambrose's classroom.

"You can't breathe inside things!" he said, his heart still racing.

The other three just looked at one another. "Are you usually able to?" Jia asked him.

"Well, no," he said, turning red. "It's all just strange. Like how are we breathing now, if we're insubstantial and can't touch anything? How do our lungs take in air?"

"It's magic," Rachel said. "If we couldn't breathe, the spell would have killed the first people to try it."

"Maybe it's ingrained in the spell," Jia said. "But can we discuss that later? We still have a bunch of floors to go, and I don't want to get caught." She glanced around. "The only thing on this floor other than our classroom is the Healing bandage storage. Next one down should be the stronger magical items."

"I really like this side of you!" Rachel said, nodding with respect.

Now it was Jia's turn to blush. "I had to practice somewhere."

"So *bad*," Rachel said, laughing lightly. "How can you even live with yourself?"

Jia didn't answer; she just sank slowly down through the floor again, steadily avoiding Rachel's gaze. Rachel waited for a moment, then dove through after her, and this time Cyrus offered his hand to Fort.

"Maybe floating just isn't your thing," Cyrus said as Fort took his hand.

"Apparently, none of this is," Fort told him as the other boy slowly descended, pulling Fort with him.

At least Colonel Charles believed in him, that there was some power to be awakened inside of him. Hopefully he'd be better suited to whatever that was than Healing.

They landed in a room filled with filing cabinets, and Jia led the way to the door, peeking just her face through at first to make sure there weren't any guards around. Cyrus confirmed they were out of camera sight too, so Jia passed through the door and then motioned for them to follow.

They found themselves in a long hallway with metal doors to their right and the elevator to their left. The metal doors were all locked by elaborate, highly technological locks, which couldn't stop their ethereal forms from peeking into the first few rooms.

"Whoa," Rachel said, pulling her head back out of the first door. "I've never seen so many fireball bullets. There are *thousands* of boxes in there! Who had time to make all of these? There's no way we did them all."

Fort threw a look at Jia, but she ignored him.

The next door held what looked like plastic egg carton containers, each one labeled with various Telepathy spells:

MEMORY/THOUGHT SHARING, SLEEP INDUCEMENT, and more.

"She wouldn't be on this level," Jia said as Fort started to look in another door. "Too many people can come down here, especially the military. Dr. Opps doesn't like to give access to anyone he doesn't trust, so she'd have to be at least one more floor down."

After *three* more floors turned out to be empty, however, Fort began to wonder how paranoid Dr. Opps really was . . . and how far down the complex extended. Each of the floors had been filled with similar vaults to the ones holding the fire bullets, but none were in use.

Two floors later, Fort was almost ready to give up.

"Maybe she's somewhere else on the base?" he said to Jia, who seemed to be getting more annoyed with each new empty floor.

"She *has* to be here," she said, slamming her fist through a wall without leaving a mark. "There's nowhere else that's anywhere near as secure."

"What if she's really *not* here at the school?" Rachel asked. "It's not like we have any solid proof—"

"No, she's close," Fort told her, hoping he was telling the truth. "Come on. Let's keep moving."

As Jia and Rachel both disappeared through the floor, Cyrus stopped Fort for a moment. "Just so you know, we're running out of time."

"What do you mean?"

"Well, before we left, I thought I saw Sebastian still awake," Cyrus said. "So I did a quick look into his future, and he should be reaching Dr. Opps's door any minute now."

Fort's eyes widened. "He's turning us in?"

Cyrus nodded. "I probably should have mentioned that sooner, huh? I kind of forgot when Rachel showed up."

Fort squeezed his eyes closed and took a deep breath. "Yes, that might have been helpful. How long do we have?"

Cyrus's eyes unfocused for a moment. "I don't know," he said, looking nervous. "Everything is fuzzy now. Either we're too close to the books upstairs, or something else is going on." He frowned. "But I got us to the Viewing Room last night without having this problem. Weird, huh?"

"So there could be guards here at any moment?" Fort said, sighing deeply. "Great."

"Should we turn around? We could probably sneak out before they find us."

For a moment, Fort considered it. But if they backed out now, there'd be no way he was ever getting another chance, both because Jia would never agree to it, and Dr. Opps would for sure be kicking him out of the school just for leaving the dorm at night.

"Nope, we keep going," Fort said. "Our only hope is to find Sierra. Sebastian doesn't know that Jia and Rachel came with us, so at least they should be okay."

Cyrus nodded, then took Fort's hand and floated them both down into the floor. "Maybe she's on this next floor anyway!" he said optimistically.

Five floors later, even Fort was starting to wonder if Sierra actually existed, let alone was somewhere in the building. "I don't *get* it," Jia said, staring around in the darkness. "Cyrus, you can't see anything about her in our future?"

He shook his head, looking uncomfortable. "It's all just a blur from this point forward. Something's wrong."

The others shared a look. "Maybe it's time to give up," Rachel suggested.

"One more floor," Fort said, knowing he'd continue on even if the others all left. "We can't give up now."

"Okay, but if we don't find anything, we're going to Dr. Opps and telling him everything," Jia said. "Especially about how you stole my spells."

Why bother, when he'll be catching us down here any minute now? Fort thought.

They descended through the floor, expecting more empty vaults . . . but this time they found just one door at the end of a very short hallway, mirrored by the elevator on the opposite side.

"*Finally*, something new!" Rachel said, and advanced to the door. She pushed her face through slowly, only to pull back suddenly, her eyes wide. "You guys have *got* to see this."

Fort tried to move past her, but Rachel held him back. "Let me go first," she said. "Just in case it's dangerous. And don't argue about it. We don't have time."

He started to object in spite of her words, but then stopped and nodded, waving her ahead. She was right, they *didn't* have time. As soon as she was inside, he leaped into the door, his meager list of spells at the ready just in case he had to cast one quickly.

But instead of anything dangerous, the warehouse-sized room was filled with huge wooden crates. At the far end, a small set of stairs led down to a lowered floor, adding height to the ceiling for some of the taller crates.

"See?" Rachel said from across the room, pointing at the wall behind her. "Now *this* is the good stuff."

Fort looked where she was pointing and felt his knees go weak.

Behind Rachel were large glass cases set into the wall, almost like the kind found in a museum. And just like in a museum, the cases were filled with skeletons.

But not the skeletons of dinosaurs or prehistoric animals.

"Are those . . . ?" Jia asked.

"Yup!" Rachel said proudly, pointing at what looked almost like a *Tyrannosaurus rex* skeleton with wings. "They're *dragons*."

- THIRTY-FIVE -

THEY'VE BEEN KEEPING THEM DOWN here this whole time?" Jia said, walking over to the glass cases slowly, almost reverently. "Look at those wings!"

Fort followed her over, not sure if he should feel terror or awe. The dragon skeletons were *immense*, and even with their wings tucked behind them, they still barely fit in the cases. They weren't the only items on display, though. Next to the two enormous dragon skeletons were four human ones, and Fort got a chill just looking at them.

"These are the magicians they found on Discovery Day," he said softly. "The ones with the books of magic. I saw one of them in Dr. Opps's memory."

Two of the magician skeletons were displayed next to a dragon, while a third hung to the left of an enormous feline-like skeleton, almost like a sabertooth tiger or something. The fourth, though, was alone. Maybe that magician didn't have a ride?

"I can't tell if they're male or female," Rachel said. "Either of you healers have a guess?"

"Two of them were women," Jia said, looking closely. "There are a few indicators that tell us based on bone shape and size. This one here, and there." She pointed at one of the skeletons next to a dragon, and the one next to the feline monster. "The other two are male."

"Nice," Rachel said, giving the dragon-riding female magician an approving nod. "Too bad they didn't dig up any dragon eggs or something."

"I wish we knew the history," Jia said. "Where the books actually came from. Who wrote them? Why were they in the hands of these magicians at the end? Why did we find them all on the same day? So many important questions—"

"Look! Dwarves!" Cyrus said, a little ways to the left. The others turned to where he stood before two half-sized skeletons, these broader than a normal human, and much more stout.

"Are you sure they're not just children?" Rachel asked.

"The bones are too dense," Jia said after giving Cyrus a dirty look for interrupting her. "Whatever they are, I don't think they're human."

"Okay, but dwarves aren't real," Rachel said.

The others all stared at her for a moment, before she realized what she'd said and then laughed. "Right, okay, I just heard it myself. Yeah, yeah." She pointed at some taller, thinner skeletons next to the half-sized ones. "So, what, those are elves?"

"Look at how narrow and thin the bones are," Jia said, pointing at the tall creatures' arms. "They would have been so delicate."

Fort stared up at the skulls of the taller creatures, which were more elongated than the magicians' skulls. What would they have looked like before they died? "Don't elves have pointy ears?"

"Ears aren't bones," Jia pointed out. "They're made of cartilage, which decomposes. You really *do* need to study, don't you?"

"Hey, I just got here, like, two days ago," he said, touching the glass in front of the elves. "So do you think they dug all of these up on the same day as the dragons and books?"

Rachel shook her head, pointing at a plaque. "Not according to the date here. See? This is later the same year as Discovery Day."

"And these they found almost two years later," Cyrus said, pointing at two slightly thinner half-sized skeletons. He leaned in, squinting at the plaque. "In Europe."

"The elves were dug up there, too, looks like," Jia said.

"Look at this," Cyrus said, pointing at a smaller case that had been covered in a thick black cloth, which he held up so the others could see. "Is that a sword?"

Fort peered in closer, feeling a weird chill as he did, like this area of the room was ten degrees cooler. It did look like some kind of sword, but it wasn't made of metal. Instead, it seemed almost like it was made of crystal, a foggy quartz or something. Next to it were an armored glove and a jaggedly sharp crown both made of the same material. The crown looked like it'd been broken in half, while the glove looked relatively intact.

Not that Fort even considered putting it on. All three items gave him a weird feeling in the base of his spine, like watching someone in a horror movie walking into a dark basement.

"Does the sword light on fire or something?" Rachel asked. "'Cause otherwise, there's better stuff in here."

Cyrus leaned down to read the plaque on the case. "These were found in the middle of some kind of battlefield," he said.

"Surrounded by hundreds of skeletons. Wow. Who do you think wore the crown?"

Fort frowned, knowing he'd seen that crystal somewhere before. The odd sense of fear he felt from the items made it hard to concentrate, though. Where would he ever have. . .

And then it hit him. The officers' mess. The creature had been wearing armor made of that same material.

His eyes widened, and he quickly pulled the black cloth back down over the case. "Let's not play with that," he told Cyrus, his heart racing.

Cyrus gave him a smile and nodded, thankfully not asking any questions, because Fort wasn't sure he could answer them anyway. Had those things left the sword and crown on this world when they went . . . wherever they were now? And more importantly, how could they use a glove that looked like it fit a normal human hand? Had the items belonged to a human in their service?

Or what if the Old Ones had once looked . . . human?

Just to calm himself down, Fort paced along the displays to stand before the dragon-riding female magician. He stared at her for a moment as his heart slowed to a normal speed.

The skeleton almost seemed to stare back at him, but unlike

with the crown and sword, he didn't feel any creepy feelings coming from the bones. He slowly put a hand up to the glass and looked at the empty eye sockets in her skull. The things she could have told them about magic. Jia was right, asking all of her questions. Why *had* the books all shown up on the same day? Why now? Where had they come from? And why had magic disappeared to begin with?

"I wish we could talk to them," he said quietly.

Jia moved closer to Fort, staring up at the same skeleton he was. "There's a Healing spell that can do that, actually. I've seen it, farther in the book, but never even thought about learning it."

"How does that work?" Rachel said, looking confused. "You heal their voice box or something?"

"No, it's called Communicate with the Dead," Jia said. "I think you talk to their spirit." She shivered. "Definitely creepy, and nothing we're going to be messing with."

"I don't know, it could be useful," Fort said.

Jia glared at him. "Don't even *think* about it."

"So what's in these crates?" Rachel asked. "More things they dug up?"

Fort's eyes widened. "All of this? There must be thousands of crates in here. And some of them are huge!"

"If these dates are true, they've been digging things up for over a decade," Jia said, looking at the boxes as well. "Who knows what other sorts of things they've unearthed?" She sighed, shaking her head. "*This* is why we should never have come down here."

"We still haven't found Sierra," Fort said. And the more time they wasted here, the sooner Dr. Opps would find them. "This is fascinating, but we need to keep moving."

"You said one more floor," Jia told him. "We can't keep searching all night."

"But look what we found!" Fort said. "This is probably where Dr. Opps is hiding all of his secret things. She's probably just waiting on the next floor!"

Rachel frowned. "I don't know, Fort. Jia might be right. I don't want someone hitting the bathroom and noticing I'm gone."

Fort gave Cyrus a quick glance, then sighed. "I'll just look ahead. If there's another empty floor, then you can all head back."

"*We* can?" Jia said as Fort dropped to his knees and pushed his head through to the next floor.

Like the storage area they were in, the floor below held only one large room as well. But instead of a warehouse, this one looked just like the Viewing Room on the ground floor, including a podium right in the middle of circular descending stadium seats.

And on the podium were two books, both wrapped in chains as thick as Fort's wrist.

He slowly pulled his head back up, his eyes wide. "You're going to want to see this."

"See what?" Jia said.

Fort swallowed, taking a moment. "Um, two more books of magic."

The others all exchanged looks. "This is a really *bad* idea," Jia said, shaking her head. "We *can't* go down there."

"Too late!" Rachel shouted, and dove through the floor. Jia cursed, then followed right behind.

"Little help?" Fort asked, and Cyrus quickly pulled him through the floor to follow the two girls.

Rachel and Jia were already examining the books as the boys arrived. *"Don't touch them,"* Jia warned as Rachel reached a hand out to the chains. "There's probably a ton of alarms on these things."

Rachel snorted, then ran her hand through the podium below the books. "What alarm are *we* going to set off?"

"This explains the blurriness," Cyrus told Fort quietly. "The books always disrupt my magic, and our future led right to them."

"Can you see what they say?" Fort asked, moving closer.

Jia glanced at him quickly, then turned away. Rachel gave her a confused look, then nodded. "Yeah, sort of," she said, pointing at the first. "This one's *The Magic of Extrasensory Perception, and the Art of Mind Reading*, but the other one's title is kind of burned off." She moved in closer, squinting at the text. "It's definitely *The Magic of Sum* . . . something."

"Some something?"

"Like what you get when you add two things, S-U-M," she said, leaning in. "*The Magic of Sum—*"

A blaring alarm filled the room, cutting off whatever else she was going to say.

They all stared at Rachel, who quickly held up both her hands. "Not me!" she said. "I never touched it!"

"I'm guessing Dr. Opps found out where we went," Cyrus said to Fort, then turned to the girls, who were staring at him incredulously. "Sebastian saw us leave and turned us in. So, should we go, or . . . ?"

- THIRTY-SIX -

"RUN!" JIA SHOUTED, THEN LEAPED upward, soaring into the ceiling.

Fort stared helplessly at Cyrus, who also started floating upward, though more slowly than Jia. "I can't even sink through the floor. How am I supposed to float up?"

"I've got you," Rachel said. "Hold on tight." She grabbed his ethereal hands in hers and tried to float up with him, but their progress was even slower than Cyrus's by two or three times.

Fort shook his head and pulled his hands out of hers, dropping back to the floor. "That's not going to work. It'll just get you caught too. Go. I'll be fine. Just get out of here!"

Cyrus and Rachel both stared at him for a moment, looked at each other, then started floating toward the ceiling. "Try the elevator!" Cyrus called as he rose. "There might be time to—"

But whatever else he tried to say was muffled by his head disappearing into the floor.

"Good luck, Fort," Rachel said, crossing her fingers for him as she too passed into the floor above.

Fort sighed, alone now in the room with the alarm still blaring. There was only one door out, and that probably led to the elevator, like Cyrus had suggested. But if he tried that, the guards or Dr. Opps would catch him for sure. They were probably coming down in the elevator at that very moment.

But maybe . . . that could work in his favor?

Fort took off at a sprint, leaping through the door to find a short hallway leading to the elevator. This elevator door didn't have an up or down button next to it; instead, three keypads and two black badge boxes covered the wall. To call the elevator, he would have needed pass codes and probably Dr. Opps's security badge, at a minimum.

At least there weren't any cameras here. That was something. For once, Dr. Opps's paranoia was actually helpful.

A blinking light caught his attention, and Fort glanced up to find the floors counting down above the elevator. He'd been right: The guards were on their way down. And that meant he had no choice.

Taking a breath, Fort dove through the elevator doors, hoping this was the bottom floor, so he wouldn't fall to his death. Unfortunately it wasn't, and he almost screamed as he sailed over what looked like a never-ending elevator shaft below him, but fortunately his momentum carried him over and halfway into the wall beyond.

Passing into the outer wall slowed him down to the point that he managed to stop completely just before he reached the dirt on the other side of the wall. He pulled himself back out enough to breathe, then looked up into the shaft, where he could just barely make out the descending elevator car.

This was *not* going to be easy. But if he could time it right, he could jump onto the roof of the elevator, then wait and take it all the way back up to the top. There'd still be guards and cameras and a million other things to deal with, but with his Ethereal Spirit spell, maybe—

NO. COME.

Fort gasped at the intensity of the call in his head. The command was so strong that he doubled over, grabbing his skull to keep it from bursting open.

More importantly, he recognized the voice.

"Sierra?" he whispered, one of his eyes twitching through the pain.

COME. *NOW.*

This time the thought was so powerful, he couldn't even question it. Without a second thought, he leaped out from the wall just ahead of the elevator car. He soared across the shaft, falling as he went, and passed through the door one floor down. A small part of him realized he wasn't in control, that Sierra had taken over his body again, but there was nothing he could do about it.

Just like when she'd forced him to run, back in D.C.

And to leave his father behind.

COME.

Without slowing, Fort's ethereal feet reached floor level, and he sprinted down a long hallway. There were multiple doorways on this floor, some of which were open with lights on, oddly. As he passed them, he noticed a man and a woman in white lab coats with their backs to the door, going over some kind of paperwork. He wanted to stop, to see what they were doing down here where no one else was allowed to come, but he couldn't even slow himself down. The command was just too strong.

COME.

The door at the end of the hallway was open and had what looked like a doctor's chart hanging in a transparent plastic folder on the wall next to it. Fort slowed down to a fast walk as he neared the door, so he was just able to make out a bit of the chart as he passed.

Patient 1, Patient 2.

Week 27, Day 4: Patient 1, no change. Patient 2 frequent somniloquy.

Fort briefly wondered what that last word meant before he passed through the door and found himself in a darkened room, lit only by the red and green lights of several monitors and machines surrounding two beds. Both were occupied, but it was hard for Fort to see in the dark.

COME.

The pull in his mind took him to the side of the bed on the right, and as he neared, he saw that a girl lay on it, a girl around his age, or maybe a bit older. Her brown hair was long, down past her shoulders, while white plastic pads were attached to her head in various places beneath her hair, with wires running from them to a machine.

Sierra. He'd never actually seen her before, since he'd always been viewing her memories through her own eyes.

He reached out and touched the girl's hand, not sure whether this was his doing, or her voice in his head.

As soon as he touched her finger, his mind exploded.

"Hi, I'm Jia Liang," a girl said with an uneasy smile.

Sierra smiled back and shook her hand. "I'm Sierra Ramirez. Nice to meet you."

Jia looked around. "Are you nervous? Or is it just me?"

Dr. Opps patted their shoulders. "No need to be anxious. We've got a lot to celebrate. Today is your birthday, both of you. How old are you again?"

"Ten," both girls said together.

Fort screamed, dropping to his knees, but he couldn't pull his hand away from hers. Image after image popped into his mind, too fast to understand, too intense to control.

"Damian, what are you doing?" Dr. Opps shouted, leading Sierra back into Damian's room, where a green portal filled one wall. On the other side, three creatures waited, wearing dark, crystalline armor. All floated in midair, almost too horrible to even look at. One even appeared to have screaming human faces up and down its armor.

The closest one floated just on the other side, its relatively less horrific tentacles reaching toward them. "Close this portal now! I told you not to contact them again!" Dr. Opps told Damian.

"I didn't," Damian said, quickly throwing his arms out almost protectively to block them from the portal. "They came to me once again, Dr. Opps. But I did use my Summoning magic to open the doorway. It's promised to show us where the last two books are. You know what the prophecy says."

"Who cares about that?" Sierra shouted at him. "The world is fine, it doesn't need saving! At least not unless you let those things back here!"

The Old One on the other side of the portal slowly turned to look at Fort/Sierra, and Fort felt a shudder go through him, though whether it was him or Sierra, he couldn't be sure. And then, in his thoughts, he heard it speak.

CHILDREN OF HUMANITY, it said, the very "sound" of it making Fort's head almost burst. YOU HAVE NO IDEA WHAT YOU'VE UNEARTHED. THOSE BOOKS WILL DESTROY YOU WITHOUT GUIDANCE. LET US SHOW YOU HOW TO PROPERLY USE THE POWER WE CREATED.

"I've used my Telepathy spells on this Old One," Damian

said, smiling slightly, though he winced at the sound of the creature's voice too, and a small trickle of blood drained from his nose. "It's not lying, I can tell. They really only want to come home!"

"Shut it down, Damian," Dr. Opps said, then raised his radio to his face. "I need guards down to room 826, right now."

YOU HAVE BUT FIVE OF THE SEVEN, the creature said, and from the way Dr. Opps stiffened in surprise, Sierra/Fort knew that he could hear the voice now too. WE CAN LEAD YOU TO THE LAST TWO. THE POWER OF THE SEVEN ECLIPSES THE SUM OF THE INDIVIDUAL BOOKS. TOGETHER, THEY HAVE THE POWER TO RULE THE WORLD.

"Damian, close this portal!" Dr. Opps shouted, his voice pained.

Damian ignored him, taking a step closer to the creature. "This is the only way to find the last two books. What damage might whoever found them do in the meantime? We don't even know what the other types of magic are. We need them here, just to keep ourselves safe. And the prophecy says that one of us has to learn from all seven if we're going to save the world." He raised his hand up to match the tentacles on the other side of the portal.

ONE WITH THE POWER OF THE SEVEN NEED FEAR NO OTHER BEING IN THE UNIVERSE, the creature said, slowly moving its hand toward Damian's. WE CAN GIVE YOU THAT POWER.

Outside, Sierra heard the arrival of several soldiers, followed by a loud beating on the door that abruptly went silent. She reached out with her mind and gasped. Damian had put them to sleep using his Telepathy magic.

Are you insane? she thought into his mind. *You're going to get us all killed! Look into that thing's head!*

I'm not naive, Sierra, Damian said in her mind, using his own Telepathy spells. *Of course the Old Ones have their own agenda. But between you, me, Michael, and Jia, we can handle them. We'll learn everything they know, then send them back to their dimension when we're done.*

"Where are my guards?" Dr. Opps shouted into his radio, his eyes moving quickly between Damian and the creature.

YOU WILL REGRET IT IF YOU REJECT THIS

OPPORTUNITY, the creature said in all of their heads. It slowly pushed its tentacled hand into the portal, and Sierra gasped as it passed through into their world. WE OFFER PEACE, FOR NOW. IF YOU REJECT THAT, YOU WILL LEARN WHAT HAPPENED TO YOUR ANCESTORS WHEN THEY TRIED TO REBEL AGAINST US.

"Damian!" Dr. Opps shouted.

"I've got this, Dr. Opps—" Damian said, only to grab his head and scream in pain. He doubled over, then slowly lifted a hand toward the portal, mumbling several unintelligible words under his breath.

Immediately, the creature began to hiss, and Damian screamed again, this time in pure agony. But the monster retreated, pulling its tentacles back through the portal a moment before it disappeared entirely, leaving just a blank wall behind it.

Sierra slowly lowered her hand and released Damian from her control as he turned to her with anger and betrayal in his eyes. "I'm not going to apologize for that," she told him. "There's no way I was going to let that thing into our world."

Damian stared at her for a moment, then stood up, shaking his head. "You don't know what you've just—"

But his voice cut off as he went extremely still, and his eyes widened.

And then he whispered the words to a spell, and the portal on the wall started to reopen.

Fort screamed again and yanked his hand away from Sierra's. Instantly the images disappeared, and he collapsed to the floor exhausted as the two lab-coated doctors he'd seen earlier rushed in.

They shouted something at him, but Fort couldn't understand what they were saying. He slowly slipped into unconsciousness, unable to process most of what he'd just seen. But one thing rang clearly through his mind, and he latched onto it like a drowning person to a life preserver.

He finally knew who'd caused the attack on his father. And from what he had seen as he fell, the person to blame was lying just feet away on a hospital bed.

- THIRTY-SEVEN -

WE HAVE TO WIPE HIS MIND AND send him home. That burst of activity shorted out any last protection we have from that creature."

"But Dr. Oppenheimer, he almost woke her up! Her brain activity jumped dramatically when he touched her, and it's been elevated since he arrived. We can't just ignore that!"

Fort slowly opened his eyes, not sure if the voices he was hearing were in his head or actually real. A bright light above him almost blinded him before he looked away, discovering he was in a room much like the one where he'd found Sierra, touched her hand, and . . .

The memories came flooding back, and he had to stop himself from flinching, not wanting to let the two people standing at the end of his bed know he was awake. He closed his eyes again and kept listening.

"And look what that contact did to him," Dr. Opps said to the female doctor Fort had seen earlier in the room nearby Sierra's. "I'm sorry, this has gone much too far. Charles can remove me from my post and destroy my career, I don't care anymore. You know he won't stop until Damian's awakened."

Colonel Charles wanted to awaken Damian? But why?

"Damian's brain activity is basically nonexistent," the doctor said. "But if Sierra awakens, we could see if she can access Damian's memories, if they still exist. That could tell us everything we need to know about . . . whatever these creatures are. She might be able to find a weakness."

"I won't allow it," Dr. Opps said, moving toward Fort. "What I want to know is whether wiping Forsythe's mind will destroy this connection between him and Sierra."

Wiping his mind? Fort's heart began to beat faster. That sounded a lot more intense than just making him forget some things. If that was going to happen, he had to get out of here!

"Do we know yet how it came about?" Dr. Opps continued.

"We have no way of knowing for sure unless she wakes up, but if I had to guess, she was spread so thin while evacuating the civilians during the D.C. attack that when Forsythe struggled against her, he sent some sort of feedback into her brain, and it shut her down. Her last word before she slipped into the coma was his name, and that's all we've gotten from her since."

"Yet she's clearly still using her magic. She sent him my thoughts, and from what Ambrose said, implanted spells in his head to help him pass his test."

Fort tried to keep his face perfectly still even as his mind reacted to these incredible revelations, finally explaining everything that had been happening. Somehow, Sierra's unconscious mind was still accessing her magic?

And they might wipe his mind to keep her from doing it again.

"Her scans don't show any conscious activity," the doctor said. "Whatever connection they have, I'd guess that his emotional state probably triggered each of those instances. But who's to say? There's so much we don't understand about the brain as it is. Throw in magic, and I'm completely in the dark."

Before Dr. Opps could respond, someone else entered the room.

"Dr. Oppenheimer, Dr. Magellan," said a voice that sounded like Colonel Charles. "I see things have gotten completely out of control down here?"

"Colonel, now is not the time—" Dr. Opps started to say, but the colonel interrupted him.

"I'd say this is *exactly* the time, Oppenheimer. How could Forsythe have gotten down here? He doesn't appear anywhere on our cameras, and we've had increased patrols since that creature showed up."

Dr. Opps sighed. "We don't know yet. When he wakes up, we'll question him, and then wipe his memories and send him home."

Fort's hands clenched into fists before he could stop himself.

"*When* he wakes up?" Colonel Charles said, and Fort froze. "I think our patient has been listening to our conversation."

And that was it. If he was going to escape a mind wiping, this was his only chance.

Before the others could move, Fort bolted up, clambered over the bed, and tried to leap between the woman in the white lab coat and Dr. Opps for the exit.

Unfortunately, he didn't take into account how fast Colonel Charles was. The colonel grabbed Fort's arm as he passed, then yanked it behind Fort's back painfully. Fort immediately stopped short, groaning in pain, as two guards ran into the room.

"If he says even one word you don't understand, Taser him,"

Colonel Charles told the guards. "Don't let him even start a spell. Am I clear?"

"Yes, sir," both soldiers said at once.

"Colonel, this is my patient!" Dr. Magellan said, leaning down next to Fort and putting two fingers on his neck. "Are you okay, Forsythe?"

"I've been better," Fort admitted.

"How much did you hear?" Dr. Opps asked, his face red with either embarrassment or anger.

"Enough to know you want to wipe my mind!" Fort shouted, then groaned as Colonel Charles pushed up on his arm, sending pain radiating up into his shoulder.

"Respectfully, Colonel, I disagree with Dr. Oppenheimer," Dr. Magellan said. "Sierra almost woke up when Forsythe came into contact with her. Think of what she could do with her magic if she came back to us."

"Her power could also destroy the minds of everyone on this base!" Dr. Oppenheimer yelled.

"Oppenheimer, there's a student present," Colonel Charles practically spat. "Watch what you *say*."

"This *student* broke into a secure facility just to find the girl,"

Dr. Opps shouted back. "Think of what that could lead to!"

"Damian," Colonel Charles said, his voice cold and distant. At least he seemed to have turned his attention away from Fort, as the grip on Fort's arm lessened slightly. If he could just break away quick enough . . .

"And if he does wake up?" Dr. Opps said. "Look at what happened six months ago! You of all people should be against this—"

"I'll take that under advisement," Colonel Charles said. "Doctor, is our patient ready for discharge?" The grip on Fort's arm tightened again, and he sighed, realizing he'd missed his opportunity. If he'd ever had one.

"He seems to be doing fine," she said. "We can move him now, if you'd like."

"I would," Colonel Charles said, then nodded at the two soldiers. "Bring the boy to the disciplinary barracks and stand soldiers on guard. I want to speak to him alone." He handed Fort over to the guards, who each took ahold of an arm, though at least they weren't twisting them behind his back.

"This is *insane*!" Dr. Opps said. "We're sending the boy home now, for his good *and* ours."

"I'm afraid your failure tonight was the last straw, Oppenheimer," Colonel Charles said as another group of soldiers entered the room. "Sergeant, escort Dr. Oppenheimer to the disciplinary barracks as well—separate from the boy, of course."

Whoa. Dr. Opps was being thrown into . . . well, whatever the disciplinary barracks were, too? At least that meant Fort wouldn't have his mind wiped.

"Don't do this, Charles!" Dr. Opps shouted, struggling against two soldiers who grabbed his arms. "You don't know what you're dealing with!"

"You should have been thrown in jail for your part in the attacks, Doctor," Colonel Charles said. "I can't believe you held on for this long. But tonight gave me plenty of justification to see you relieved of your duties. I've already spoken to the committee. The school is now under my authority. I imagine they'll want your mind wiped as well, but that decision has yet to be made."

"Please!" Dr. Opps shouted. "You weren't there, not when it all happened. I saw how easily it controlled the boy—"

"Sergeant, if he continues to resist, you have my permission to use force," Colonel Charles said.

"No!" Dr. Opps shouted, but the soldiers pulled him from

the room, followed by Colonel Charles, and the closing door cut off any further sounds.

"I'm sorry about all of this," Dr. Magellan whispered to Fort as the two guards waited a moment to give the other group time to leave first. "I don't know how you got down here, but I'm glad you did. You could be the key to waking up Sierra, and if that's the case, you have my thanks. Her magic is just too powerful to be locked away down here."

"Yeah, I think we're both on the same page there," he said. Whatever connection he had with this Sierra girl, he did need her awake. At this point, she might be the only person at the school who knew what was going on and might actually tell him.

One of the guards at his side held up a pair of handcuffs. "Are you going to be trouble?" he asked, looking far too eager to use them.

"Nope, I surrender," Fort said. And that was true; he'd definitely be going along quietly. If Colonel Charles wanted to talk to him, that was fine. He'd have some questions of his own for the good colonel too.

- THIRTY-EIGHT -

FORSYTHE," COLONEL CHARLES SAID, sitting down outside Fort's cell in the disciplinary barracks, which apparently was just a nice name for a military jail. "I'm sorry for the accommodations, but I'm sure we won't need to keep you here for very long. I just have some questions I need answered, and then we'll try to replicate your experience with Sierra from a few hours back. But this time, we'll ensure your safety and monitor the entire process."

Fort nodded. He already expected this, given who'd won the argument between Colonel Charles and Dr. Opps earlier.

"First, an easy one," Colonel Charles said, smiling in a friendly manner. "How exactly did you get into that room without being seen? Did someone help you?"

Fort paused before answering. No one else was going to get

in trouble for this; that was the least he could do. "No, I got there all on my own."

"That's simply not possible."

"You should talk to your guards," Fort said with a shrug. "None of them were paying any attention, I guess. I just walked right in."

Colonel Charles narrowed his eyes, his smile fading. "This isn't the time for jokes, Forsythe. I can have you sent home with your memory wiped if I need to. But I know you want to serve your country just as much as I do. I remember your testing a couple of days ago; you're a fighter, just like I am. So help me on this, and maybe we can keep you at the school, transferred to the Destruction classes. I just need to know how you got down there, and who helped you."

Fort paused, taking that in. It was everything he'd wanted from the first time he'd even heard of the Oppenheimer School. And all he had to do was sell out his friends to get it. To abandon them, just like he'd abandoned his father.

That was never going to happen.

"Why do you want to wake up Damian?" Fort asked. "Everything that happened is because of him."

Colonel Charles leaned back, then looked over Fort's shoulder. "How much did you see in Sierra's mind?"

"I saw him open a . . . a portal or something, to another dimension," Fort said, staring at the colonel. "Whatever it was, it led somewhere dark and awful. And out of it came the same monsters that attacked Washington."

"Then you also are aware that he wasn't in control of himself?" the colonel asked, turning back to Fort.

"Maybe not, but I saw him try to let that same tentacle monster through before that, too," Fort said, his heart racing at the thought of it. "That makes all of this *his* fault. And since that's the case, I want to know how you think you can control him this time, if that thing comes back and takes him over again?"

"The blame lies with *Oppenheimer*," Colonel Charles hissed, his face contorting with anger before he regained control of himself. "Dr. Oppenheimer was the one in charge of Damian's education," he said more calmly this time. "He allowed, even encouraged Damian to experiment with Summoning magic, as it's called. And because of him, not only your father, but other people's loved ones are now gone."

Fort gritted his teeth at the mention of his dad. "That's not true, though, is it?" he said quietly. "Only *my* father died in the attack."

Colonel Charles narrowed his eyes, and Fort could see his anger building again. "On the National Mall, yes. But *my own son* Michael was killed at the National Security Agency headquarters, boy. Another student of Oppenheimer's that he *failed.*"

Fort's eyes widened, and suddenly a bunch of things began to fall into place. The Destruction student in Sierra's memories was Colonel Charles's son? And he had lost his life in the NSA attack?

"I'm . . . I'm sorry," Fort said, knowing exactly how useless that was to hear from someone else. "But doesn't that just mean we definitely shouldn't bring Damian back?"

"I'm not here to answer to *you*—" Colonel Charles started to say, then sat back and rubbed his forehead. "Forget about Damian for the moment. I need to know how you made your way down to Sierra's room. You bypassed our entire security operation. How did you do it? Who helped you?"

"I told you, no one did," Fort said. "It was all me."

"Using magic?"

"What, my Healing spells?" Fort said, forcing a smile. "Yeah, I cured a few diseases, and there I was."

Colonel Charles's lips curled in anger. "I'm going to give

you one more chance to tell me how you reached that floor, Forsythe," Colonel Charles said. "I won't tolerate this another minute longer."

"Or what?" Fort said. "You won't send me home. You need me to awaken Sierra and Damian, so he can put the entire world in danger."

Colonel Charles leaped to his feet, his chair crashing down behind him. "How about if I expel all your friends, then? Oppenheimer tells me you've been hanging out with our resident clairvoyant. Why don't I arrange to have him sent home, without his magic?"

"Good luck with that," Fort said. "He'll see you coming a mile away."

"Then how about Sebastian? Jia? The entire Healing class?" He sneered. "I'm happy to send them all home and start fresh if you'd like. Maybe just cancel the entire program?"

Fort dug his fingernails into his palms, trying to stay strong. Sebastian going home would be great news, but the rest of the healers hadn't done anything wrong and didn't deserve to lose their magic. And Jia . . . well, he still had a lot of questions for her, not to mention her spells were still in his head.

"Or how about your family?" Colonel Charles said, squeezing the bars with both hands. "Should I arrange for your aunt to lose her job? Her apartment? Whatever happens next, it'll be on *you*, Forsythe."

"Don't you hurt her!" Fort roared, slamming his hand against the cell bars.

"Then tell me how you evaded our security!"

Fort growled in frustration, wanting to scream at the man, even attack him through the bars, but knowing he couldn't risk anything that might set the colonel off. *"Fine,"* he said through clenched teeth. "I'll tell you the truth."

"It *better* be the truth!"

Fort cursed the man silently. "I heard Sierra in my head, commanding me to come to her. I couldn't stop myself. I had to do what she said."

There. That was the truth. Not the full story, no, but he hadn't lied.

Colonel Charles slowly blinked. "She had no conscious brain activity at that time. She couldn't have commanded you in such a way."

"Then you tell *me* how I knew she was there," Fort said, turning back to glare at the colonel. "I'm not a doctor, but I know what it's like to have my body taken over. And this was the second time she's done it to me."

"Assuming that's true, that only explains how you knew *where* to go. But how did you get in unseen?"

Well, Fort had *tried* being truthful, but that was all he could say without getting his friends in trouble. So now it was time to lie. "I don't know. She must have used her magic on the guards and had me avoid the cameras. I barely knew where I was. Before the guards brought me here, I didn't even know I was underground."

Colonel Charles stared at him for a moment, and Fort began to sweat, wondering if the colonel could see how nervous he was. But then Colonel Charles smiled slightly. "If she's *that* close to waking, we might not actually require your services any further, Forsythe." He stood up and turned to go.

"Hey, wait!" Fort yelled, jumping to his feet. "Don't do this. You *can't* wake up Damian. You haven't seen what happened, what he did!"

"Enjoy your time here, Forsythe," Colonel Charles said. "It looks like you'll be heading home after all today, with no memory of the school. Your country thanks you for your service, such as it was."

And with that, he left, and a soldier closed another barred door behind him.

Fort screamed in frustration and punched the pillow on the cell's bed a few times before calming down. That wasn't helping. But what else could he do? He didn't have the power to stop Colonel Charles from waking up Sierra, and no one else would believe him, other than maybe Dr. Opps, who wasn't any better off than Fort was.

Except there *was* someone with the power to fix everything. Someone who could wipe people's memories herself, or even take over their minds. Wipe the magic from Damian's head before Colonel Charles could make the boy use it, even.

And all Fort would have to do was get to Sierra first—and hope that waking her up didn't destroy his own mind in the process.

He watched the door for a moment and counted to one hundred, just to be sure Colonel Charles was gone.

Then he cast Ethereal Spirit on himself and left the disciplinary barracks through the wall behind him.

- THIRTY-NINE -

FORT MADE HIS WAY THROUGH THE ground as if he were swimming, each stroke pushing him forward against the slight pressure from the dirt. He came up every minute or so for air, carefully pushing as little of his face above ground as he could while still taking in a deep breath. It wasn't quick, but at least no one would see him unless they happened to be staring down at the exact right moment.

He made it to the boys' dorm without being discovered and crawled up through the floor. "Cyrus?" he said as quietly as he could, hoping the other boy would be waiting for him.

But the barracks were empty. Either all the other kids were in class, or something else was going on. Would Colonel Charles have interrogated Cyrus, too? If so, would the other boy know not to give Rachel and Jia up? Fort wasn't sure how his future magic might work with getting stories straight, but it didn't seem like the most approved usage.

He cursed as he looked around one last time, then dove back into the floor, just like he'd seen Rachel do.

The Training Hall wasn't that far by foot, but swimming through the ground was exhausting, especially while trying to stay out of sight. Whenever there was a hiding spot out of the security cameras' view, Fort pulled half his body up above the ground and just lay there, like he was propped up against the side of a pool, letting himself rest a bit before diving back in.

Finally he arrived at the outer wall to the Training Hall, breathing a huge sigh of relief as he stopped, exhausted. Before just jumping inside, he moved slowly around the building until he found the elevator shaft leading down. Here, he pushed himself through the wall, then slid down the shaft with one hand inside the wall, the friction of the solid material slowing him down just enough to keep him from falling uncontrollably.

As he descended, something occurred to him: Why *should* he fall in the shaft, when he didn't through floors? The air of the shaft was only a bit less substantial than the floor would be. Was his sense of reality really that strong that it kept him standing on floors and falling in elevator shafts?

A noise above him derailed his thoughts before he got an answer. The elevator was descending rapidly from above, coming straight at him. He yipped and threw himself into the wall just as the car passed, then threw himself out after it, landing on top of the elevator as it descended. Again, that shouldn't have worked; the roof of the elevator wasn't any more real to him right now than the air was. But whatever logic the magic had, at least he hadn't fallen through the ceiling.

The car stopped on the twelfth basement floor, the one above where the skeletons and crates were stored. Fort waited for it to unload, then peeked his head inside. Finding it empty, he pulled himself down into it and quickly pushed the B-15 button. The elevator beeped in response but didn't move, and Fort noticed for the first time a place to swipe a security badge next to the button.

Great. He sighed deeply. Taking the elevator would have made things easier, but whatever.

He slowly bent down toward the floor and pushed his head through, judging the distance to jump down three more floors. It was at least twenty feet below him, and he didn't like the idea of what his sense of reality might feel the need to do to his legs if he landed hard. Granted, he could heal himself with his magic, but that didn't mean he *wanted* to break a leg.

Instead, he settled for jumping back to the wall and sliding down farther using the trick he'd been using before the elevator arrived. This brought him safely to basement level fifteen, where he poked his head through the elevator doors to the hallway beyond. No one was around, just like the night before.

Okay. He could do this. All he had to do was reach Sierra, wake her up somehow without losing his mind in the process, then convince her to wipe Damian's magic. Easy.

Fort crept down the hallway, keeping close to the wall in case someone came out and he needed to hide in a room along the way. As he reached the room where the doctors had been the night before, he stopped and pushed himself into the wall, just to check to see if they were still there.

No doctors, but two soldiers were sitting in chairs, talking quietly.

They seemed distracted enough that Fort could potentially make it past the doorway without being noticed, but he wasn't about to get caught this far in, so instead he did a shallow dive into the hallway floor, just in front of the door. He swam beneath the door like a dolphin, kicking his whole body several times, then pushed himself up on the other side, emerging at the end of the hallway, right at Sierra's room and peeked inside.

Fortunately, the room was empty, other than its two patients. Fort moved through the closed door and slowly approached Sierra again, this time mentally preparing himself for what was to come. The pain had been immense, when her memories had flooded his mind uncontrollably, but maybe if he was ready for them, he could handle it better?

He reached out a trembling hand toward hers, then paused, wondering if there was a better way. Could his Healing magic bring her back, somehow? Or maybe just screaming her name, really close to her ears?

No, he knew what he had to do, and the only thing stopping him right now was fear of what might happen. But if he waited much longer, he'd be caught. It was only a matter of time before—

As if to finish his thought, alarms began clamoring throughout the room and hallway outside.

"Oh, you've *got* to be kidding me," Fort whispered, whirling around. Had they found him already?

But no. Out in the hallway, he could hear the two soldiers from the other room running toward the elevator. If they weren't coming this way, then what was the alarm about?

Oh, right. They must have discovered him missing from the disciplinary barracks, but they would still be checking for him down here next.

Which meant he didn't have any time left to worry about what might happen.

"Please don't fry my brain," Fort whispered to Sierra, then grasped her hand tightly.

"Damian!" Sierra shouted, staring in horror as the Old Ones began making their way to the portal. "Have you gone insane?"

Damian looked back at her without recognition, and from his mind, a horrible darkness emanated. YOUR FRIEND NO LONGER EXISTS, the presence said in her mind, sending waves of agony through her skull.

"Damian, stop—" Dr. Opps shouted, but Damian raised a hand and sent a magic missile flying into the doctor's chest. Dr. Opps went flying, slamming into the nearest wall, groaning as he landed on the floor.

Sierra immediately cast Mind Blast, sending it at the creature's mind, but Damian waved his hand as if batting aside an annoying insect, and the spell seemed to have no effect. DO NOT INTERFERE, the Old One's voice exploded in her head, and she dropped to her knees in pain.

Before she could stop him, Damian began to whisper more words of power, and somewhere, she could almost feel something horrible had just happened.

YOU KNOW NOTHING OF THE TRUE POWER OF MAGIC, the voice said in her head again, just as the floor began to shake beneath her feet. YOUR KIND REBELLED AGAINST US, TRICKED US WHEN WE RULED THEM MERCIFULLY EONS AGO. EVEN EXILED US FROM OUR TRUE HOME.

"Sierra, shut him down!" Dr. Opps yelled.

"I don't know if I can!" Sierra shouted, not sure what to do. The darkness was just so strong . . .

"Do it! Or we'll all die!"

Sierra gritted her teeth and reached out with her mind, flooding Damian's head with her magic. Damian smiled as the darkness inside his head pushed back, and Sierra knew she had no chance against it. Instead, she slipped around its presence in his mind, even as it struck back, taking control of Damian's body instead, just like she'd done the last time he'd communicated with the creature.

But then, she'd just been dealing with Damian. She'd never be able to hold the creature off, not for more than a second or two. But maybe that was enough?

THIS CHILD SPOKE OF THE PROPHECY, BUT IT HAS ALREADY COME TO PASS, the creature continued. ONE OF YOUR KIND MASTERED THE SEVEN FORMS TO HIDE MAGIC AWAY, TO ENSURE WE COULD NEVER USE ITS POWER TO RETURN. BUT MAGIC COULD NOT STAY LOCKED AWAY FOREVER. IT DESIRED THE RETURN OF ITS TRUE MASTERS, AND SO HAS REAWAKENED NOW, TO WELCOME US BACK.

"Close the portal," she hissed out loud, commanding Damian's body to do the same. Using his voice, she picked the words to the spell from his memory and cast it, just as the first Old One reached the portal. The gateway collapsed, and both she and Damian screamed, though his scream was from anger, not pain.

IF YOU INSIST ON INTERFERING, YOU SHALL KNOW *PAIN*! The creature's voice roared in her head, and she shrieked. Damian started whispering another spell, then another, and the room began to shake violently.

Fort shouted in pain and collapsed to his knees. A drop of blood fell from his nose to his hand, and he stared at it in surprise, then wiped his bleeding nose. Sierra moaned beside him, her eyes fluttering, and he hoped she was going to wake up soon, before this killed him.

Because he knew what came now. He'd already lived out the memory of the next few minutes.

This was when the monsters attacked.

Please, Fort whispered in his mind. *Don't make me watch that again.*

Whether she heard him or not, her memory jumped forward a few minutes in time.

"Sierra!" Dr. Opps shouted from across the room as the giant black clawed hand retreated, yanking down half the building with it. The outside wall crumbled, and sunlight poured into the room, fighting with the shadows pouring from the portal to the Old One's realm. "There's no time left. Free Damian's mind now!"

Sierra's skull felt like it was about to burst, but she nodded. Half her mind she left at the National Mall, trying to get the civilians out of harm's way, while the other half she turned back to Damian. But the Old One in his head wouldn't even let her get close. It turned its attention down to her, and she screamed as it turned Damian's mental spells back on her—

"What is going on?" she heard someone yell, and abruptly the attack on her mind ceased.

"Michael!" Dr. Opps shouted. "Take Damian down! He's possessed by a supernatural creature. Do it!"

"Damian?" Michael said. "Really? But how can I do that without hurting him?"

WE GROW WEARY OF THIS, the Old One said in their minds, and they all screamed in reaction.

Even through the pain, Michael launched a fireball at Damian, only for Damian to raise a hand and stop it in midair. The fireball suddenly grew to three times its size and turned from bright orange and white to a sickly yellow, then whirled back toward the Destruction student who'd created it.

With no way to protect himself against his own spell, Michael took the fireball right in the chest, letting out a piercing scream.

His clothes on fire, he dropped to the floor, rolling to quench the flames, but the magical blaze refused to go out, and the boy continued to cry out in pain.

"Jia!" Dr. Opps shouted, and the previously possessed healer crawled to Michael, a hand raised to put out his fires, until she was slammed out of the way as the giant black hand pushed up through the floor once more.

The creature's hand enveloped Michael's burning body and pulled him away screaming, down into the darkness.

"NO!" Sierra shouted, and rage filled her mind, giving her some remaining energy where she'd all but run out of strength. She gathered her will, then put everything she had into one final Mind Blast. It exploded out of her and straight into Damian's head, and this time, it was too strong for the Old One to deflect it.

The Old One shouted in agony. And as it did, its cry turned from a shriek in their minds into Damian's actual voice.

"What . . . what is happening?" he said.

"Damian!" Dr. Opps shouted. "Close these portals, now!"

"I . . . I'll try," Damian said. "But it's still inside my head. I don't know how long until it takes control again!"

"Sierra, burn that thing out of his mind!" Dr. Opps shouted.

Almost too tired to even breathe, Sierra struggled to call

forth another Mind Blast. Hoping for more strength, she withdrew her commands on the National Mall, releasing all the tourists who were now far enough away to be safe.

And then, something strange happened. One of the tourists still in danger pushed back against her control. Almost in annoyance, she looked into his mind and saw that his father was in the other creature's grasp.

"No," she whispered, feeling the boy's terror and anger. But it was too late, and if she didn't get him out of there, he'd die too. As she cast the Mind Blast at the Old One in Damian's head, she sent her control back at the boy on the Mall, forcing him to leave.

But he refused, and just as her power struck the Old One, the boy fought back. The struggle split her mind, filling it with the boy's overwhelming fear and anger, and she couldn't think about anything else.

She screamed, and Damian did too, connected to her now, just like she was connected to this one last civilian at the National Mall, the only one who refused to run.

And then her world collapsed in around her, blackness filling her vision, and she fell to the ground, not sure of anything except for one last word. . . .

"Forsythe?!"

Fort writhed on the floor in agony as Sierra bolted up in bed, her powers radiating out of her mind like a hurricane.

And then, even through the pain, Fort heard another voice, and he realized that after all of that, he'd managed to do the one thing he'd been trying to prevent.

"Sierra?" Damian said from the bed next to hers.

- FORTY -

DAMIAN!" SIERRA SAID, LOOKING OVER at the other boy. "Are you . . . yourself?"

Fort slowly pulled himself up to the bed and watched Damian pat himself on the arms and chest. "I think so?" Damian said, sounding relieved. "Whatever you did, I think it pushed the Old One out of my mind." He pulled his legs out from under the covers and placed them on the floor, then tried to stand up, only to wobble shakily. "What's . . . what's wrong with me?"

"You've been . . . unconscious," Fort said, not very stable himself as his head continued to pound. "In a coma. For a while. I'm not sure how long."

"I have?" Damian asked, leaning back against the bed while giving Fort a suspicious look. "Who are you?"

"Fort, what are you doing here?" Sierra whispered, turning

back to him with a concerned look. "Does that mean everything I've been dreaming . . . oh *no*. No no no! I'm so sorry. I didn't mean . . . what have I . . . oh *no*." She dropped her head into her hands. "I saw you come to the school, and you were so worried, I tried to help. But everyone had secrets, things they wouldn't tell you. I wanted you to know what they knew . . . but you kept thinking about the attack in D.C., too, and I couldn't help it, I couldn't stop remembering—"

"There was an attack?" Damian said, trying to stand again. "Did something happen?"

Sierra's eyes widened. "You don't remember?"

"The last thing I remember is you making me close a portal," he said. "Then the Old One took over, and . . ." He started to look sick. "Oh, what did I do?"

Fort pushed to his feet, for once just letting the rage build, not even caring. "Everything that happened . . . it's because of you," he yelled at Damian. "There was an attack. Two, actually. One of them killed Michael, your friend. And the other one killed my *father*."

Damian's face lost all its color, and he fell back to the bed, shaking his head. "I . . . I'm so *sorry*. I didn't . . . I never would have—"

"Fort, it wasn't him," Sierra said quietly, also trying to stand, but her legs were too weak. "You saw my memories. The Old One had control, not Damian. He couldn't help it. It wasn't his fault."

"Except you were the one who let it in," Fort said to Damian, slowly rounding the beds, trying to stay calm so that the other boy wouldn't run. Fort wasn't sure he'd be able to keep up in his current shape, and there was no way he was letting Damian escape, not now. "Even when Dr. Opps told you not to communicate with them. But you thought you could handle it. And because of you, people *died*."

Damian looked up at him, his mouth hanging open. "They could have taught us so much," he said, his voice almost too quiet to hear. "I saw it in that thing's mind. They *discovered* magic! I knew it couldn't be trusted, but I thought that we could learn from it and send it back. And the risk would be worth all the good that would have come from it. . . ."

"Fort, back away," Sierra said, holding out a hand toward him, and he felt a gentle pull on his mind, less an order than a suggestion that he move away from Damian. "You . . . you shouldn't be here right now."

"*I* shouldn't be here?" Fort said, his voice rising. "The attack in D.C. was his fault! My father *died* because of him. And you want me to just go back to the dorm and forget about this?"

"It wasn't *me*," Damian said, his voice sounding more gravelly now, like he was about to cry or something. But Fort barely noticed, trying to decide if he should cast his Paralyze spell on Damian first, or just use his fists.

"Fort, *STOP*!" Sierra shouted, and this time, her voice echoed in his mind, a telepathic command he couldn't ignore. His legs froze to the ground, so he slowly twisted around to look at Sierra, who was trembling wildly from the effort of holding him in place. "You don't know what's happening here. You don't want to do this!"

"You don't know me," Fort growled at her, pushing back against her command. "You have *no idea* what I want!"

I know everything about you, she shouted in his mind, slowly sinking back to the bed as her magic took a toll on her. *I've been inside your mind for months, Forsythe Fitzgerald. I was in it during the attack, just like I was in everyone's mind there. But you wouldn't leave! The rest of them ran, but you stayed, for your father. I had to push you harder, and I saw everything, everything you did! Don't you think I wanted to help him too?*

Fort clenched his jaw, exerting all of his might to break her spell, and he could see the effect his struggle was having on Sierra. But her thoughts in his head just pushed him onward. She didn't get to just explain away her role in his father's death. If she hadn't pulled him away, his dad might still be alive!

It wasn't your fault he was taken! she thought in his head. *If I hadn't made you run, you would have been on the steps with your father when that monster grabbed him, and the only difference would be that you'd be gone now too. The creature is the one to blame for all of this!*

"You're wrong!" Fort shouted. "I could have saved him. All it would have taken was one extra minute, maybe even less. But *you* made me run!"

"The Old One knew so much," Damian said, sounding even worse now, his voice fading in and out. "It promised it would open my mind to the universe and all of reality. It could teach me things about magic that no book could possibly contain. Humans wrote our books of magic, it said. And for that reason, they were all flawed . . . we never understood the true power, it said. We put limits on it. . . ."

"I'm so sorry," Sierra said out loud, almost flat on the bed now, one hand clasping her head like she was trying to hold it together, the other pointing at Fort. "Everything had gone wrong, and I couldn't let anyone get hurt. We had no idea what we were doing! We just wanted to *help* people!"

"And what about him?" Fort shouted, pointing at Damian. "Was he helping people when his creature killed my father?!"

"You know what it's like, trying to learn from the books!" Sierra said, groaning from the pain now. "And look at how I helped you get ahead. Think what you would have done in Damian's place, just to learn the first three Healing spells! We didn't understand what the Old Ones were, that they'd been waiting for us, waiting for magic to return!"

"It was in my head," Damian said, and now Fort barely recognized his voice at all. "I . . . I couldn't take it. It had seen the beginning, and will be here until the end. Thousands, millions of years. I felt its hatred for us, that humanity betrayed them, exiled them from their home. But it told me that I could . . . MAKE UP FOR . . . HUMANITY'S MISTAKE, IF I JUST UNLOCKED THE DOOR—"

Fort slowly turned back to Damian, disturbed by the boy's words, but even more so by the fact he'd heard the last part in his head. And that was when he saw something that made his heart stop.

Damian wasn't alone in his body anymore.

The shadowy, half-transparent Old One from the officers' mess pushed its way into Damian's body, overlapping him completely, and opaque crystal armor slowly began to grow over Damian's hospital gown. The boy's hands and feet stretched out and split into a mass of tentacles, as did his teeth, now protruding from a skull-like helmet. And within seconds, where there had once been a human boy, now there was only an Old One, Damian's body transformed by the creature into its own form.

"No!" Sierra shouted, trying to run to Damian, but Fort quickly grabbed her, holding her back. "I thought I expelled it from him. I didn't know!"

Fort stepped in front of her, his hands raised and his Healing spells at the ready. "You might have," he whispered, as the creature rose into the air, its attention seemingly taken with its transformation. "I think this one's been searching for him but couldn't find him while he was asleep. Sierra, you need to wipe the magic from his mind *right now*. Before it figures out how to access it."

"I'll try," she said, and pointed her raised palm at the Old One. But the creature just stared at her for a moment and she collapsed to the floor, her body shuddering as shadows played over her eyes.

And just like that, Fort's legs were free. He leaped at the

Old One, the only spell he could think of that might actually hurt this thing at the front of his mind: Cause Heavy Wounds. Without having mastered it, he'd just have the one chance, but maybe that'd be enough.

"Mon—" he started to shout, only for the Old One's tentacle to snake out and wrap around his throat. The tentacle squeezed, cutting off Fort's air, and with it, the rest of his spell.

WE HAVE FOUND THE ONE WE SEARCHED FOR, the creature's voice erupted in Fort's head as it and Sierra both rose a few feet off the ground. WE WILL TOLERATE NO FURTHER INTERFERENCE.

Fort's air began to run out, and he struggled to free himself, or even just to breathe, but the Old One held him tightly as another tentacle moved toward Fort's head. It gently brushed against him, and his mind filled with the presence of something too large to be contained by such a small skull.

Millions of years of memories flooded into Fort's mind. Stars appeared, lived out their lifetimes, then exploded, while billions of species winked in and out of existence. Nothing in his own life mattered now, not in the face of such an existence. To the Old One, Fort lived for less time than an insect, and had just as much impact.

And the creature's knowledge! It understood concepts that humans wouldn't discover for thousands of years. Its senses weren't contained to three dimensions, and Fort couldn't take the overload of information coming from the tenth, fifteenth, twentieth dimensions.

Tears rolled down his face as the creature's presence filled his mind, and he wanted to laugh, to scream, anything to stop the madness he was forced to see, the millennia of life that he couldn't comprehend. He couldn't contain this much time, this much awareness of the universe.

Please, stop, he whispered in his head, willing to do anything if it just released him, let him never have to witness these horrors again.

And strangely, it did. The Old One abandoned Fort's mind and dropped his body, and his awareness crumbled back to just three dimensions, his own life, his own memories, his own time. He collapsed to the floor, gasping for breath.

The thing that had been Damian turned its attention from him to now stare at two shaking soldiers standing in the doorway.

"Stop!" one shouted, aiming his weapon at the Old One.

The creature just stared at them for a moment, then raised several tentacles. YOU HAVE NO TAINT OF MAGIC

IN YOU, AND SO WILL MAKE FOR PERFECT SERVANTS, AS IS HUMANITY'S DESTINY. AND THIS TIME, THERE WILL BE NO *REBELLION.*

Tentacles exploded out from the Old One's hand, piercing the two soldier's minds. They screamed, their bodies shaking violently, only to abruptly go silent and stand up straight.

And then they turned their weapons on Fort.

- FORTY-ONE -

DESTROY THE BOY, THE OLD ONE COMmanded, and the two soldiers took aim.

Barely able to think, Fort threw his hand out toward the men and shouted, "Phon t'cor!" The soldiers' bodies instantly turned ethereal, and the weapons fell out of their insubstantial hands to the floor.

The Old One hissed. WHAT SPELL IS THIS? IT WAS A MISTAKE TO ALLOW YOUR KIND MAGIC, WHEN YOU WERE SERVANTS. YOU BETRAYED US AND TOOK THE POWER FOR YOURSELVES.

A tentacle swept out over Fort, and he tried to dodge but couldn't move fast enough. The tentacle just hovered over his head, though, then retracted. What had it done?

WE WILL NOT ALLOW HUMANITY THE POWER TO REBEL THIS TIME, the creature said, and launched a different tentacle at him. Fort managed to sidestep it, but it sliced through the sleeve of his uniform. A second one snaked toward him, and he knew he couldn't avoid them all.

Fortunately, he didn't have to. All he needed to do was cast Ethereal Spirit, and . . .

And the spell wasn't *there*.

Fort gasped as a tentacle cut into his shoulder, sending lightning bolts of pain up and down his body. "You . . . you took my spell," he gasped, falling back against the floor.

YOU ARE A CHILD PLAYING WITH FLAME, the creature said, pulling its tentacle free of Fort. Then it slowly rose higher in the air—Sierra with it—as the two soldiers collapsed, unconscious. YOU KNOW NOTHING ABOUT THE TRUE POWER OF MAGIC. The Old One glanced upward, and a magic missile slammed up through the floors above, all the way up through the building, revealing blue sky above. NOW, IT IS TIME TO GATHER AN ARMY TO SERVE US. THOSE HERE SHALL DO FOR A START.

Fort fell back against the wall, writhing in pain from the wound in his shoulder. He quickly healed himself, gritting his teeth as the Old One and Sierra continued to rise through the room. He couldn't just let them go, but what choice did he have? The few spells he still knew didn't seem likely to help, and anything he cast, the creature could apparently just steal right from his head. Was it using Damian's Telepathy spells, just like when Sierra had stolen Jia's spells for him?

Sierra! Fort looked up at the floating girl, her eyes covered in shadow. If only *she* was free, her magic could push the creature out of Damian again, just like he'd seen her do in her memories of six months ago. But how could he free her without using mind magic himself? If only he had some spell that could heal someone's mind, or . . .

Wait a second. *Headaches.* Jia had pointed out that healing a headache was dangerous, because the magic would restore the brain to a previous point, and could wipe out memories.

What if it could also wipe out magical possession?

"Hey!" Fort shouted, pushing off the wall and waving his uninjured arm. "I'm not done with you yet!"

The Old One paused in its flight and turned its skull-helmeted head back to Fort. YOU ARE OF NO CONSEQUENCE.

"That's probably true," Fort said. "But I know someone who *is*." Before the creature could take another spell from him, he launched himself at Sierra, the words to Heal Minor Wounds on his lips. He had more powerful Healing spells available, but he didn't want to restore her mind to months or years in the past and cause her to forget all of her magic, too.

"Mon d'cor!" he shouted, reaching out for Sierra's foot with his hand.

But the Old One was too fast. Its tentacles intercepted Fort's hand before he could reach Sierra, and the Healing energy dispersed into the creature instead. Fort's momentum crashed him against one of the hospital beds, but he pushed to his feet immediately, figuring the Old One would try to wipe this spell too.

But instead, the Old One shrieked in agony. And where the creature's skull helmet had been, Fort saw Damian's human eyes staring back at him for a brief moment.

But the tentacles quickly reappeared, and the creature took control once more.

PAIN, it screeched in Fort's head, which felt like it would explode from the force of the creature's distress. YOU KNOW CORPOREAL MAGIC? YOU HAVE NO IDEA OF THE POWER YOU HOLD.

What kind of magic? And Healing magic . . . hurt it? Or did it just feel pain from being pushed out of Damian, like Fort had hoped would happen with Sierra?

Either way, this was something he could use.

Fort held his hands up toward the Old One in what he hoped was a threatening manner. "That's right," he said, bringing Heal Minor Wounds back to mind. "I know, um, corporeal magic. And if you don't let her go, I'll use it on you again!"

The Old One shuddered at that, then sent several tentacles flying over Fort's head. He jumped for the nearest one, ready to cast his Healing spell on it, but the tentacles were too quick, and Heal Minor Wounds disappeared from his mind.

YOU HAVE *HURT* US, the Old One said, and the force of its anger sent Fort to his knees. FOR THAT, YOU SHALL SUFFER YOUR WORST FEAR.

Out of nowhere, images of the attack in D.C. began playing through Fort's mind, and he froze, fear and rage filling him. This had to be the Old One's mind magic. But why was he searching Fort's memories?

YOUR GREATEST PAIN SHALL BE INFLICTED ON YOU ONCE AGAIN! the creature shouted.

When he looked up again, though, the Old One and Sierra had both disappeared.

"No!" Fort shouted, pushing back to his feet. "*No!* Come

back!" He slammed his fist against the bed, then again, screaming in frustration. This was all his fault! If he hadn't forced Sierra to wake up, none of this would have happened. Dr. Opps had been right the whole time.

Now the creature had to be using its mental powers on the rest of the school above. He could already hear shouts through the hole the creature had made, and what sounded like explosions. Would the Destruction students or the soldiers be able to stop it?

Not if they didn't know its weakness. Healing magic could hurt it, but right now, only Fort knew that. He had to tell someone. There might still be time!

Fort leaped across the nearest bed and ran to the door of the hospital room, only to stop as the entire room shook. Shook in a familiar way.

Almost like a truck had just passed by.

Fort froze, terror flowing like ice water in his veins. Could the Old One have . . . ? *No.* He was just paranoid after reliving the memories a moment ago. It couldn't—

A second tremor sent Fort crashing to the floor. Bits of the ceiling and the floors above began raining down through the hole the Old One had created. Something slammed into his back, and he groaned, then quickly scrambled under one of the nearby beds to avoid getting hit.

"No," he whispered, hiding his face in his arms and squeezing his eyes shut as the building shook around him. "This can't be happening. Not *again*!"

As the quake intensified, the floor jumped beneath him, tossing both Fort and the bed into the air. Fort landed hard on his healed shoulder, but even that pain didn't cut through his fear. The entire building felt like it was collapsing around him.

Could this be another dream? Another one of Sierra's memories?

A giant black claw exploded through the floor beneath him, throwing the bed against the nearby wall as a second and third finger rose up around him.

A roar echoed up from below, just like the one he'd heard in D.C., and in his nightmares ever since the attack.

And then the creature closed its enormous clawed fingers around him, and just like his father before him, Fort was pulled down into the depths.

- FORTY-TWO -

EVERYTHING WENT PITCH BLACK AS the creature pulled him down, and Fort began to hyperventilate, not able to move, not even able to think. He was going to die. Just like his father had. There was nothing he could do. The creature had returned. He had nothing to fight it with. No Destruction magic. Nothing.

He screamed, out of fear more than any hope for help. But the only response was another roar from the monster, and Fort knew then that no one would be coming to rescue him.

Everything began to get hazy as his breathing grew faster, and part of him knew he'd pass out if he couldn't slow it down. But what did that matter? Maybe it'd be better to be knocked out if he was going to be . . . to be eaten?

"NO!" Fort screamed at himself. "Not again. *Not again!*" He couldn't let someone else down, not like he'd failed his father, even if that someone else was him. But what could he do? The fear was too much, and there was no way to overcome that. . . .

Except there was. A spell he'd found in the Healing book.

"Nen timo!" he shouted, and his hands began to glow blue, lighting the darkness inside the creature's fist as they descended. Fort quickly pushed his hands against his chest and felt the cold magic flow into him.

Immediately his breathing slowed, and the haziness dissipated, though he couldn't see anything outside the monstrous hand clutching him. Still, he could even think clearly again.

That Remove Fear spell really worked!

Okay, Fort thought. *Get it together. There has to be a way to escape this.*

Yes, he might get eaten, but right now, he was still alive, and he still had *some* spells. He rose to his feet, using the creature's nearby finger as leverage, and steadied himself as best he could against it.

Strangely, his heart began to race again, and he wondered if the fear was coming back already. But no, this was something . . . different. Frustration and anger began to rise in his chest, and he clenched his fists, wondering if he could punch his way right through the creature.

This thing killed his father and now was trying to eat him, too! Rage pounded in Fort's veins, and he bared his teeth. "That's not going to happen!" he shouted, slamming his fist against the monster's scaled finger.

Oddly, their descent stopped immediately.

Fort stepped back in surprise as the creature's fingers slowly spread open, revealing two red sources of light in an otherwise pitch-black cavern. The red light lit the walls of the cavern, showing uneven claw marks where the creature had dug up from below. Much farther down, a hint of a weird, greenish glow suggested that maybe the portal to the creature's dimension was still open somewhere in the depths.

The creature's red eyes stared at him from what looked like dozens of feet away, and it roared again. The blast of its breath sent Fort crashing backward into the monster's scaled fingers, but he didn't stay down long.

"Come on!" he shouted, leaping to his feet and waving the creature toward him. "Attack me! I dare you! You've got *nothing*!"

The hand jolted beneath him as it moved closer to the monster's head. Its eyes reflected off yard-long teeth, each one glistening with saliva as it opened its mouth.

Fort knew he should escape, if he could. The fingers were open. Maybe he could jump off the monster's hand and climb up out of the cavern, back to the surface.

But right now, escape was the last thing on his mind. All Fort cared about was revenge, both for himself and his father. He wanted the creature to feel *pain*, as much as or more than what it had put him through when it had taken his father.

It didn't even matter anymore if this was the same creature. As far as Fort was concerned, this one would pay for its people's crimes.

As he drew closer to the razor-sharp teeth, a practical question filled his mind. Even in his rage, he knew punching the creature wouldn't exactly do much. He wasn't afraid to attack it physically, of course, not now. But he needed to put it through agony! If only he'd ever learned Destruction magic . . .

Wait. There was another spell still in his mind. He'd forgotten about it after considering using it on the Old One.

Cause Heavy Wounds. The spell he'd taken from the Healing book before Jia had caught him.

Perfect.

As its hand reached the creature's head, it tried to toss Fort into the air, straight at its wide-open mouth. But Fort wrapped both hands around the nearest of the scaled fingers, holding on tightly.

Then he grinned.

"Mon d'rexenen cor!" he shouted, casting the Cause Heavy Wounds spell, expecting the usual cool Healing energy in his palms.

Instead, his hands began to burn white hot, sending pain shooting up through his arms and into his shoulders. He screamed in agony . . . but so did the creature. As it did, he felt both the pain and the magical energy leave him and flow into the monster.

The giant monster roared in anguish as the finger Fort held began to wither away, the muscle dying and the bones crumbling beneath his hands.

It was *working*! Fort screamed in joy as the monster moved its hand back away from its mouth, and he dropped off the wilted finger. For a moment, the bloodred eyes almost seemed confused, like the creature wasn't sure what had caused its pain.

"That was *me*!" Fort shouted at it, bashing his fist against his chest. "I did that to you. And I'm going to do it *again*!"

Except, he *couldn't* do it again. Not having mastered the spell, he could only use it the once.

The monster paused another moment, then moved Fort back toward its mouth once more. Apparently, as bad as the pain had been, it wasn't enough to stop the creature completely.

Fort quickly clambered over to one of the still-healthy fingers and held himself in place as the creature tried to toss him into its mouth again. In spite of the air whistling around him and the force of the monster's arm, Fort managed to hold on.

But the creature wasn't done. It tried throwing him over and over, getting more frustrated with every attempt. Fort's arms began to tire, and he slipped a bit on the last toss, but the monster had had enough and instead drove its palm toward the nearby rock wall.

Fort shouted in surprise, barely managing to climb around to the back of the finger as the monster slammed its hand against the wall, sending huge boulders crumbling down into the nothingness below them. A second hit knocked one of Fort's hands loose, and a small bit of fear began to worm its way back into his heart. "Oh, *great*," he said, his hands now starting to sweat. The spell couldn't have lasted longer?

But it wasn't another Remove Fear spell he needed here. The Cause Heavy Wounds spell had *worked*, but once just wasn't enough. He needed to cast it again and again until the creature was *destroyed*. But he couldn't do that, not without having mastered the spell. . . .

The monster's hand bashed into the wall once more, and this time Fort lost his grip completely. He frantically grabbed for whatever he could as he fell into nothingness, barely managing to grab onto the scales on the back of the creature's hand to avoid tumbling into the depths below.

The monster lifted its hand for another hit, and Fort tumbled off the side of the hand, crashing into the creature's thumb. He slammed into it hard enough to knock the air from his lungs, and spots began exploding in her vision. Even woozy, though, he managed to wrap his weak arms and legs around the thumb and hold on tight.

Not that he'd be able to hold on much longer. One more hit, maybe two, and that would be it. If the creature didn't eat him first.

Why couldn't Cause Heavy Wounds have been one of the spells he took from Jia? One instance of the magic just wasn't enough! And it wasn't like he could work out the words on his own. . . .

. . . Could he?

A memory of studying with Rachel floated through his

mind, and something about how the words to a spell and its opposite were really close, only one word apart. Could he use that with the Heal Heavy Wounds spell he *did* have?

The creature slammed its hand into the wall again, and the hit sent a shock wave through Fort's body. That was it, he wouldn't last another one.

Fortunately, the monster seemed done with smashing its hand against the wall.

Instead, it brought its thumb straight up to its mouth, ready to pick Fort off with its teeth.

- FORTY-THREE -

FORT'S MIND RACED FRANTICALLY AS he neared the monster's gaping mouth. Remove Fear had run its course now, and he could barely think, now that he was about to be eaten. He took a deep breath as he tried to think of other spells he knew. "Utri cor" were the words to Cause Disease, and "*nen*utri cor" was Cure Disease. Did that word "nen" negate the spell somehow?

"Nen mon d'rexe cor," he shouted, adding the word to the Heal Heavy Wounds spell. But no magic filled his hands, and now he'd reached the monster's mouth.

"Monnen d'rexe cor! Mon d'nen rexe cor!" he shouted in a panic, trying anything.

But nothing happened, and the creature brought its giant razor-sharp teeth down toward him. He screamed and dove away, landing back in the palm as the teeth scraped against the scales on its thumb, then moved down toward him.

Covering his head with his hands, Fort curled up on the palm, squeezing his eyes shut.

He had to try, just once more.

"Mon d'rexenen cor," he whispered.

And there it was. The same white-hot pain filled his arms, and he immediately threw both arms above him, almost in defense. His hands struck the monster's teeth, and the magic passed right into the creature.

This time, its shriek lasted for almost a minute.

Wrapping one arm around a finger, Fort watched triumphantly as the creature wailed in agony, its head slamming back and forth against the cavern walls. Fort wanted to laugh, to shout, to celebrate at the top of his lungs as it threw its hand far away from its face, like it didn't want him anywhere near it.

And for good reason. But that wasn't going to save the monster. Not anymore. Because Fort had figured out the language of the magic instead of reading it in the book. And somehow, he could still remember the words he'd used. There they were, still in his memory, fresh and ready for another casting.

Above him, the creature writhed in pain, roaring in anger and now fear. "You *deserve* this!" Fort shouted up at it from its hand. "You're going to *suffer* for what you did to my father!"

With that, he brought his own hands down onto the scales and cast the spell again, then again, and again.

Each time, the pain radiated over Fort, making him scream, but the effect on the creature was exponentially greater. With each new spell, the magical energy passed farther up the monster's arm and into its chest. From there, it spread out over the entire massive body, withering away its muscles and sending scales dropping from its skin like rain.

"Are you enjoying this?" he shouted as the monster shuddered, its body wasting away to the point that it couldn't even lift its hand anymore. "This is for my *father*! I hope you feel every ounce of pain he did!"

The monster quaked, and the motion almost buckled Fort right off, but he managed to latch onto another of the withered fingers, and he attacked again.

"Come on!" he shouted as the magic filled the beast. "Is that all you can take? I've got enough for hours of this!"

The monster roared again, but instead of attacking him further, it began to descend again, back into the ground, using its still-healthy opposite hand.

"That's it?" he shouted as the creature lowered them both down toward the glowing purplish portal. "You're running away? You coward! *Face me!*"

WHAT HAVE YOU DONE TO MY MINION? came the Old One's voice in Fort's head, and he winced at the force of it. IT HAS BROKEN MY CONTROL. YOU ONCE AGAIN CAUSE US PAIN!

As the voice subsided, Fort readied another spell but paused for a moment. The Old One *controlled* the monster? So had the magic Fort cast been somehow channeled back up into the Old One too?

Somehow, that made his revenge even sweeter.

The monster was now actually digging itself back down toward the portal, the hand Fort held on to hanging uselessly at its side. It whimpered as it increased its speed, sounding almost like a wounded animal, and the sound nearly tugged at Fort's heart.

But it *wasn't* an animal. This was a bloodthirsty, raging monster that had killed his father! Sneering, he cast another Cause Heavy Wounds spell into it, and the creature squealed, hastening its descent once again. They were getting close to the portal now, and its light reflected up on the cavern walls.

But with each new terrified squeal, Fort's rage seemed to lessen. Even trying to remind himself of his father didn't seem to help—it was hard to even think over the creature's loud whines. As the light of the portal intensified, the rage disappeared entirely, leaving Fort feeling both empty and nauseous.

He'd been dreaming about getting revenge for so long, and now that he had the power, it somehow felt . . . wrong.

But no! He couldn't stop now. This was for his father. This was *justice*!

Is it? his father's voice said in his head as Fort watched the portal get closer. *Why are you doing this, Fort? This isn't the boy I know, the one who's going to grow up to be the first astronaut president. You're just torturing this creature. What does that accomplish?*

The monster's lower body passed through the portal, just seconds ahead of its hand holding Fort. If he didn't escape now, he'd be taken through to the creature's dimension.

But if he let go, the creature would escape. He might never have another chance to face it.

"It *deserves* this," Fort whispered, staring at the approaching purple light. "It . . . it hurt you! It took you from me!" He whispered the words of the Cause Heavy Wounds spell, cringing against the white heat, then moved his hand over to the now-charred flesh of the creature's finger he was wrapped around.

But this won't bring me back, said the voice in his head. *That thing wasn't even in control. The Old One was making it do this!*

Fort winced, knowing the imagined voice of his father was right. The creature *wasn't* here by choice. All its actions had been under the control of the monster in Damian's body.

Just like when it had stolen his father.

"I can't just let this go!" he shouted to no one. "This is all I have left!"

And soon you won't even have that, because you'll be taken to the monster's dimension, the voice said to him. *Just like I was.*

Fort growled in frustration, feeling both shame at the pleasure he'd taken in the creature's pain a moment before as well as a primal *need* not to let this go, not to let his father down again.

You could never let me down, Forsythe, he heard his father's voice say in his head.

Something wet fell on his cheeks, and Fort shuddered, releasing the spell he'd been holding in. The white pain disappeared into nothingness, and he quickly cast another spell.

This time, his hands glowed a cold blue, and he healed the creature, allowing the muscles, scales, and bone beneath his arms and legs to begin to grow back, replacing what he'd taken so horribly moments before.

That's my boy, his father's voice came to him.

Again and again, Fort cast his Healing magic into the creature, and as its muscles and sinew re-formed in its arm, it slowed its descent, right as Fort approached the portal. On the other side, he could just make out more of the monsters, all equally as horrific as the one he'd been torturing, but somehow, at this moment, he could only feel sorry for them.

They weren't to blame here. This was the Old One's fault. The Old One and Damian, who'd unleashed it on the world.

"I'm sorry for what I did," Fort whispered to the creature, who seemed to be shaking less now. "I, um, don't suppose you'd let me jump off before you go home?"

The creature looked down at Fort with its red eyes, and he wondered if it actually understood a single word he said.

"Maybe not," he whispered. "Either way, I really am sor—"

The air around him started to shimmer, and he froze, not sure what was happening. Had the monster pulled him through the portal?

But no. There were no giant creatures surrounding him now. Instead, he floated above what looked like the ruins of a battlefield.

The ruins that had once been the Oppenheimer School.

- FORTY-FOUR -

BELOW HIM, THE OPPENHEIMER SCHOOL lay in ruins. The boys' and girls' dorms were rubble, and the Training Hall had half collapsed. Here and there, a few soldiers lay unconscious on the ground, but the vast majority of guards had lined up in formation directly beneath Fort, looking straight ahead without moving.

Beside him in the air, the Old One floated, Sierra at its side.

YOU CAUSED US PAIN AND DESTROYED OUR CONTROL OF OUR MINION, the creature's voice pounded in Fort's head. Some sort of invisible force slowly turned Fort around to face it, then pulled him closer. Fort flinched away, but the thing didn't seem to notice.

WE HAD THOUGHT CORPOREAL MAGIC TO BE GONE, the creature continued, each word like a spike in Fort's brain. NOW IT SHALL BE.

The creature's tentacles reached out to surround Fort's head, but this time, they pushed into his ears, nose, and mouth. He tried to scream but couldn't get any air. He felt like he was drowning as one by one, all the spells in his head disappeared, leaving just darkness behind, the Old One's shadows, the same terror he'd felt in Sierra's room earlier from the inescapable fact that humanity had lived to serve these ancient creatures, and there was nothing he could do, *nothing*—

And then the connection broke, and Fort almost fainted from relief as the tentacles pulled away, letting him breathe again. He looked up at the Old One, who floated silently at his side.

"You . . . haven't won," Fort said, barely able to speak. "I'm not . . . the only . . . *healer*."

The magic holding Fort slowly rotated him to look down below, and he almost cried out in despair.

There, lined up behind the soldiers, were his classmates from Dr. Ambrose's Healing class, as well as the rest of the students from the Oppenheimer School. All of them were under the Old One's control, just like the soldiers.

Now that he was being forced to stare, Fort also found the teachers at their students' sides. Dr. Opps was there, and

Colonel Charles. Even Dr. Ambrose stood next to Bryce, who looked much less evil now that his mind was being controlled.

Fort looked down at everyone he'd met in the last three days, wanting to scream, to fight back, *anything*. It was *his* fault the Old One had escaped, after all. Everything he'd done had led right to this moment. *He'd* woken up Sierra, and that in turn had brought Damian back.

All because he couldn't let his desire for revenge go.

"Please, don't do this," he whispered, knowing the Old One wouldn't listen.

HUMANS NEVER UNDERSTOOD WHAT EACH TYPE OF MAGIC TRULY MEANT, the Old One said, waving its tentacles out over the assembled crowd below. WHAT YOU CALL DESTRUCTION IS BUT A FRACTION OF THE POWER OF THE TRUE *ELEMENTAL* MAGIC. YOU USE MAGIC OF THE BODY TO HEAL WOUNDS, WHEN YOU COULD USE IT TO RESHAPE YOURSELVES AS WE DID.

Reshape themselves? Fort gasped, remembering the glove he'd seen in the storage warehouse beneath the Training Hall. It'd been made from the same type of armor the Old One wore now, but shaped as if for a human.

Maybe he'd been right before, that the Old Ones *had* once been human? Or at least something closer in appearance.

THREE OF US REMAIN OF THE SEVEN THAT ONCE RULED, the Old One continued, and his tentacles formed multiple patterns in the air, a complex weaving dance that Fort could barely follow. As it maneuvered its tentacles, a tear formed in the sky before them, like a rip in the fabric of space and time. AND NOW, THE THREE OF US SHALL RULE YET AGAIN.

The tear widened, then solidified, forming a shimmering green portal. And on the other side . . .

Fort dry heaved, barely able to comprehend what he was seeing but unable to look away.

Colors screamed in madness, and time wept with sorrow. Mountains of incomprehensible anger raged against a cracked and broken sky, while sinister rain fell in multiple directions at once. And standing before it all were two human-sized creatures, both wearing the same crystal armor as the Old One within Damian.

But that was where the similarities stopped.

One of the Old Ones was covered in shrieking human faces, as if its body was filled with terrified souls. The second looked to be formed from pure flame, though it burned black at the edges and white at the center.

OUR TIME HAS COME TO RETURN TO OUR WORLD, MY BROTHER AND SISTER, the Old One said to the figures on the other side of the portal. COME. RETURN HERE TO OUR HOME, AND LET US MAKE IT OUR OWN ONCE MORE.

Fort frantically tried to free himself, struggling against the magical force holding him in the air, but it was like pushing against a mountain. He yelled in frustration, unable to imagine what was next to come.

If one Old One could so easily take control of an entire army base, three of them could surely take over the world.

But what could Fort do? He had no magic, not even Healing spells. Sierra was just as broken, controlled as she was by the Old One.

But maybe she was still conscious, somewhere within her mind? Could she hear him, through whatever connection they shared?

Sierra? Are you . . . still in there?

The Old Ones approached the portal, and Fort could almost feel the magic radiating off them. The one made of flame gestured, and a geyser of lava shot into the air just outside the school's walls, setting the nearby forest ablaze.

The one with the shrieking faces gestured toward the soldiers, and they all turned toward the creature, gazing up at it lovingly.

THE SEVEN FORMS OF MAGIC TOGETHER HOLD THE POWER OF ALL REALITY, the Old One said to Fort. YOU WILL WITNESS THAT POWER IN MOMENTS. AND THEN, FOR THE PAIN YOU HAVE CAUSED US, WE SHALL UNCREATE YOU FROM EXISTENCE.

Fort started hyperventilating again, not even sure what "uncreate" could mean. This time he had no Remove Fear spell to stop himself, but that worry paled before whatever was about to come.

Just like when his father had died, feelings of helplessness washed over him, but the memory of his dad woke something in him, and he pushed back against the despair with what remained of his will.

He wouldn't let this happen, not when it was all his fault. He *couldn't*!

A familiar voice in his mind seemed to groan. *You know, whenever you . . . you push back like that, it gives me . . . such a massive headache.*

Sierra? Fort thought, suddenly feeling the slightest bit of hope. *You're still there?*

Barely, she said. *It's all I can do to . . . just talk to you. I don't . . . I don't have the power to . . . fight those things.*

And just like that, the hope slipped away as quickly as it came. Fort watched as the students below now joined the soldiers in turning toward the screaming-faces Old One, like it had taken over not their minds, but their spirits.

But then Fort noticed something odd. Not all the students turned at the same time, like the soldiers had. Instead, four of them seemed almost surprised by the movement and had to hurry to catch up.

And they were four students that he recognized. Cyrus, Rachel, Jia, and Sebastian.

Fort's eyes widened. *Sierra? I need you to tell Cyrus something. He* has *to know!*

I can try, she said. *He's close by, so I should . . . be able to reach him. But what good will that—*

Trust me, Fort thought back at her. *Tell him that I said healing magic can hurt the thing inside Damian. Maybe even send it away. And that he's going to need something to protect him and a few others against mind magic. Whoever he thinks he needs to save us.*

What? What are you . . . it's too late. He's already here . . . with the rest of them.

Just, please, tell him*!* Fort thought back at her.

Sierra didn't respond, and Fort hoped she'd heard and hadn't just been overcome by the Old One.

The two Old Ones had reached the portal, and the fiery one was starting to step through.

And then from somewhere down below, someone . . . clapped.

"HEY!" a voice yelled. "Hold on one minute. We got you something. A welcome-home present!"

Fort looked down, a smile growing over his face as Rachel turned back around to face the Old One within Damian.

HOW DO YOU RESIST OUR CONTROL? The Old One's voice hit Rachel hard enough to almost knock her over, but she quickly stood back up and grinned.

"You have no *idea* how powerful I am," she said to him. "But let me educate you a bit."

Faster than Fort could see, she threw her hands out, sending a magic missile streaking toward the Old One.

With barely a movement, the Old One flicked a tentacle

out, slapping the missile back toward her, forcing Rachel to leap out of the way as it exploded into the ground.

But even as it did, the Old One screamed in agony and pulled its tentacle up to find what resembled a medical bandage now sticking to its skin.

WHAT IS THIS? it demanded, incinerating the bandage with a glance. YOU DARE USE CORPOREAL MAGIC ON US?

In front of them, the portal began to waver, and the other two Old Ones pulled away from it. The pain must have disrupted the Summoning spell, just like it had the Old One's control over the monster below the Training Hall.

"You're not supposed to burn it," Sebastian said from behind Rachel. "But don't worry." He held up two duffel bags, one in each hand, both practically overflowing with Dr. Ambrose's Healing bandages. "We've got more."

- FORTY-FIVE -

THE OLD ONE SNEERED AT FORT'S assembled friends below. YOU WILL SERVE AS AN EXAMPLE OF WHAT HAPPENS TO REBELLIOUS HUMANS, it shouted as an enormous fireball formed between its tentacles.

"Run!" Fort yelled, but there was nowhere for his friends to go, and even fewer places to hide. Most of the school buildings were now rubble, and those that weren't wouldn't offer any protection against something so destructive.

"We've *got* this, New Kid!" Rachel shouted, lightning sizzling off her fingers toward the Old One. The creature deflected the lightning into the remains of the mess hall, but the fireball it'd been creating imploded on itself, the magic absorbing back into the Old One.

"Keep it distracted!" Fort shouted. "It can't maintain all of the magic at once!"

"Stop shouting our plans!" Sebastian said, holding a bandage out in front of Rachel, who shot another magic missile into it, aimed at the Old One.

This time the tentacled creature sent the missile flying off into the now-burning forest beyond the school before it got anywhere near.

THE PORTAL, said a strange voice in Fort's head, one that was similar to the Old One's, only a different tone, less painful somehow. WE WILL DESTROY THESE HUMANS FOR YOU IF YOU SOLIDIFY THE PORTAL!

WE REQUIRE NO AID! the Old One within Damian hissed, but it turned one set of tentacles back to the portal anyway, and the shimmering doorway took shape once more.

Fort groaned deeply, feeling like they'd just missed a huge opportunity. Distracting the Old One definitely seemed to work, but just throwing spells at it wasn't the answer, not when the creature could deflect incredibly dangerous magic right back at Rachel and his other friends.

No, they needed something more, something that the Old One couldn't just flick away like an irritating bug.

Sierra? Fort shouted in his mind at her. *I know you can't free Damian, but can you reach his consciousness in there?*

No response. Rachel, meanwhile, went to fire another magic missile, but before she could, the Old One thrust its tentacles down toward her, growing them impossibly long and hideously sharp as it did. One sliced into Rachel's leg, dropping her to the ground, while the other hit Jia, who collapsed next to Rachel.

Sierra! Fort screamed. *We don't have any more time! You need to—*

I've got him! she sent back, and abruptly, Fort could feel a third presence with them, though this one felt even weaker than Sierra was. *Damian, can you hear me? It's Sierra!*

I . . . I can't fight him, Damian's voice echoed in Fort's head. *Sierra, I'm so sorry, I should never have let it into our world in the first place. This is all my fault!*

So Damian was ashamed for all that he'd done? *Good.* But now wasn't the time for that. Fort needed Damian fighting back, pushing against the Old One just like Fort had done against Sierra back in D.C. And for that, he needed Damian angry, not feeling sorry for himself.

Damian, it . . . it wasn't your fault, Fort said, clenching his fists just to get through it. He hated lying like this, but if that was what it took to save his friends, then fine. *You're not to blame. But right now, we need you to fight against the Old One's control. Push back with everything you've got. If we can divide his attention, we might actually land a hit and free you of him!*

From where she lay on the ground, Rachel sent dual sizzling lightning bolts at the portal, one from each hand. The fiery Old One inside the portal deflected the first, sending it into the Training Hall, which quickly caught on fire. The Old One within Damian stopped the other bolt in midair, then slowly turned it around and shot it back toward Rachel.

She screamed, but the bolt stopped just inches from her face.

REVEAL HOW YOU RESIST OUR MENTAL CONTROL, HUMAN, the Old One said.

Her leg still injured, Rachel tried to push herself out of range of the bolt, but the lightning followed her, never moving from its spot right over her eyes. "I'll *never* tell you," she whispered, and the bolt sizzled dangerously.

Damian, we need you now! Fort shouted.

There's nothing I can do! Damian said back. *My magic is useless against it.*

It's not about *magic!* Fort screamed, his heart racing as the bolt slowly pushed toward Rachel. *It's about* you, *your will-*

power, your own strength. Use that! Take all the anger, the injustice, everything that this creature has done to you, and use those feelings to fight*! You can* do *this!*

THEN YOU SHALL PERISH, the Old One declared, and raised a tentacle to release the lighting bolt. Rachel covered her face with her arms as the bolt sizzled again. . . .

But then the Old One hissed in pain. WHAT ARE YOU . . . YOU CANNOT RESIST OUR CONTROL! WE WILL WIPE THE REMNANTS OF YOU FROM YOUR MIND IF NEED BE!

With the Old One distracted, Rachel rolled out of the way a moment before the Old One turned its concentration inside, unconsciously releasing the lightning bolt. The electricity exploded into the ground just beyond her, and Rachel cried out as her back was burned from the hit, but that didn't stop her from readying another spell.

"Rachel, now's your chance!" Fort shouted, watching as the portal shuddered again, forcing the other Old Ones back within. *Sierra, push back against the Old One too! The more we can distract it, the better chance Rachel has of hitting it with a Healing spell!*

Back on the ground, Cyrus grabbed bandages from the

duffel bags and held one in front of both of Rachel's hands. Two magic missiles launched from her fingers, sweeping the bandages along with them, straight at the Old One, as the creature hissed again, louder this time.

It's fighting back! Sierra shouted in Fort's head. *I can't . . . it hurts so much!*

It's . . . killing me! Damian shouted, then yelled in pain. His scream in Fort's head matched the one from the Old One as Rachel's twin missiles struck home. One of the bandages hit its chest and burned up on contact, but the other passed right through the opening in the skull helmet and into the mass of tentacles where the Old One's face was.

A shriek like nothing Fort had ever heard exploded in his head, and he almost blacked out. Through the agony, he could barely see the portal violently waver in place, then finally wink out of existence completely.

And then Fort was falling, whatever magic holding him in the air now gone as well. He crashed hard against the ground, pain shooting through the arm and leg he landed on and into the rest of his body.

Sierra landed at the same time, groaning loudly as she hit. A moment later, the creature itself slowly touched down, its descent wildly at odds with the screams of agony in their heads. It now had its tentacles frantically reaching into its helmet, trying to retrieve the bandage within, only to get burned by it.

"Now!" Cyrus shouted, and two bodies sprinted past Fort and tackled the creature, slamming it to the ground. Jia first, then Sebastian slapped their hands onto the Old One's tentacle hands, each one furiously casting Healing spell after Healing spell.

NO, STOP! the monster shouted in all of their heads, and though Fort could see the pain its voice caused both of the other healers, neither paused in their spellcasting.

The tentacles began to burn away beneath their Healing hands, slowly revealing human fingers, human hands, human arms. The opaque crystal armor crumbled at their touch, and human legs appeared below it.

THE MAGIC RETURNED FOR *US*! the Old One shouted. IT SERVES US, NOT HUMANITY! THERE IS NOTHING YOU CAN DO. WE *WILL* RULE HUMANITY ONCE MORE, OR WE WILL WIPE YOU FROM THIS EARTH FOR ALL OF—

And then the voice in their heads went completely silent

as the last tentacles disappeared, leaving behind a very uncomfortable-looking boy in a hospital gown.

"YES!" Sebastian shouted, leaping to his feet. He turned and smirked at the others. "I just saved the whole world. You're *welcome*."

- FORTY-SIX -

JIA KNELT AT FORT'S SIDE AND RAN HER hands over his broken arm and leg. Cool healing energy flowed into him, and the pain instantly disappeared. "That should feel better now," she said, looking down at him with a mix of anxiousness and worry.

"You lied to me," he said, glaring up at her with a bitterness he was too tired to really feel. "I mean, not about the healing just now. It *does* feel better. You *knew* Sierra was here!" He pushed himself to a sitting position, but even that effort took more energy than he had.

"I didn't know she was here," Jia said quietly, looking away for a moment. "I really thought she was sent home. But either way, I couldn't tell you what happened, with the attack in D.C. and all. Do you know how many times Dr. Opps told me he'd wipe my memories if I said anything about what happened?

If I shared one word, he'd have kicked me out. And while this school is pretty messed up, it's also the only place I've got. At least until my parents come back, if they ever do."

Fort grunted, trying to stay annoyed but just thankful he was alive. "Oh, and you've been here since you were ten? No wonder you're so far ahead."

"What?" Sebastian shouted from a short distance away where he was healing Sierra. He snorted. "I knew I wasn't second best."

"No one's better than Jia," Sierra said, sitting up. "Thank you, by the way."

Sebastian just looked at her suspiciously. "And *you* are?"

Sierra paused for a moment, staring at the bright medallion around his neck. "Did Dr. Opps give you that?"

"No, Cyrus brought them to us an hour ago," Jia said. "He said we'd need them: me, Sebastian, and Rachel. If the three of us didn't follow him, we'd lose. Or that's what he told us."

"And I was right," Cyrus said, waving a hand at Damian. "I ran all the scenarios using my magic, and this was the only one where we had the slightest chance to stop the Old Ones from dominating the entire world within the next few days."

"Wait," Rachel said, looking at him strangely. "I thought you said we'd win for sure if it was the three of us."

Cyrus winced. "Well, I didn't see us *winning*, exactly. Everything was so chaotic, and the future got really hazy right around when the Old One attacked you and Jia. But I had faith!"

"You *what*?" Rachel said. "The only reason I wasn't terrified was because you had seen us defeat that thing!"

"See, but that was good!" Cyrus told her. "If you hadn't been so confident, maybe we'd all be serving Mr. Tentacles there for the rest of our lives."

Rachel just stared at him.

"I did tell you that you'd save the world," Cyrus admitted, blushing a bit. "Admittedly, that was just a guess. But if we lost, then none of us would have known it anyway, since our minds would have been taken over! Doesn't that help?"

Her mouth fell open at this, and she shook her head. "You and me, Future Boy. We're not done here."

"Can I see this for a second?" Sierra said to Sebastian, then pulled the necklace off his neck. "Yours too?" she asked Rachel, who still indignantly glared at Cyrus. She shrugged, though, and tossed the medallion to Sierra.

"What do you want them for?" Sebastian asked.

"Shh," Sierra said, then patted him on the cheek.

He instantly collapsed to the ground, sound asleep. Rachel shouted out in surprise, only to follow a second later.

"What are you *doing*?" Fort said, his eyes widening. "Those are . . . Rachel is my friend! They saved us!"

"And now they're getting a good nap," Sierra said, tossing one of the necklaces to Damian, who caught it. She then turned to the slowly reviving soldiers and students all around them and held up her hands. Instantly, the murmurs and groans went quiet, replaced by light breathing and snoring.

"What are you doing?" Fort repeated, slowly raising his hands to stop her . . . except how would he? He had no spells left. They'd all been removed by the Old One.

"Jia," Sierra said, stepping closer to the Healing girl and taking her hands. "It's *really* good to see you. I feel like it was just a couple of minutes since we last talked, but it's been . . . a while, hasn't it?"

"Six months," Jia said sadly, then hugged Sierra. "It's good to see you too, Erry. They never told me if you were okay, or what happened. I was so worried, and then everything started happening with Fort. I didn't know what to think!"

"You didn't miss *me*?" Damian said with a half smile, carefully standing up in his hospital gown.

Jia glared at him. "You, I never liked."

Damian shrugged. "Yeah, that's fair. If it matters, I did always like you. Sierra, any chance you want to give us some clothes?"

Sierra nodded and murmured something. Out of nowhere, jeans, T-shirts, and jackets suddenly appeared on both of them. "Just a Telepathy spell," she told Fort. "People will see this until we can find some actual clothes to put on."

"I'll get you some uniforms," Jia said. "If any survived, at least." She ran off, and Fort turned to Sierra for answers, but she had moved next to Damian and had her hand on his shoulder, her eyes closed.

"The Old One is completely gone, Damian," she told him, loud enough for Fort to hear too. "I think you're actually free of it."

"For now, maybe," Damian said, looking away. "They won't rest until they find a way back into our world. And I'll always be their first target."

"That's why we're going to hide you," Sierra said, tapping his medallion. "No one will find you if you've got this protective medallion on. I should know, since I created it. Dr. Opps insisted once he figured out I could read his mind at will. With that on, no one should be able to sense your presence, let alone read your mind."

"Good," Damian said. "This will help me track down the remaining books of magic."

Sierra frowned, staring at him. "You can't still be taking all of this 'chosen one' stuff seriously."

Damian shrugged. "Who else is going to do it? We need the power to destroy the Old Ones if they come back. And that's going to take all seven books. You heard it. Anyone with that power can save the world."

"I think it said *rule* the world," Fort said, his anger rising again in spite of his exhaustion. "And who said you're going anywhere? You can't leave, not after everything that happened. The attack in D.C. happened because of *you*."

Damian gave him a confused look. "That's not what you said in my mind, back during the battle there."

"I was *lying*," Fort shouted. "I needed you to fight back, and that meant you couldn't sit there feeling guilty, no matter how much you *should* feel that way!"

Even as he yelled, part of him felt guilty *himself*. As much as he wanted to blame Damian for everything, the boy wasn't any more responsible for the attack than the creatures had been.

Damian's face fell. "You're . . . you're right. I can't begin to say how sorry I am. But you *know* it wasn't me in control. You felt the Old One in your mind just as much as I did. I don't—"

The sounds of several helicopters in the distance interrupted him, and they all turned to look. Fires still raged in the forest around the base and in the Training Hall within the fences. Someone had either noticed the smoke, or reinforcements had been called before the Old One had taken control of everyone.

"These might be big, but they'll do the job," Jia said, returning with some uniforms.

She handed them to Damian and Sierra, who both put them on over what looked like their jeans and jackets. But the uniforms just disappeared into the illusion, and a moment later, two hospital gowns lay on the ground in front of them.

"I need to go," Damian said, and turned toward the broken gate out of the base. "If they find me here, they'll imprison me, and then I'll never find the power to destroy those things."

"You can't just leave, not with that magic," Fort said. "It's too dangerous. Sierra can erase it from your mind instead. That's the only way we'll really be safe."

Fort, Sierra said in his mind, and he turned to look at her in surprise. *What if he's right? What if those things find another way through, and no one knows how to send them back this time?*

What? he sent back. *This all happened because of him and that magic!*

Partly, she said. *And partly it happened because of me. And because of Dr. Oppenheimer. There's enough blame for everyone. But maybe this is how we all start making up for it.*

We? He looked at her in confusion. *You don't mean that you're—*

I'm not letting them lock me up either, she said, and outwardly gave him a small smile. *You know that Colonel Charles wouldn't let a telepath wander around the school, not anymore. He's seen the kind of power I have, and I know that's why he brought you here, to wake up me and Damian. Well, he's not getting either of us. He wants revenge just as much as you do, since his son was the first one who . . . who lost his life, in the attack at the NSA.*

I get it, Fort responded. *I'm not saying Damian's responsible, but what if one of those things takes him over again?*

That's why we have the medallions, Sierra said. *Besides, now that I'm awake and healed up, I can keep us out of sight. We'll be safe, from them and the TDA.*

"They're almost here," Jia said quietly. "If you're going, you need to go *now*."

"I'm going to use my Telepathy to make sure none of you remember where I go," Damian said, giving them an apologetic look. "I'm sorry, but it's for your own safety. That way you can honestly tell the soldiers you don't know."

"Don't bother, I'll get it," Sierra said, stepping over next to him.

Damian looked surprised, but she just tilted her head like she was speaking to him in his mind. Finally he nodded and turned back to the rest of them. "Thank you all, for everything. And again, I can't begin to express how sorry I am for what happened."

He turned, and with Sierra's hand in his, started to walk toward the edge of the base. But Fort moved to block them, not sure he could stop them, but unwilling to let Damian just go, not with such a dangerous magic, not after . . . everything. "Think of what could happen if you lose control again," he growled at the boy. Mostly, he wanted to add, *Think of what happened the last time you did, and who suffered for it.*

Damian sighed, then raised his hand, and it began to glow a dull red. "I don't want to fight you," he said. "But right now, you need to let us go, for the good of everyone."

Please, Fort, Sierra said in his head. *We will talk again, and soon. But we need to go now, if we're going to have a chance.*

Above them, the helicopters began to circle, moving in for a landing.

Fort gritted his teeth, wanting nothing more than to refuse. If he could just keep Damian on the base until the soldiers arrived, the soldiers would lock him up and take his magic away, and then they really *would* be safe. . . .

Fort, his father's voice said in his head. *What did I tell you about living in fear? I'm pretty sure this isn't North Carolina.*

That's not what I'm doing! Fort shouted in his mind, knowing it was a bit ridiculous to talk to his own imagination.

Are you sure? his father's voice said. *Is this about safety . . . or just more revenge?*

Fort sighed deeply. *I don't even know, honestly,* he thought. And he realized that if he couldn't even tell the difference, then that was an even bigger problem.

I hope you're right about this, he told the imaginary voice of his father in his head.

I'm you, his father's voice said. *And when have* you *ever been wrong?*

Fort rolled his eyes internally, then stood aside and let Damian and Sierra pass. "You can go, but keep your magic *under control*," he said to Damian. And then, just for his father, he added, "Because you won't always have a master magician around like me to fix things."

Damian nodded gravely, then pulled Sierra into a run. She threw Fort one last slight smile before they both headed into the woods.

"Whoa, did they just disappear?" Jia asked.

Fort, though, watched Sierra and Damian run out of the base. "I guess so," he agreed, as the helicopters started landing all around them.

- FORTY-SEVEN -

"WELL, FORSYTHE," COLONEL CHARLES said, sitting across from Fort in a small room with a long mirror on one side. "This feels familiar, doesn't it? Was it just yesterday I was talking to you in the disciplinary barracks? It can't have been. So much has happened."

Fort shrugged, staring down at his hands, which were handcuffed to the table.

"I've spoken to the other students already and heard their versions of things," Colonel Charles said. "And obviously I know much of yours. Is there anything you'd like to add?"

Fort paused, then nodded. "I have a question. How much do *you* remember?"

Colonel Charles looked away. "You mean, what did the Old One let me remember? All I know is that I heard an explosion at the Training Hall a few minutes after I sent my guards after you. Then, the next thing I knew, I was hearing a voice in my head, telling me to fight back against whatever was inside my brain. I did, and then woke up in the middle of the destroyed school." He winced. "I'm told by Lieutenant Moynahan that several of the men were able to put up a fight, and the Old One displayed his power before taking over their minds."

"I think that was its power," Fort said. "The Old One said that they discovered magic, and each of them was a master of one kind. That one had to be the best at Telepathy magic, considering."

Colonel Charles nodded. "That doesn't exactly explain how we all fell asleep a moment after being freed from the creature, however. Do you know anything about that?"

Fort swallowed hard. "Nope. I woke up out there, same as you."

"You and your friends managed to drive it off," Colonel Charles said, giving Fort a serious stare. "And for that, we can't begin to thank you."

"So you're going to do that by sending me home?" Fort knew it was coming. Even if he knew more of the truth than Colonel Charles did, he'd still seen far too much to be allowed to stay. Besides, the only reason he'd been invited was to wake up a telepathic girl that was now gone.

Colonel Charles paused, then gave him a confused look. He reached across the table and unlocked Fort's handcuffs. "Ah, no. You'll be remaining here, in the Oppenheimer School, for the foreseeable future."

Fort blinked once, then again. "Um, what, now?"

"You have proven beyond any doubt that there's a need for healers," Colonel Charles said. "Without you, we might not have figured out the Old One's weakness. In that vein, we'll also be increasing the number of students in the Healing program. Given that Destruction magic had little to no effect on the Old One, we'll need powerful healers around for . . . protection."

Fort just stared at him in astonishment. "So I can stay? And learn magic again?"

"I'd even allow you to learn Destruction magic, if you wanted. Though from what we've seen, your powers seem to lie elsewhere."

"I think I'm okay sticking with Healing," Fort said, and smiled. He stood up, rubbing his wrists where the handcuffs were. "So . . . I can go?"

Colonel Charles shook his head and waved at Fort to sit back down, which he did. "There's someone else here who needs to speak to you. After that . . . well, I'd say you could head back to class, but we'll need to find a new base soon. In the meantime, I have to go. We're pretty well hidden out here, but there were some dramatically large explosions, I'm told, as well as some other mystical elements. I need to speak to the press about what happened here. Rumors are running wild already."

Fort narrowed his eyes. "Who else am I supposed to speak to?"

Colonel Charles gestured at the mirror, then left through the door.

A moment later, Dr. Opps walked in.

Fort clenched his hands into fists as the doctor sat down across from him, not able to look at the man who'd been at least indirectly responsible for his father's death.

"I know you have questions, Forsythe," Dr. Opps said quietly.

"Like how you could lie to me, and bring me here even though you never wanted to?" Fort said, his voice rising in spite of trying to stay calm. "About how there was a whole class of students before this one, and that *they* caused the attack in D.C., not some other group, some other country like you let us all believe? Questions like *those*?"

Dr. Opps spread his arms. "All fair, and many more besides. I've made . . . many mistakes, Forsythe. Those you just listed wouldn't even make a dent in the overall total. But yes, I do owe you . . ."

"An apology?!"

"Yes, and I *am* sorry, but that couldn't begin to cover it," Dr. Opps said. "I thought founding a school beneath the headquarters of the NSA would keep the students safe, and the civilian population in blissful ignorance. I had no idea that when the Old One took over Damian's mind, it would send one of its creatures to the closest heavily populated area, hoping to cause as much destruction as possible. The fact that it turned out to be where you and you father were, well, I can never be forgiven for that."

"No, you *can't*," Fort said quietly. "So . . . you remember them? Damian and Sierra?"

"Sierra, yes," Dr. Opps said. "Colonel Charles doesn't remember them, and I think he might be better suited staying in the dark. I can't imagine he'd let our fugitives run free for long." He sighed. "But apart from that, I want to ask you something: You wanted revenge when we first spoke. Yet from what Colonel Charles tells me, you could have killed the creature who attacked you in the basement. But you didn't. Why?"

Fort dug his fingernails into his palms, then slowly unclenched his fists. "I just want to make sure that what happened to my father never happens to anyone else, ever again."

"You want to protect people."

Fort nodded. "From creatures like that . . . and from people like you."

Dr. Opps sighed. "I deserve that. Before the accident . . . before Damian unleashed the Old One, I should say, the military only had access to my school in a purely advisory role. But afterward, the committee in charge of the school gave Colonel Charles equal control over the students. I'd hoped that he would listen to me about keeping the students safe, but clearly that hasn't happened."

"Clearly not," Fort said, his anger threatening to bubble out of him.

"I guess I thought at least I could keep the school from turning into a weapons factory, spitting out child soldiers wielding magic instead of weapons. I still think that's possible. But to do so, we'll need students like you here, leading the way." He held out a hand. "In that vein, I want to extend a permanent invitation to stay, with no ulterior motives. You've more than earned your place here, Forsythe."

"I'm not going to stay here just so you feel less guilty," Fort hissed at him.

"No, and you shouldn't," Dr. Opps said, staring down at the table. "You should stay here because you have the best of intentions. And I think we need as much of that around here as we can get. I just have one request."

"What?" Fort said, completely indignant. "You want a *favor* now?"

"Try to always keep in mind what you just told me," Dr. Opps said, rising from his seat. "The moment you forget you're here to protect people . . . well, we both lose."

He turned and walked toward the door, then paused. "You could have stopped Damian and Sierra from leaving, I'm guessing. Why didn't you?"

Fort turned away. "I haven't known Sierra that long. But I've been inside her mind, and she's seen far too much of me. So I guess . . . if she thinks we can trust Damian, then I'm willing to be proven wrong about him."

Dr. Opps nodded, then left the room, closing the door quietly behind him.

- FORTY-EIGHT -

"HELLO, CYRUS," DR. OPPS SAID, SITTING down next to the clairvoyant boy as he watched Colonel Charles at a press conference via satellite on television, assuring the public that not only had the TDA stopped another attack, but this time they had no casualties. "I'm glad you weren't hurt."

"Me too," Cyrus said, his eyes on the television as the reporters all began shouting questions. "Though I probably would have known that was coming ahead of time. I *do* check my personal future quite often."

"Do you know what caused the attack this time?" a reporter asked on the television.

"Yes, an outside group that calls themselves the Gathering Storm," Colonel Charles said. "We have good leads into their whereabouts, however, and are currently tracking them down."

"The Gathering Storm?" Cyrus said to Dr. Opps.

"I thought we'd picked the Rising Tide," Dr. Opps said with a shrug. "The military focus-tested a few different names. They wanted one that came across as ominous, yet not threatening enough to demand immediate action. A good nonspecific group to blame instead of our students."

Cyrus nodded, not responding.

Dr. Opps leaned in closer. "Did you know this was all going to happen when you found out I'd brought Forsythe to the school? I know you and he are close, and you most likely looked into his future."

Cyrus smiled. "Of course I knew. If he hadn't been here, Sierra would have woken up eventually, and Damian with her, and nothing would have stopped them. But I knew Colonel Charles wouldn't wait much longer, not with Sierra saying Fort's name over and over downstairs."

Dr. Opps pulled away in surprise. "You knew about . . . but why didn't you tell me any of this ahead of time?"

"Because if I had, you'd have insisted Fort go home, even if it cost you your position," Cyrus told him, still watching the television. "And you'll still be needed in the months to come."

Dr. Opps's eyes widened, and he shuddered a bit. "You scare me at times, Cyrus."

"I get that a lot," Cyrus said, grinning slightly.

"So what happens now?"

"Now?" Cyrus said. "The Old Ones won't stop, and eventually they'll find their way home. You need to make sure these students are trained, and soon, or the world will suffer like you wouldn't believe. The Old Ones brought humanity magic, Dr. Opps. Unless we have it mastered by the time they return, that's it. We'll be wiped out for good."

"And you've . . . you've seen this?"

Cyrus looked at him, still smiling, but didn't say a word.

Dr. Opps sighed, rubbing his eyes. "Okay. And Damian and Sierra? Is Damian the one who's going to learn all seven forms of magic? Will he be the one to save us?"

Cyrus paused. "That's too far for me to see."

"But he *is* the chosen one that the books referred to?"

Cyrus shrugged. "I thought so at first, just from what you'd told me about him. But then Fort told me what he learned from the Old One, that a magician who mastered all seven types shut magic away on earth, to make sure the Old Ones couldn't return. The books might be referring to that person."

"Let's hope not, or they really will wipe us out when they return," Dr. Opps said. "And Fort? Is he going to play any further role in all of this, or is his job done now?"

This time, Cyrus laughed. "Oh, he's got a lot more to do, trust me. And it all begins right now, actually."

"What do you mean?" Dr. Opps asked as on the television Colonel Charles thanked the reporters and left the podium with a curt smile, while the reporters continued shouting questions for him.

Cyrus shrugged. "Nothing," he said.

Dr. Opps sighed. "I'm just glad Sierra's gone. I never felt comfortable with someone who could read my thoughts. No telling what secrets could be leaked."

"Secrets like what?" Cyrus asked.

Dr. Opps smiled and leaned back, looking away. *Secrets like how the creature in D.C. was being controlled by that Old One,* Dr. Opps thought, *and it wouldn't have taken a human back with it unless it was ordered to. Which means Forsythe's father could still be* alive.

"There's a reason they're secret," he said out loud, then stood up. "Always good to chat with you, Cyrus."

"Hey, Bandage!" someone yelled to Fort as he walked toward the temporary shelter the army had put up in the middle of the base. He looked over and sighed as Trey, Chad, and Bryce walked over to him.

"Can we not do this right now?" Fort asked. "I'm really pretty exhausted, honestly. There was a whole thing with a monster, and, well, another monster—"

"We know what you did," Trey said, narrowing his eyes. "And I for one just wanted to say, um, *thanks*."

Fort's eyes widened as the boy stuck out his hand for a shake. "Is this a prank?" he asked, staring at Trey's hand.

Trey laughed. "Nope. I have to admit, for a healer you did pretty good, what with destroying that monster and all."

"He also destroyed the school," Bryce whispered, not looking at Fort.

"And saved our lives," Chad said, patting Fort on the shoulder. "Just don't ever sit on our cot again."

"Fair enough," Fort told them, then smiled to himself as the other boys kept walking. That had been unexpected. But maybe now that all the secrets and hidden intentions at the school were revealed, things would finally be improving here. Or at least, wherever they ended up, since there was no way the school could stay at the now-destroyed base.

Even in spite of his tiredness, Fort let himself feel almost relaxed for the first time in six months. It just felt really good to have all the secrets out of the way, and . . . .

Secrets like how the creature in D.C. was being controlled by that Old One, Dr. Opps's voice said in his head. *And it wouldn't have taken a human back with it unless it was ordered to. Which means Forsythe's father could still be alive.*

It took a moment for Fort to realize what he was hearing. When it sank in, he dropped to his knees in the middle of the courtyard, barely breathing.

I just thought you should know, Sierra said in his mind. *Please, Fort, don't do anything dangerous with this information, okay? I . . . I don't want you to get hurt.*

But Fort couldn't respond to her, couldn't even think straight.

His father . . . might still be *alive*?

At his sides, his fists slowly clenched. It couldn't be true, could it? After all this time, his father could have been held captive, suffering in the creature's dimension, or held by the Old Ones somehow?

If it *was* true, if there was even the slightest possibility of that being true, Fort had only one choice.

He'd have to learn Summoning magic.

ACKNOWLEDGMENTS

Uh-oh. *That* doesn't sound like it's going to lead anywhere good. Hopefully someone will stop Fort before he causes a lot more trouble!

Ha, just kidding, he's totally going to ruin everything. But even if the world is destroyed, isn't the true magic the friends we made along the way?

Nah, in this case, it's definitely the magic.

Thank you to all my readers, especially those who followed me from the Half Upon a Time and Story Thieves series and are taking a chance on something new. I know *Revenge of Magic* feels different from my other work, but I think if you'll trust me, you'll find it's going some fun, awful, fun, horrible, and fun places.

And thank you to everyone who made this series possible to begin with, starting with (in chronological order) my fiancée Corinne, my agent Michael Bourret, and my editor at Aladdin, Liesa Abrams. Also thanks to my publisher Mara Anastas; and to Chriscynethia Floyd; to Caitlin Sweeny, Alissa

Nigro, Christian Vega, and Anna Jarzab in marketing; Nicole Russo and the publicity group; Elizabeth Mims in managing editorial; Sara Berko in production; Laura Lyn DiSiena, who designed the book; Michelle Leo and the education/library team; Stephanie Voros and the sub rights group, too; Gary Urda, Christina Pecorale, Jerry Jensen, Karen Lahey, Christine Foye, Victor Iannone, and everyone else in sales; and the amazing Vivienne To, who brought Fort's horrible day to life with her cover.

Come back for the next book. I promise, things are just gonna get worse. So it'll be fun!

James